Chasing
THE
SUN

Praise for
KATY COLINS

'Brilliant, life-affirming story of a jilted bride who heads off to explore Thailand. Perfect escapism.'

– Heat

'Katy writes with humour and heart. The Lonely Hearts Travel Club is like Bridget Jones goes backpacking.'
– Holly Martin, author of *The White Cliff Bay series*

'The perfect first-sunny-afternoon in the garden book!'
– Kathleen Gray on *Destination India*

'I cannot recommend this book enough. It is beautifully written with a brilliant plot and fantastic characters. READ IT!!'
– Blabbering About Books on *Destination Thailand*

'Imaginative, fascinating, and funny!'
– What's Better Than Books? on *Destination India*

'If you're looking for an escape from the cold, winter nights, the drudgery of day to day life and love to read about exotic locations then Katy Colin's debut novel is the book for you.'
– Ellen Faith on *Destination Thailand*

'A great book to pop in your holiday/weekend bag that will make you just want more.'
– The Reading Shed on *Destination India*

'*Destination Thailand* had me hooked from the very first page and kept me up til 2:30am as I was dying to know what happened next.'

– Books and Boardies

'I loved this book.'
– For the Love of Books on *Destination Thailand*

Chasing THE SUN

KATY COLINS

ONE PLACE. MANY STORIES

This novel is entirely a work of fiction. The names, characters
and incidents portrayed in it are the work of the author's
imagination. Any resemblance to actual persons, living or
dead, events or localities is entirely coincidental.

HQ
An imprint of HarperCollins*Publishers* Ltd.
1 London Bridge Street
London SE1 9GF

This edition 2017

2
First published in Great Britain by
HQ, an imprint of HarperCollins*Publishers* Ltd. 2017

Katy Colins asserts the moral right to be
identified as the author of this work.
A catalogue record for this book is
available from the British Library.

ISBN: 9780008202194

Printed and bound by
CPI Group (UK) Ltd, Croydon, CRO 4YY

KATY COLINS

Katy sold all she owned, filled a backpack and booked a one-way ticket to south east Asia and never looked back.

The acclaimed travel blogger's experiences inspired her to pen 'The Lonely Hearts Travel Club' series and saw her labelled the 'Backpacking Bridget Jones' by the global media.

When she's not globe-trotting, writing about her adventures and telling anyone who'll listen to grab life by the horns, Katy loves catching up with her family and friends and convincing herself that her cake addiction isn't out of control - just yet.

You can find out more about Katy, her writing and her travels on her blog www.notwedordead.com or via social media @notwedordead.

enough of a profit for us not to worry about the bold move to open it, and many customers were returning from their group travel adventures with praise, five-star reviews and great word-of-mouth recommendations. Until now, we'd been juggling the workload of our flagship store in Manchester with a fairly normal home-life routine, but the time had come for us to take the plunge and buy a place in London, as commuting was taking it out of both of us. I was excited about being a homeowner with the person I loved most in the world, and as much as I adored Manchester, I couldn't wait to embark on a new life in the capital. Plus, I was sick of the sight of these bloody boxes, crates and bubble wrap in every room of our flat.

Ben turned and spooned some Bolognese into my mouth. 'Well, life will be perfect, once you've tasted this.'

I licked my lips and swallowed the tangy tomato sauce. 'Hmm, maybe a little more black pepper,' I teased, as he tickled me in my side.

'Oi. This is seasoned *exactly* right, you horror!' He laughed and began plating up dinner as I topped up our wine glasses. 'Perfection in a bowl, I'd say.'

We negotiated our way around the boxes and wandered through to the lounge. I flicked on the television. 'Netflix or Sky?' I asked, as he gently put the steaming bowls down on the coffee table. It had been ages since we'd snuggled up on the sofa together. Sadly, I would have to limit myself to one hour of relaxing, then I needed to have another read-through of things for tomorrow.

'Babe?' I repeated.

Ben was staring intently at his mobile phone. 'Sorry?' He glanced up.

'What do you want to watch?'

He hurriedly flicked off his phone and put it in his pocket. 'Oh, err, Netflix? We've not finished watching this season of *Narcos*, remember?'

I faffed around with the TV and settled back into the sofa, trying not to feel put off by how distracted he'd been recently. It wasn't just work; there was something else on his mind, but whenever I asked him he said everything was fine.

'Oh, I heard from Jimmy today, said Shelley is like a kid at Christmas waiting for you to get over there,' he said, pulling me from my thoughts. 'You ready to head down under?'

I rolled my eyes. 'Ready' was not *exactly* how I'd describe it. I was working flat out to get things finished before I took annual leave, and we were hoping to finalise the house move before we left, but it had been dragging on unresolved for what felt like months. There was still so much to do before I could let myself get properly excited for my trip to Australia.

'I'll take that as a no then.'

'I can't wait for a holiday, but until tomorrow is out of the way, I haven't been able to give it my full attention.' I flicked on to the right episode and loaded up my fork.

Our diaries were a military operation to organise at the best of times, but it felt like things had ramped up even more in the last few months. A lot of our popularity had to do with the public support that we'd received since appearing on *Wanderlust Warriors*, a TV show that I'd persuaded Ben to take part in last year in Chile. I still had to pinch myself at how things had developed since we'd first started both the business and our relationship. It was exciting, stressful, hectic and nerve-wracking all at the same time, but there was no one other than Ben who I wanted by my side through it all.

'You still okay that I'm not flying over with you?'

I smiled and shook my head. 'Babe, it'll be wedding central from the moment we both arrive. It's not that long till you're joining me and, anyway, you'll only be roped in to help out. Plus, we need someone to keep an eye on things here with the move; well, specifically with chasing the waste-of-space estate agent.' I took a sip of my wine to calm down. Although I couldn't wait to see Shell, I was secretly worried that this trip would be less sightseeing and more wedding planning.

'For a girl who's ticking Australia off her travel bucket list soon, you don't exactly sound like you're that excited, babe.'

I scrunched up my nose. The question was innocent enough, but I felt like I wasn't sure if I had the correct answer. So much had changed since I had been jilted by my ex-fiancé, and even though it was a few years ago, I still felt unsure what my feelings were about weddings. Part of me loved the fact we were going to be hanging out together for a big knees-up with our best mates, and another part of me knew it could easily blow out of control. I'd learnt so much since I'd planned a wedding and been in Shelley's shoes of balancing budgets and family expectations, wanting it all to be perfect. I wasn't what you'd call ecstatic at getting back into that world again.

'Mmm, I just know what it can get like when you're in that bubble.'

'Oh, yeah, sorry.' He fidgeted. 'You and marriage aren't exactly best mates.'

'You could say that.' I finished off my glass of wine. How had we got through a bottle already?

'Did I tell you that I've got a pre-wedding meet-up with some of Jimmy's mates who can't make it over for the big day, but wanted to give me some stories for my best man speech?'

I rolled my eyes. 'Shelley's going to love that. Just run them past someone before you tell the whole room how he got his arse tattooed when you went to Laos.'

'How do you remember that?' He gasped dramatically.

'I remember *everything*.' I grinned, waving my fork in his direction, and tucked my feet under his legs.

'Like an elephant,' he laughed, spooning a mouthful of pasta into his lopsided grin. 'Also, don't stress about the house stuff. I'll be on to them as soon as I get back from this trip.'

'Thank you, babe. God, it really feels like the end of an era,' I mused, nodding my head at the mountains of bubble wrap and flattened crates filling most of the room.

'Yeah, I guess.' Ben smiled and gave my knee a squeeze. 'Or the start of a new adventure.'

'I'll drink to that!' I laughed. 'Right, less talking and more eating, this is delicious.'

'Told you, perfection.' He grinned and turned the volume back up.

CHAPTER 2

Ardent (adj.) – Enthusiastic or passionate

'Here you go.' Kelli passed me over a Styrofoam cup of coffee before perching on the edge of the chair opposite, smoothing down her tailored charcoal-grey dress as she sat. The girl who'd come to us for work experience wearing Avril Lavigne's wardrobe circa 2005 had blossomed into this confident and competent businesswoman, dressed for success. She was killing it in the office-wear style stakes. I self-consciously tugged on my own deep purple pleated skirt, hoping I didn't let the team down. I'd read this thing in a magazine a few years ago that if you wanted to be remembered for all the right reasons, then you should wear a pop of bright colour in corporate environments. I was hoping that *Cosmo* never lied.

'That machine is more complicated than the one Felix has installed.' She nodded her head to an intimidating neon-blue and stainless-steel coffee machine emitting strange grinding and beeping noises in the corner of the tastefully decorated waiting area. 'You need a bloody PhD in barista-ing just to figure it out.'

'Maybe that's our first test,' I whispered, stealing a glance at the bespectacled-wearing receptionist. I craned my neck to see if she was surreptitiously observing us and making notes to pass on to the panel of bankers we were about to meet.

'Well, luckily all those years of making you and Ben coffee means I'm more than qualified.' Kelli grinned and poured a sachet of sugar into her steaming drink. We'd been sitting here for ages, running through our presentation, and now I just wanted to go and shine. I was about to ask her how she was getting on with the new team of designers she'd been managing when my mobile rang.

'Georgia, I know you're just about to go in, but I wanted to let you know that we've been given sign-off on the content for *Lonely Planet*,' the high-pitched and excitable tones of my PA, Erin, rang down the line. 'I've also seen that Ben has just passed over Germany and thought you might like to know.'

'Sorry?'

'Oh.' She let out a tinkly giggle. 'I mean, I've been watching his flight on this app to see where he was. To make sure there weren't any delays,' she hurriedly added. 'It's so cool, it even shows you the view from the camera underneath the plane so it's like I was there with him!' she babbled.

I tucked the phone between my neck and my ear, sipped my coffee, and noticed Kelli roll her eyes in mirth. She'd openly admitted that she didn't have the patience to deal with Erin; their working styles were worlds away from each other.

'Erm, great, anything else?'

I heard papers rustling. 'I've rearranged all your meetings for when you're away to be sure that you don't get hassled on your holiday. Oh, and I've set a reminder to check you in online for your flight to Melbourne when it opens. You know that journey takes twenty-three hours!' She blew air through her teeth.

'I'm sure it will be fine,' I said, repeating what was fast becoming some sort of mantra for me.

'Well, rather you than me. Actually, scratch that, I'd swap places for a break in Australia compared to London. Wait – is Oz even sunny this time of year? Isn't it their autumn if it's our spring? No matter. Compared to here I'd give it a go. Did you know there's another tube strike planned for next week?'

'Erin?'

'Whoops, sorry, I went off on a bit of a tandem then.'

'Tangent,' I corrected her and smiled to myself.

I'd warmed to her when we'd hired her as she was so bubbly and chatty, but there were times, like when I was about to go and pitch for a huge investment deal and needed to stay focused, when I willed her to wrap things up this side of the decade.

'Listen, we're just about to go in so I need to get off the phone.'

'Ah, of course! Sorry! Oh, one more thing, the estate agents have called because they couldn't get hold of you, I'm guessing because your calls are diverted to me and then with Ben on a flight too. They said that they have finally sorted a moving date. I'll add it all into an email for you.'

For a moment I forgot about preparing myself for this pitch and allowed myself a frisson of excitement. No matter how many times I thought about the fact that Ben and I would soon be homeowners, it still didn't feel real. Life was almost too good to be true. I didn't dare think about it too much, otherwise I'd convince myself that something just had to go tits up.

'Got it. Thanks, Erin. Now I do need to go. I'll catch up with you tomorrow.'

'Great! Good luck with the pitch. Break a leg! Is that what they say? Well, don't literally do that otherwise your trip down under will have to be called off and, from what you've told me, Shelley wouldn't appreciate that one bit!'

'K, thanks. Bye.' I hung up, cutting her off.

'All good back at the ranch?' Kelli asked, stifling a smile.

I nodded and popped my phone back into my bag. 'Fine. You need to get used to her; she'll be the one helping you while we're both away.'

Kelli let out a faux groan. 'I'll soon have her working efficiently.'

'She is efficient, just a little excitable sometimes.'

'A little excitable? A hardcore Justin Bieber fan finding out they've got a meet-and-greet in his bedroom is less excitable than her!' She laughed. 'So, the big wedding of the year, huh? On a scale of one to ten, how likely are they to play Kylie and Jason at the evening disco?'

'Hmm, a solid zero I'd say.'

'What no "Especially for You"? What about "Come On Eileen"? If *that's* not blasted out and you're forced to dance with some drunk uncle with bad breath, then the marriage is fair game to be legally annulled,' she said sagely.

'Shelley's already said she doesn't want anything super cheesy; she was vetting the DJ's collection a few weeks ago to make sure.'

'What! But it's a wedding! That's like saying you don't want to say any vows because they're a bit old-fashioned. I mean I'm all for making it "your day, your way", but there are some things you don't mess with, and doing "YMCA" with wedding cake crumbs in your hair and some bloke's tie around your head is one of them.' Kelli shook her head in disbelief. 'I'm guessing she's gone all bridezilla then?'

'If you call a daily updated WhatsApp group with me and her cousin Cara, who's the other bridesmaid, slightly over-the-top, then yeah. Every morning I wake up to at least fifty unread messages from the pair of them. Photos of table centrepieces, links to wedding blogs where there was a real-life shaman performing the ceremony, and conversations back and forth over the preferred height of heels the bridesmaids should wear. The worst thing is they live together, so why there needs to be a text group, I don't know. I mean, I'm happy to be involved, but I'm just too busy to be as into it as they are.'

'Not to mention what happened to you with your own wedding.' Kelli winced.

'Yeah, that too, I guess.' I absent-mindedly picked at my nail. It had felt like it had been constant wedding chatter since Shelley had sent out her 'save the date' cards.

'Seriously though, a shaman?!' Kelli struggled to hold herself together; even the receptionist kept looking over to see what was so funny. 'A shaman! Oh, I've heard it all now!' she said through chokes of laughter.

'Don't, it's not a joke!' I flashed the receptionist a nothing-to-see-here-type smile.

'Sorry. Okay, game face on.' She tried to straighten her mouth and wafted her hands at her eyes to compose herself. 'God, you poor thing, going all that way down under to spend time with this marital monster. Tell her from me she needs to get a grip. It doesn't sound like it's going to be much of a holiday for you and Ben.'

I was about to say that I'd given up trying to remind Shelley that it was for one day, ONE DAY, and instead

was making sure not to tip her over the edge when she
was so fraught with nerves and constantly consumed
by stress. I also secretly hoped that once I got over
there she would be a lot calmer and on top of things,
but I was pulled from sticking up for her as we were
beckoned over to head into the lions' den.

'Miss Green? They're ready to see you now.'

Here goes.

*

*We're nailing this. It literally could not be going any better.
They're eating out of our hands, loving what we have to
offer, and quite rightly so.*

'So, ladies and gentlemen, if you turn to page fifteen
in your packs, you will see our year-on-year growth,
which I'm sure you'll agree is pretty impressive in this
current market.' I beamed proudly at the corporate
faces spread around the mahogany desk in front of me
as a rustle of papers filled the pine-scented room.

The past twenty minutes had flown by in what felt
like a whirl of PowerPoint presentations, marketing
stats and business buzzwords. Kelli had given a
breakdown of our figures and projected financial
targets, all of which had been met with subtle eyebrow
raises and the slightest of smiles.

I confidently stepped forward, enjoying the spotlight
and opportunity to talk about how unique my business
was.

'I wanted to tell you a little about how Lonely
Hearts Travels came about. I only discovered the
joy that comes from booking a flight and jetting off
after I was jilted, and found the courage to turn my
devastating break-up into a whole new life, thanks to

the opportunities that travel gave me.' I paused for effect. 'I now get to work with broken-hearted singles who, just like I was, are looking to find themselves by changing their scene and embracing a sense of adventure. After being dumped it can be all too easy to sit back and feel like the weight of the world is against you, that your hand has been dealt and there's nothing you can do about it. Well, travel is something you *can* do. Go to that country you've dreamt about visiting, hang out with like-minded people, taste new food and take envy-inducing photos showing how you are having the best life. By getting out there you get a new perspective on the world; it can even show you that your ex wasn't this perfect person you'd built them up to be. No one's perfect, after all, and don't get me started on the pedestal that I'd put my ex-fiancé on.' A weak laugh floated from the room, spurring me on.

'They say that travel is pure escapism, which is why it makes sense to turn to your backpack when you're at a time in your life that you want to escape from. On the tours we run, we encourage guests to talk about their break-ups in a healthy way, so that they don't return home still carrying the weight of their sadness with them. It's like shedding a skin, a heavy fur coat that you didn't realise you were lugging around, and that's the most refreshing and amazing feeling there is.'

Kelli was smiling at me to continue.

'At Lonely Hearts Travels we believe that—'

I was cut off by the shrill ringing of someone's mobile phone. The suits shifted in their seats as I paused and waited for the culprit to turn it off. I was half tempted to remind them that the sign in reception said all phones were expected to be placed on silent

when in the presentation room. Nobody moved.
I let out a little laugh as the tune rang on, increasing
in pitch. The awkwardness grew as they exchanged
confused glances as to who was being so ignorant as to
let their phone ring for this long.

'Anyone going to fess up?' I smiled. They stared
back at me blankly.

'Georgia,' Kelli hissed, violently nodding her head
towards my handbag placed under the table, which
I now realised was the source of the repetitive ringing.

Crap. If it's Erin, I'll bloody kill her. She'd been
messing about with my phone to make sure my calls
transferred to her and must not have done it correctly.

'Oh!' I flustered. 'I am sorry! I was sure I'd put it on
silent, I…' I leant down and fumbled in my handbag,
feeling my cheeks flush and heartbeat quicken. I
muted the call, without checking who it was, and
stood up, brushing my hair from my face and trying to
compose myself.

'So sorry.' I cleared my throat. 'So, as I was saying,
at Lonely Hearts Travels we pride ourselves on offering
unique trips to fabulous destinations that will get even
the most broken-hearted guests back on top form.'

I paused to check that I still had a captive audience.
Kelli had a slightly manic smile fixed on her pale
face. The only other woman in the room, bar Kelli
and me, had her piercing green eyes narrowed into
a pinched frown. She'd been the only one to shake
my hand limply and fail to raise a smile during the
introductions. *So much for sisterhood solidarity*, I thought,
nodding at Kelli to press play on the short video she'd
created. It was a montage of clips filmed by various
tour guides showing our guests having the time of
their lives. From a woman laughing and waving in

the back of a colourful tuk-tuk in Bangkok to groups of smiling tour-goers trekking in the lush rainforest of Brazil, from guests practising yoga poses on a beach in India to dancing at a festival in Berlin, all set to a Florence + the Machine song, that uplifting one with lots of clapping; it never failed to give me goosebumps. This sense of pride that I'd started a business that meant something, that these people were getting on with their lives and, often, *changing* their lives because of being on one of our tours really was incredible. With my life being so fast paced, I didn't stop to take in what we'd achieved as often as I probably should. I made a mental note to take a step back before rushing on to the next project in the future.

Just as the crescendo hit and my throat felt clogged with emotion, my phone rang again.

Green-eyed woman coughed loudly and purposefully as the gentleman next to her shifted in his seat in embarrassment for me. I avoided Kelli's eye but sensed her bristle. If the shoe had been on the other foot, I'd be livid too; we'd worked too hard to look unprofessional like this. I scrabbled to the floor and delved my hand in my bag to shut it up. I thought I'd turned the bastard thing onto silent, so why was it still ringing!

My finger was pressing on the off button when I noticed that the persistent caller was Shelley, my best friend and current Australian bridezilla. Why was she calling me? We always pre-arranged our Skype sessions because of the time difference. It must have been the middle of the night there. I pressed decline and was just about to turn my phone off when a text pinged through from her.

'Call me ASAP! Everything ruined!!! Jimmy's gone.'

Jimmy, her fiancé and Ben's best friend, had gone? Gone where?

I stood up and brushed some fluff from my skirt. My bold purple skirt that in a sea of neutrals they'd fail to forget. Stupid *Cosmo*. Stupid skirt. I apologised once more and thanked Kelli for jumping in where I'd left off. I cleared my throat and continued with my pre-rehearsed speech, except I was struggling to concentrate. What did she mean, Jimmy had gone? I knew we'd been chatting before about how stressed she was over the wedding and how some of her ideas were a little – well, a lot – farcical, but this was serious. Super serious. I felt this scratching at the back of my mind as what I refused to believe wouldn't stay restrained. It had happened again. I knew only too well the pain, humiliation and heartache of being jilted, and now it was happening to my best friend.

'Excuse me, do you mind if I just…' I picked up a glass of water from the table in front of me and gulped it back in one, feeling Kelli's confused eyes trained on me. 'Something in my throat,' I laughed lightly, and tried to get back on track with what I was saying.

The rest of the pitch went by without a problem or interruption, and thankfully Kelli took centre stage, doing an excellent job in wrapping it up. I felt like I was going through the motions as I was desperate to get out of this stuffy room and speak to Shelley. It had taken all my concentration to stick to our script, answer their questions and keep my head in the game, when all I could think was how heartbroken and sick I'd felt when my ex-fiancé, Alex, had left me. She must be beside herself.

'Excellent, well, I think we have everything we need for now. We are very keen to get things up and running as soon as possible, so we'll call you tomorrow afternoon with our decision.' The deep, monotone voice of the man opposite pulled me from my thoughts.

'Thank you so much for your time, and apologies again for my phone.' I blushed and shook their hands, giving the green-eyed lady an overly officious smile as Kelli quickly passed out our business cards. I kept that smile fixed rigidly to my face until we were back in the plush corridor waiting to be escorted to reception.

'I'll be two minutes, just nipping to the loo!' I hurriedly told Kelli, before rushing into the bathroom.

I clocked my face in the brightly lit mirrors; all the colour had been washed from my skin and the lipstick that I'd patiently applied, matching lip liner and all, had been absent-mindedly chewed off. I shut the door of one of the stalls, sat on the closed toilet seat and pressed FaceTime; within seconds, Shelley's face filled most of the screen.

'Hey! What's happened?' I garbled, taking in her appearance and feeling that familiar sinking sensation in the pit of my stomach. Dark, heavy bags sagged underneath her bloodshot eyes, stringy strands of dull blonde hair were stuck to her frowning forehead, and a cluster of angry spots lined her chin. Shelley shook her head. That's when I realised that in her sleep-deprived-looking eyes were tears threatening to spill.

Oh God, it was true, Jimmy had left her. The wedding was off. She'd been jilted before her big day, just like I had.

She started to sob loudly.

'Shelley! Oh hun, please stop crying. Tell me what's going on.'

She looked like she hadn't slept in weeks, judging from her ghostly pale skin and the trembling hands that wiped at the snot from the tip of her nose.

'It's...it's...' She grabbed a tissue from somewhere off screen and loudly blew into it. 'It's Jimmy. He's gone.'

A cold chill ran up my spine. 'But why? What's happened? How could he do this to you?'

Shelley shook her head and grabbed another tissue to dab at her eyes, leaving white flakes of Kleenex on her sallow cheeks. 'We've had a row. A huge row!'

They never rowed.

'A row about what?'

'The wedding, yet again.' She tried to catch her breath. 'He told me that he hates the table centres I've picked out and that he really doesn't want us to have a photo booth, even though I told him that this was the *one thing* I wanted.' With that, she was off again, sniffing and wiping her snotty nose.

'Wait.' I paused, trying to understand correctly. 'Table centres and photo booths?' I repeated slowly, just to make sure I'd heard her. These two innocent things were the reason that her patient and loving fiancé had dumped her and called off their wedding? I didn't get it.

'Yes! But that was just the start. I feel like he's not supporting me with the whole thing. I feel so stressed out. I mean just look at me, Georgia. LOOK AT ME!'

I winced and hoped the quality of this call wasn't good enough for her to see my reaction.

'I need about a year of sleep. I've never felt so stressed out before. If it's not wedding planning, it's managing everyone's expectations, treading carefully between the views of his mum and my mum. Oh my God, we've got less than a fortnight to go and there's still so much to do, it's just a complete nightmare!'

I pinched the bridge of my nose, still trying to make sense of it all. 'Hang on – so the wedding is still on?'

She jolted back in her chair, looking confused. 'Of course. Why? You're still coming, aren't you? Oh God, don't tell me there's been a problem with your flight. I knew you should have come out here earlier!' she wailed.

'So where has Jimmy gone? You said that he'd gone?' I asked, through slightly gritted teeth.

'He's gone to see about getting a photo booth, like I asked him to do weeks ago.'

I didn't know whether to laugh or cry. I was desperate to bark that she could have ruined a really important meeting for me, but judging by how on edge she seemed, it wasn't worth it. It wasn't her fault; I was the one who should have turned my phone to silent and not jumped to conclusions, remembering that she'd been struck down with a case of bridezilla-itis meaning rational decisions were few and far between. I sighed and tried to be the supportive best friend, grateful that she hadn't suffered the same fate I had.

'Why don't you just take a break from it all for a bit?' I said soothingly. 'Then we've got our hen-do road trip to look forward to!'

Originally, Shelley had insisted that she didn't need a hen do, despite me reasoning that with all the stress she felt she was under, a night out to let her hair down was *exactly* what she needed. Then one day, out of the blue, she'd announced that she wanted us to go on a road trip. She'd suggested starting in Melbourne and ending in Adelaide. We'd take a few days to drive up the coast, stopping at cool little beaches and quaint coastal towns as a sort of hen-do/pre-wedding relax time. She was then further insistent that she would plan out the exact route, ignoring my offer to help.

'It can't come soon enough.' She'd caught her breath now and seemed a lot brighter as she was back on her favourite topic of conversation.

'You know, I really wish you'd let me help you organise that; you need to let others in to take some of the burden off you doing it all.'

She wafted her hand at the screen. 'It made sense for me to plan the route, being an Aussie and all, plus Cara has helped.' Cara was a wannabe pro-wedding planner by the sounds of it. She was only trying to help, but whenever I'd mentioned ideas they never seemed to be as good as her suggestions. 'I'm leaving the fun festivities up to you though!'

'Don't you worry about that.' I'd already stocked up on everything and anything penis-shaped as hen-do props.

'God, Georgia, there's *so* much to do and so little time to do it.' She shook her head skywards, as if hoping for divine intervention to help her with making favours and finalising seating plans.

'Well, maybe explain to Jimmy how much you'd appreciate his help. A job shared is a job halved, or whatever that saying is?'

She sniffed. 'He is good, well, most of the time.' She plastered on a smile that was more like the Shelley I knew. 'Sorry, Georgia, for just unloading then!'

I smiled kindly, hoping that her mini freak-out hadn't messed up our pitch. 'Hey, that's what I'm here for.'

'Well, I appreciate it. I can't bloody wait to see you. Listen, I'd better go and try and get more sleep like you suggested. Speak soon!'

With that she hung up, leaving me looking into the black of my phone screen, wondering how I was going to get through Planet Wedding once I got over there.

CHAPTER 3

Temerity (n.) – Excessive confidence or boldness

'Ah, here she is!' Conrad smiled as the bell dinged my arrival into my small but beautiful travel tour agency in Manchester. 'I wasn't expecting to see you today; thought you'd be out celebrating still. I heard your pitch went really bloody well.'

'News travels fast then.' I grinned. 'I'm just waiting for their call with the final answer, but I was going mad trying to work from home, surrounded by all our boxes. Plus, I feel like I'm hardly ever in this store nowadays.'

'And I thought you were only here for my rugged good looks.' He acted mock-offended. 'Speaking of ugly men, Ben not around to entertain you?'

I shook my head. 'He's in the London office today, overseeing a recruitment drive.'

'Didn't he just get back from Finland?'

'You know there's no rest for the wicked.'

'Then you both must have been terrible in a past life.'

'Maybe next time I'll be reincarnated as a pampered house cat or something, but right now there's too much to do, so sleep can wait.' I smiled at him and shrugged off my jacket. 'I'm guessing you've spoken to Kelli then?'

He shook his head. 'I doubt she's surfaced yet, judging by the photos she was tagged in on Facebook in some very swanky-looking wine bar quaffing on champagne last night. I figured she was out toasting your success.'

'Well, technically we still haven't got it all signed off.' I hoped we weren't all getting carried away with ourselves. 'Their decision should be coming through any moment now.' I pulled my phone from my bag and checked I hadn't missed any calls since I last looked, three minutes ago.

'Pfft,' Conrad blew out through his lips. 'I read the pitch, remember. Solid gold.'

'Let's hope they think so too.' Why was I doubting myself this morning? We had this in the bag. 'Anyway, there's nothing that a strong cup of coffee won't fix.'

'I guess I'd better stick the kettle on then, shall I?'

'You superstar.'

The Manchester store had flourished in the hands of Conrad, a brusque but brilliant Yorkshire man who had taken to our company like a duck to water. Having him on board meant less stress for me, though I did miss the old days of us all squished into this room, as well as the daily banter, office gossip and the camaraderie that came with it. Because we had expanded so rapidly, Ben and I had hired Felix to oversee the day-to-day running of the London store; he was perfectly lovely and still learning the ropes, but in my opinion lacked the charm and likeability that Conrad had in bagfuls. Flitting between the two places, as well as trips away, networking events, conferences and everything else that filled my hectic diary, it was the people I missed the most.

'I've got everything crossed, not that I need to. I just know that this is what we've been waiting for.' He gave a knowing smile and generously poured coffee granules into matching mugs. Since the start of the year we'd been obsessing over what the business was missing, this spark of an idea, a revelation, an X-factor decision that would push us further than our competitors. 'Lord knows we need something, as yesterday's meet-up was *not* our answer.'

'Oh, what happened?' I asked, flicking through my diary to check that I had time for a quick catch-up before my next call, which Erin had set up. Realising I had an unexpected free half an hour, I settled onto the comfy sofa next to the bookcase, stacked with glossy brochures advertising exotic destinations and trips that we offered.

'Well, I mean, we had a few new clients interested, but most of them just wanted to eat Val's cakes and nick a few of our pens,' he grumbled.

'Maybe it will be one of those things that takes a little time to pick up?' I offered, sensing how disappointed he was that his latest idea hadn't taken off exactly as planned. Conrad was always coming up with ways we could increase our client base and spread the word about what we do, from holding Thai cooking classes to promote our Southeast Asia trips, which ended in two people getting food poisoning, to an outside Australian barbecue that fell victim to the unpredictable Manchester weather.

'Hmm, maybe. I think we'll have to shelve the "pin the tail on the llama" game for the Chile trip – almost took a poor lassie's eye out,' he confessed, cringing. 'But, I'll keep trying. You know the sales figures speak for themselves, but I can't help thinking there's something that we're missing out on,' Conrad said, as he poured in milk, his face growing serious for a moment. 'I haven't quite put my finger on what it is yet, but I've been sending my spies into our rivals' businesses and hopefully they'll be back with ideas.

I just have this sense that there's some trick we're missing, something we could offer our customers that would knock the competition out of the park.'

He was right. As great as our reviews were, the profits healthy and customers going home happy, I often had this niggle in my head too. To keep moving the company forward, we needed to make sure we moved with the times and offered over and above what other travel agents or tour companies did.

'Well, we can only keep trying.' I gratefully took the steaming mug he handed me.

'Aye, that we will do.'

I glanced around the small room as Conrad picked up his ringing phone and smiled. In the corner, they'd set up a snack station for customers with hot drinks and complimentary cookies, which came from Val's café over the road. This had gone down well, but it wasn't like a free slice of banana bread or homemade Eccles cake was going to be the trailblazing idea we'd imagined.

'So, how are things with the lovely Val?' I asked, absent-mindedly picking up a cookie and breaking a piece of buttery biscuit off as he got off the phone. 'She could put Mary Berry to shame.'

His ruddy cheeks broke into a wide grin at the sound of her name. 'Well, it's not gone tits up between us yet.'

I laughed. 'And I'm sure it won't either. Tell her from me that she makes the best cakes in town; in fact, I'm surprised you've not put on ten stone since meeting her.' I brushed crumbs off my shirt.

It was probably for the best that the snack station hadn't been implemented when I'd worked in this shop full time. With this much temptation in my way, there'd be nothing left for the customers. I tried not to think about how snug my work clothes had got since Ben and I had moved in together. There was something about the comfort of being in a happy relationship, eating a lot more takeaways, not wanting to leave the warm bed for an early morning run, and sharing a bottle of wine most evenings, that was a hell of a lot of fun but did nothing for your figure. Sexercise only burnt a fraction of the calories I was indulging in.

'Keep it to yourself, but I've started this new fitness regime.' He leant forward, dropping his voice to a whisper, even though we were the only ones in the shop. 'She's had me join a gym.'

'You? At a gym? I never thought I'd see the day!'

'Mock all you want, but it's the only way I don't balloon. Anyway, that's not the worst part.' He lowered his voice even more. 'She's got me taking a few evening classes.'

'Oh yeah? Like what?'

He grimaced, as if locked in a mental disagreement over whether to tell me or not. 'Dancing.' He sat back in his chair, waiting for my reaction. I couldn't help but let a giggle escape at the thought of Conrad pirouetting in a fetching pink tutu; he ignored me and carried on. 'Well, first it was Zumba, then it was this salsa beat workout, and now it's sodding ballroom with a twist.'

'Ballroom with a *twist*?' I repeated, quite enjoying the blush rising on his face.

'Yep. The twist is that you break into this flaming difficult hip-hop routine midway through.'

I couldn't help but let a snigger escape. 'Hip-hop? You do hip-hop?'

'Don't.' He placed his reddened cheeks into his large hands. 'I've not told anyone else and I'm making you swear that you won't either.'

I held up my fingers in a Brownie Guide salute as he continued.

'You know those YouTube videos of couples, usually a bride and groom on their first dance, who start off all formal and then the music changes halfway through to some irritating dance song, and they perform this well-rehearsed but bloody ridiculous routine?'

I nodded, my cheeks aching from smiling.

'*That*'s ballroom with a twist.'

'Oh, wow. So, you going to show us a move then?'

'Don't hold your breath. I only agreed to it to make her happy. The things you do for love.' He grunted and began shuffling through some brochures on his cluttered desk.

'Love?' I raised an eyebrow.

'Yeah, I love her,' he mumbled. I had the urge to start clapping but kept my emotions in check. Conrad wasn't usually this forthcoming with his personal life so I didn't want to stop his flow. 'Lord knows why she puts up with me, and trust me there's nothing I wouldn't do to keep her happy. But flaming dance classes?' He shook his head at what he had become. 'Seriously.'

'Well, I think it sounds adorable, and don't be putting yourself down. You're a catch; she's lucky to have you in her life too.'

He shrugged and cleared his throat. 'So, back to you, I still can't believe you and Ben are finally taking a holiday. He's promised me that you'll both turn your work phones off and step away from your emails.'

'Nice subject change. Don't expect me to forget that you owe me a dance at the Christmas party,' I teased and took a slurp of my coffee, double-checking my phone again for when the bank called. 'I'm not sure how much of a holiday it will be with helping Shelley out, but I am looking forward to ticking Australia off my list and spending time with Ben.'

'Your first trip down under! Be prepared for the jet lag as it can be a bit of a killer, you know. Why don't you ask Shelley to delay the trip for a few days so you can adjust?'

I shook my head. 'No way. I don't want to do anything to make her already dangerously high anxiety levels rocket even more. I'm sure I'll be fine.'

'You're just going to have to have a coffee drip inserted in your arm and be prepared to ride the jet lag waves more like.'

'Oh come on, it's not that bad, is it?' I'd taken enough long-haul flights by now to realise he was overreacting.

Conrad raised his bushy eyebrows. 'You've never done the London–Australia route before. I know you think you may be superwoman at times, but, trust me, that can really mess your head up.'

I dismissed his scaremongering and flicked my head back to my laptop screen. 'I'll be fine, really.'

'Well, good luck. I just hope I won't be saying I told you so when you're feeling like a zombie for your first few days.'

'I'll be *fine*,' I repeated. 'Anyway, even if I do, there is no way I'd tell you and give you the satisfaction of saying I told you so!' I teased, and ducked when he flicked a paper clip at me.

'We'll see; also, unless you've changed your phone screen to a topless photo of Ben, you need to stop checking that phone of yours.' He nodded, as I glanced at my mobile phone, again.

'I know. I'm just…Don't tell anyone…but I'm just a little nervous. They said they'd be calling us today and, judging by how they spoke yesterday at the pitch, I thought I would have heard first thing.'

'They're probably telling everyone else they didn't make the grade and saving the good news for last.' He shrugged just as a customer walked in who he then went to help.

Suddenly, my phone chirruped to life, making me jump and Conrad spin his head over to the noise. *Oh God, oh God, oh God. Here goes!*

'Georgia Green speaking,' I said in my most professional phone voice.

'Georgia, you're there!' The harassed-sounding voice of my best friend Marie rushed down the line. 'I called your London office and Erin said you were in Manchester. I'm not interrupting some super-fancy important meeting or something, am I? Can you talk?'

'Marie, slow down, is everything okay?'

I could hear banging in the background and some irritatingly high-pitched nursery rhyme, probably coming from the TV.

'No!' she said in a gulp of what sounded like tears.

Before I could ask another question, she'd turned her mouth from the phone and began telling off her son, Cole, for not sharing with his sister.

'Marie?'

'Oh, Georgia. I am *so* sorry to have to do this but I need your help.'

'Sure what's happened?' I flicked my eyes off my emails and focused on her breathless, anxious voice, bracing myself for the worst.

'I really, *really* don't want to have to ask you as I know how busy you are. Trust me, I've tried every other option but I'm desperate.' She let out a chirp of a laugh that fell flat. I tried not to take offence.

'Are you okay? Are the kids okay?'

'*Cole. Give that to your sister!*' she barked distractedly. 'Yeah, they're fine. It's just, I need you to watch them. I've got to be at this audition and Mike's mum was going to have them but she's not well and then the childminder we sometimes use is booked up and...'

Marie was a part-time actress slash hairdresser, always waiting for the big break that never seemed to come. Before her daughter Lily was born she had been going to quite a few auditions, and had mentioned contacts who were hoping to break her into the big time, but it had all gone very quiet since then.

'Is that it?' I let out the breath I hadn't realised I'd been holding and laughed lightly. 'Of course I can look after them.'

'Really? Are you sure?' She sounded surprised, which hurt a little. I hadn't been that bad in helping her out with her children, had I?

''Course! I love spending time with them.' I heard her breathe a sigh of relief as I flicked open my diary and ran my finger down the packed pages. 'So, when do you need me? Remember, I'm off to Australia in two days, but I can look for a day when we get back?'

There was a brief pause. 'No, Georgia. I need you now, like right now.'

'Now? Oh,' I stuttered. 'It's just I've got this call to tell me about this deal and...' Everything else on my list could be rearranged with Erin's help but this, this was a biggie.

Marie picked up on my apprehension. 'You know I wouldn't normally ask at such late notice but I can't cancel. Please, Georgia.' The desperation in her quiet voice was painful to hear.

I sat up in my seat. What was I doing even hesitating? I didn't have to choose between helping out my oldest friend in her hour of need and signing off this deal, I could manage both.

''Course. I'll grab a taxi over right now.'

'Thank you!' She sighed with relief. 'I *really* owe you one.'

I hung up and turned off my laptop, feeling Conrad's eyes on me as he made a hot drink for the customer who was sitting at his desk, flicking through the Moroccan brochure.

'I'm just heading out for a bit.'

'Wait – what about the call?'

'Don't worry. Will you just drop Erin a line telling her to cancel my afternoon meetings? I won't be long!'

I just had to entertain two small children *and* do my job. It couldn't be that hard; people on TV did it all the time. In fact, they made it look easy. I could so handle this.

CHAPTER 4

Incongruous (adj.) – Lacking in harmony; incompatible

I sucked in a short, sharp breath as I saw what looked like blood staining my wrist. *How the?* I hadn't felt a thing, more preoccupied with covering my head as I body-rolled across the ground to safety, shielding my vulnerable frame from yet more attacks. I swear it felt like they were growing in numbers. My heartbeat thrummed in my ears, my voice sounded strangled as I pleaded for them to let me go, to show some sort of compassion, to realise that I was at their mercy – only, my cries fell on deaf ears. I sniffed and tried to keep my emotions in check. This wouldn't go on for ever, the end had to be in sight soon. Then again, what had I expected? It wasn't like they were going to calmly sit down and discuss our issues over a nice cup of tea.

And then, as quickly as it had started, it stopped. Only this time the silence was deafening. I wasn't sure what was worse – the relentless barrage of flying missiles or not knowing what was coming next. What were they planning? I'd never heard it so quiet in here. Blood rushed to my head and I dared to peek out from my hiding place. They knew I was here, so why didn't they advance and try to capture me to put me out of this nightmare?

Calm down, Georgia, you can't let them win, I scolded myself, desperate to get some sort of control over this situation I'd found myself in. I needed to think straight and use my brain to try to come up with an escape plan. They would be getting tired soon, surely; that had to be to my advantage. I hadn't exhausted myself the way they had. *How had today led to this?*

I rubbed at the dark, crimson mark on my wrist, which instantly slicked to my fingers, tensing my body and preparing to wince at the pain an open wound would bring. But there was nothing. My skin was perfectly intact under the thickened gloop of what looked like blood.

The smell of strawberry jam hit my nostrils at the exact moment the attack started again, with more force and vigour than before. But I wasn't taking it any longer. I rolled to my feet and stood tall, emitting a roar that bellowed from the depths of my stomach. The movement shocked them into silence for a moment before a petrified wail filled the air. *Oh balls.*

'Shush, it's all right. Just Aunty Georgia being silly!' I pleaded, as I leapt over the back of the sofa that had been my base camp. One of my captors was now crying, with the other on the verge of tears. *Nice one, Georgia.*

'Don't cry.' I scooped up Lily, whose tiny face had crumpled in on itself. Her small shoulders juddered with heart-wrenching sobs.

'You made Liwy cry! I'm telling Mummy of you!' Cole pouted, then threw a stuffed elephant at my feet for good measure as I cradled his younger sister, feeling her warm soft skin touch my jam-stained arms.

'No, no. Don't tell Mummy. We were just playing a game, remember? You were protecting her from the monster. Remember?' My voice was in that irritating sing-song style that people seem to use when speaking to small dogs, gurgling babies or bartering with sullen toddlers.

I knelt down to his height and awkwardly shifted his sister to one hip. She was still crying, but it was more of a grizzly moan than the full-on sobs from a few moments ago. Cole jutted out his tummy and put his hands on his hips. I realised that he had pen marks down one arm and something crusty clinging to his royal blue t-shirt that I swore wasn't there when Marie left us in a whirl of nerves for her audition earlier.

'You made Liwy cry,' he repeated, his young face stern as he struggled to pronounce his sister's name through gapped teeth. 'Mummy says I'm in twouble when I make her cry so you are too.'

'Well, actually if you think about it, you were invading *my* camp and I…' I trailed off, realising that you can't rationalise with a small person, especially over the game of monster warfare, as all my other efforts at entertaining them had failed spectacularly. 'I'm sorry. You're right,' I admitted, getting to my feet and hoisting his sister into a more comfortable position. 'Now then, who's for a snack?'

Cole tilted his head to one side, working out if my promise of sweet treats was genuine or not. I'd already succumbed to opening one pack of rich tea biscuits and I wasn't entirely sure if Lily was old enough to eat them, but she'd grabbed some in her chubby hand and stuffed them in her mouth before I could protest.

'I want four biscuits 'cause I'm nearly four.' He jutted his lower lip out and eyeballed me. This was clearly non-negotiable. I nodded with a deep sigh. 'But I'm still telling Mummy of you!' he shrieked, and raced off to the kitchen, knocking over a side table along with the plastic cup of juice that had been sitting on it.

'Crap.' I put Lily down on the rug and tended to the sticky orange juice puddling across the wooden floor.

'Ommm! You said a bad word!' Cole peeked his head back around the door frame. Was he holding a jar of Nutella?

'No, I said, cr—' I couldn't think of a child-friendly substitute word as Lily had started wailing again. Spinning around, I saw that she had her fingers trapped in a set of chubby plastic keys. Lord knows how she'd managed to do that. 'God damn it,' I muttered and left one task for another.

'You said a bad word. You said a bad word!' Cole sang, running around and spreading garishly bright orange footprints across the messy room. He was still clutching the jar of chocolate spread that looked dangerously precarious in his skinny arms.

'Cole, can you put that down, please. Lily, don't cry, it's okay!' I didn't know which child to attend to first. The orange juice was inching closer to my shoes but that mess just had to wait. I eased her fingers from the toy – I thought these things were made for children – and picked her up again, before running a tea towel over the worst of the fruity mess on the floor with my right foot, while simultaneously calling for Cole to stand still so I could wipe his feet. He ignored me and clambered onto the fort, sorry, sofa. Why in God's name did Marie have a beige sofa with two young children and, more to the point, how had she managed to keep it so clean?

When she'd left for her audition, Lily had been fast asleep and Cole quietly sitting at the miniature-sized table patiently colouring in. The whole scene had been calm, serene, and a world away from the chaos I found myself embroiled in right now. I glanced down at my watch, trying to work out how much time I had to turn this situation around and get the house back to the same state it had been in when I'd arrived. But I had no idea what time it was as I'd left my watch in the bathroom when I'd tried to rinse felt tip pen from the strap without success. I felt exhausted. My voice was hoarse from pleading with the youngsters, my arms were stained in syrupy jam from a previous snack attack, my hair had frizzed up with the heat of racing around after them both and my stomach gurgled for something to eat, a cup of non-tepid tea or even a bottle of wine.

The muffled ringing of my mobile phone coming from somewhere unidentifiable began playing its tune.

Shit! In the chaos of controlling two small humans, the call from the bank had completely slipped my mind. I hurriedly scanned my eyes over the mess of the room, trying to locate where my sodding phone had been buried.

'Cole, if you can find Aunty Georgia's phone you can have five biscuits.' His eyes lit up as he worked out that five was more than four, and he began flinging cushions off the messy sofa, following the chirping sound.

Oh God, where was it? I couldn't miss this call.

'Here! I win!' he boasted, holding up my phone.

'Excellent.' I took it off him and pressed connect. 'Hello, Georgia Green speaking.'

'Ah, Miss Green, it's Simon here, we met yesterday?'

'Yes! Hello, thanks for calling me. It's great to hear from you—'

Cole was tugging at my top. 'Biscuits. You said more biscuits.'

'Yes, yes, in a minute,' I loudly whispered to Cole and turned my back on him. 'Sorry, Simon, not you. Right, I'm all ears.'

'Well, we all enjoyed your pitch and believe that Lonely Hearts Travels is a very unique and interesting opportunity, but we have a few, erm, let's say concerns.'

My heart and stomach both dropped.

'Concerns? Really?' My voice had gone all high-pitched and funny.

'Biscuits!' Cole began stomping his feet.

'Cole, just one moment – yep, sorry about this, Simon, I just need to—' I snapped. What concerns could they possibly have?

'BISCUITS NOW!' Cole roared.

For the love of God. 'Cole, please. I'm on the phone, just wait a minute,' I barked, then plastered on a smile that Simon couldn't see. 'Simon, I am so sorry about this, things are a little hectic my end. What was it you were saying? Some concerns you have?'

Simon cleared his throat. 'Well, one of them is that we're worried we won't receive your full attention, as you clearly have an awful lot going on and...'

Ah, balls. First my phone interrupts the pitch and now I'm engaged in biscuit bartering with an impatient toddler. I can see how bad this looks.

'Well, I will stop you there as I can one hundred per cent promise that if we were to receive your generous investment we would be committed to ensuring that you have our utmost attention and...'

I clasped my hand over the receiver and loudly hissed at Cole to let go of my leg. He thought it was hilarious and gripped on tighter.

'Miss Green?'

I tried to angle my body away from the excitable toddler currently using my thigh as a climbing frame and focus on what I was saying.

'And…and we will make sure that you feel involved every step of the waaaaaaaaay!' Cole had used all his weight to leverage his body onto my leg, causing shooting pains of cramp to seize up my thigh. Cole found this hilarious. Simon did not.

'I think this call has only reinforced our concerns, so I am sorry to inform you that we will not be taking your application any further. I'll let you get on to whatever it is that you are occupied with. Thank you for your time.' He hung up.

We'd lost the pitch. That investment had slipped through our fingers. I felt numb. To top it off, Lily was now crying for some unknown reason, Cole was dancing on the crumpled cushions, my leg was in agony and, at the exact time when I realised he had somehow opened the jar of Nutella and had thrust a pudgy palm into the thick spread, the front door swung open.

CHAPTER 5

Chagrin (n.) – A feeling of mental unease; annoyance; embarrassment caused by failure

'What the...?' Marie was standing open-mouthed at the mess of her usually pristine front room, her smallest child screaming (I'm sure she notched up the volume just for extra effect), her oldest smearing chocolate spread on the sofa, and sticky orange juice puddling at her feet.

'Uh oh,' Cole whispered.

'Cole! Get off that sofa this instant. What on earth are you doing with *this*?' Marie pulled him to stand in front of her so she could scold him.

'You're back! How did it go?' I asked, hoping to divert her attention from what a terrible job I'd done both here and in my professional life. Ben and Kelli were going to be crushed when I told them about the bank's decision.

'Fine. I didn't get it,' she mumbled, and grabbed the jar of Nutella from her son.

'What? Oh, I'm sorry. I was sure you had it in the bag.'

Marie shrugged dejectedly. 'Nope. Apparently not. It's fine, it was silly of me to go in the first place. I'm obviously not what they were looking for, what any casting director appears to be looking for.' She tugged at her hair, pulling it out of its previously neat style and messily piling it on her head.

'Well, there'll be other auditions—'

'Cole!' Marie barked, ignoring me. 'What have I told you about eating between meals? You know that this is not for you.'

'I'm so sorry. I hadn't realised he'd picked it up or even knew how to open it. I don't know how you do it, Marie!' I laughed weakly, hurrying to chuck toys into a large wicker basket as she went to pick up Lily in one smooth and effortless move. She had thankfully stopped crying, but, judging by her wavering bottom lip, a repeat of the waterworks could happen at any second. Marie continued to berate Cole as she marched him out of the bombsite to wash his hands. I hastily cleaned up as much of the debris from our play fight as I could and straightened up the seat cushions, hoping that a quick flash of cleaning spray would get those jam and Nutella stains off, before my shoulders sank once more.

'Oh my God. What's happened in here!' I heard her cry from the kitchen.

I winced. I'd had the bright idea of making cupcakes, but it turned out neither of the children had the patience to calmly bake a surprise for Mummy. Instead, I'd burnt the mixture, as Lily had done an explosive poo in her nappy that had needed urgent attention; I'd had to wrestle an egg whisk from Cole and spilled icing sugar on every visible work surface as the bag burst in my hands. Judging from the noises Marie was making, I hadn't done the best job in cleaning them all up.

'Oh, we did some baking, didn't we?' I said, still in that irritating sing-a-long style as I rushed into the kitchen. She was right to have a face like thunder. It looked like the place had been ransacked and dusted with cocaine.

'Has Lily been eating this?' Marie asked, shaking an empty packet of sweets at me. I nodded, feeling my cheeks flame exactly like Cole's did. I'd intended to use them for the cupcake decoration, but they'd vanished before I'd managed to save any. 'Georgia, she's *way* too young for this!'

She gave me such a horrified look, as if I'd told her we had all been dancing with flaming knives. I felt Cole flick his head between the two of us; Lily was swiping her hand over the icing sugar and sticking her powdered fingers into her open mouth.

'Oh. Sorry. I, erm, I didn't know,' I sheepishly admitted.

'Mummy, she made Liwy cry too!' Cole piped up. It was my turn to deliver the death stare. He poked his tongue out and ran behind his mum's legs.

'Well, no, I…it was a game—' I made a mental note to give Cole a shite birthday present for being such a tattle tale.

'Crap, crap, crap, crap, crap!' Cole sang, in between banging one of the kitchen cupboard doors, the noise making Lily giggle.

Marie flew her head to her boisterous son. 'What did you say?'

Oh balls.

'Crap, crap, crap,' he continued to sing, banging more doors, making Lily laugh louder. The noise was giving me the mother of all headaches.

'Shit! I'm sorry,' I apologised, then clasped my hand over my mouth. What was wrong with me? 'It's not been the best of days, to be honest.'

Marie let out a deep sigh. 'Cole, stop that.' Cole nodded solemnly and slammed the door for one last time before receiving a look from his mum. 'Now, go and pick up your toys from the lounge before Daddy comes home.'

'I'm so sorry for the mess and my inability to censor myself. I honestly have no idea how you cope looking after them Every. Single. Bloody. Day.' I shook my head in amazement, only now noticing her painted lips and flick of eyeliner. It was a surprise to see her wearing make-up again. My once constantly glam best friend had slowly morphed into more of a wash-and-go girl. I'd forgotten how well she scrubbed up. Her fiery, long, red hair was freshly washed and glossy and the patterned top she was wearing accentuated her slim waist and toned arms. Probably from hours of carrying her baby girl around.

'Don't worry, it's my fault. I should have told you that he's at the stage where everything and anything you say will be repeated. Last week he thought it was hilarious to shout out "wee wee farty bum" numerous times in the freezer section of Aldi.' Marie rubbed her face, smearing her make-up. 'Hopefully he'll forget about it soon.'

Cole hesitated for a moment then pottered off, making truck noises and running a wooden bus over the walls as he went, loudly shouting, 'NO,' with every heavy step he took.

'He's more and more like you every day,' I mused, catching Marie roll her eyes.

'Don't. I may be stubborn, but he takes it to a whole new level. He's a terror, but you can't help but love him.' She followed her surly son with a look of fondness that dispelled how irritated she had been a second ago. She gently lowered Lily into her high chair, strapped her in and handed her a rusk to eat. 'Cole's going through a stage; well, that's what everyone keeps telling me. I didn't realise how hard it would be with two of them though. Luckily, Mike is amazing and pulls his weight, unlike a lot of the partners of the NCT mums I know.'

I nodded and made what I hoped were the right sort of noises, as if I had the faintest idea what NCT stood for.

'They can be a handful but it's all worth it.' She smiled adoringly at her daughter. 'Thank you so much for looking after them. Don't worry about the mess; it's part and parcel of parenting.'

I got up to fix us mugs of tea. 'Any time,' I replied, crossing my fingers that the next time would be when they were in their teens.

'What did you mean when you said it had been a bad day?'

I shook my head, focusing on a crusty piece of cake mixture that had made its way onto the kettle.

'Georgia? You all right?'

'Yep.' I plastered on a smile. 'Well, not really.' I sighed and plopped squashed tea bags into the bin. 'I just found out that we've lost out on this really important business deal. A deal that I was in charge of and had been so sure we'd get.' I picked up one of Lily's baby toys, running my fingers between the soft ears of the pink, stuffed rabbit. 'We'd worked so hard on the presentation and they seemed to love what we do, but apparently it wasn't enough.' I felt a bubble of sick rise in my throat thinking of how I was going to break the news to the team.

'That makes two of us not doing a great job today.'

'There'll be other auditions, hun.'

'It's over, Georgia. I shouldn't have gone in the first place. Who do I think I am, chasing some dream that's so far out of my reach? I need to realise that *this* is my job now.' She nodded at her baby girl, who had somehow managed to get the lurid orange paste Marie was feeding her all over her face and in her soft, downy hair. 'You've seen what it's like looking after them; it's hard work but I do love it, and I love them. I mean, just look at how far we've both come! You with your super-fantastic business, me with these two little rascals. Why can't I be happy with what I've got? Why do I have to chase some pipe dream?'

'You can't just give up though!' I turned around, not buying what she was saying. 'You're an excellent actress!'

'I can and I am, at least until they are a little older.' She nodded determinedly. 'But, thanks for watching them anyway. Waiting in the audition room with girls a lot slimmer, younger and hungrier than I am for the role, helped me to see that I'm tired of the auditions and the disappointments. I should be focused on my real job here.'

'I promise I'll be here to watch them for the next audition,' I said firmly, ignoring her change of heart. She was too good to give up. 'Just with less baking and less Nutella.'

'We'll see; anyway, try not to be too down-hearted about your deal. You'll find something bigger and better than that. I'm sure of it.' She gently patted my arm before Lily noisily filled her nappy. 'She doesn't seem to be having any trouble digesting those biscuits you gave her!' Marie laughed and scooped her daughter up.

*

By the time I arrived home I felt wrung out. My hands were sticky, my head was banging, and melted chocolate buttons were smeared over my new top, which I'd worn thinking my day would be spent celebrating our win, not playing referee between two under-fours.

'Hey, babe, how was your day?' Ben called from the bedroom. I wandered in to see him sitting on the floor, surrounded by boxes and the contents of his chest of drawers. Clothes were strewn everywhere.

'Hey,' I said, brushing off icing sugar from my jacket and picking at a dubious crusty stain on my black trousers.

'Jeezus, what's happened to you?' He flicked his head up and pulled a face at the smell of sweat and defeat clouding around me.

'Toddlers and babies is what happened.' I tried to make my way over to him without breaking my ankle on the stacks of books or the leaning tower of video-game boxes that blocked my path.

'You what?'

'Marie had a babysitting crisis so I said I'd watch Cole and Lily for her.' I saw Ben raise an eyebrow from the corner of my eye.

'So, you weren't at the office for the debrief call?'

I purposely ignored him. 'Seriously, it was like a war zone.' I shivered as flashbacks of nappy bags and tepid tea came rushing back. 'I honestly don't know how she does it. Although Cole was pretty cute just as I was leaving; he'd drawn this picture of us on an aeroplane. Future artist in the making, that one.' I let out a yawn and grumbled at the state of our room. Flopping on the bed would have to wait. 'I'll make a start on dinner.'

I padded to the kitchen and opened the fridge, then pulled out a chilled bottle of white wine.

'You want one?' I asked Ben, as he wandered in behind me.

'I'll pass, thanks. Seeing how traumatised you're acting, neither do you!'

'What?' I looked up, confused. 'I meant wine; do you want a glass of wine?'

'Oh, erm yeah,' he mumbled sheepishly. 'Go on then.'

I poured large slugs of Sauvignon Blanc into two glasses, trying not to spill a drop, and took a long sip, feeling it relaxing me as soon as the tang of grapes hit my throat.

'So, apart from watching those two, how was your day?'

I turned and opened up a cupboard, pretending to be searching for something to cook for dinner. 'Oh, fine.'

'I've been waiting for your call. The final decision on the investment was today, wasn't it?' I could sense the excitement in his voice. 'You nailed it, didn't you? I knew you would!'

I swallowed down the acidic bubble of bile that had leapt up my throat. I'd been so full of confidence that we had it in the bag when I'd left the meeting. Why did I have to jump the gun like that?

'Georgia?' He pushed, waiting for my answer, his face growing more concerned as he took in my expression.

I shook my head slowly, hoping the words would form. They didn't.

'What? We didn't get it?'

'No,' I squeaked, as a bag of pasta shells tumbled from the shelf and burst over the floor. 'Crap.'

He slapped his palm against the kitchen counter, making me jump. 'Sorry. It's just...it's just you sounded so sure, that it was a done deal. Our presentation was watertight. I don't understand what went wrong? Did they give you any explanation when they called?'

Looks like it wasn't just me who'd been spending the investment cash in our head before we'd got our hands on it. I bent down and started scooping up dried pasta from the floor.

'They just chose to go with someone else.' I didn't want to say that I'd had a toddler clambering on my leg at the time of the important business call, or that my head wasn't in the game in the pitch thanks to Shelley's confusing and panicked text. I didn't want him to blame Shelley or Marie for the distractions. I needed to take the blame; I should have had my phone on silent; I should have let their call go to voicemail; I should have said no to Marie. Who did I think I was, expecting to be a professional businesswoman whilst playing mum to two small children? I should have done all of this, but I didn't. I got to my feet and dejectedly tipped the broken pasta into the bin.

'Don't worry, there'll be something else. Something bigger that we can get on board with,' I said, hoping I sounded confident, ignoring the fact that this meant a huge loss both personally and to the business. We'd stupidly been counting on that money.

Ben closed his eyes and pressed his fingers to his temples, letting out a deep sigh. 'I hope you're right, Georgia.'

CHAPTER 6

Odious (adj.) – Extremely unpleasant; repulsive

I let the familiar thrum of the busy airport wash over me as I padded through the check-in hall, narrowly sidestepping floor polishers and rows of trolleys. I felt a funny pang in my chest as I walked past amorous couples kissing goodbye. Forget the arrivals hall scene from *Love Actually*, saying farewell to your loved ones was just as emosh. Ben was late for a breakfast meeting, so our own goodbye was more of a peck on the cheek as he rushed out the door than a heartfelt profession of love. I'd tried not to feel too disappointed he couldn't see me off at the airport, I knew that I'd see him soon, but a small part of me felt like he was still sulking over us losing the investment, probably thinking that he could have done a better job if he'd been there. I shook away these negative emotions and made my way through security, deciding to treat myself to a new perfume in duty free to cheer myself up and get into holiday mode.

I wasn't nervous about the long flight that loomed ahead of me; the fact that I was going to be travelling for the next twenty-four hours on my own actually filled me with excitement at having some well-deserved me-time. My out-of-office was on, I'd filled my e-reader up with beach reads, loaded up my iPod, and found this mini travel facial kit that the beauty pages of a magazine Kelli had been reading raved about.

I plodded patiently down the aisles of the plane, waiting for others to faff around with squeezing their bags in the overhead lockers ahead of me. A queue had blocked the path to my seat as the couple in front decided that this would be the perfect moment to have a detailed debate with their travel partners over who should take the window seat before taking off layers and bundling up jackets into the lockers.

I eventually got to my row, where a middle-aged woman wearing a hijab was ensconced in the window seat, rabbiting on a mobile phone in a language that I didn't understand or recognise. The middle seat was empty and, in my seat – the aisle seat – sat an overweight man who looked about late thirties. The type who would linger around the buffet table at a party and who shopped at Big and Mighty; his fleshy rolls hung over the armrests like uncooked pastry on a pie tin.

'Oh, excuse me. I think you're in my seat,' I said to him politely, noticing flakes of eczema around his scrunched-up, piggy eyes.

He creased up his round, bowling-ball-shaped face into a look of disgust that I'd deigned to pull his attention from the inflight entertainment channels.

'What? *This* is 24C.' He said this as a statement rather than a question. '*My* seat is 24C.'

He had one of those nasally voices that grated on you with every heavily articulated syllable. I hastily looked at my boarding card, even though I'd memorised it enough times in the wait to board. 'Yep, that's 24C but 24C is actually *my* seat.' I flashed him my card to prove that I wasn't lying.

'Well, that's just great. Great,' he said through gritted teeth, glaring at me as if I'd been in charge of the flight seating plan and messed up on purpose just to piss him off and ruin his day.

I flashed him an apologetic shrug as I waited for him to swap seats. He huffed loudly but still didn't make any effort to move and let me sit down, leaving me standing like a lemon. Passengers began tutting behind me now that *I* was the one blocking the aisle. I felt my cheeks heat up as I appeared to be in a stare-off with this flaky lump of lard.

'Everything okay here?' A pretty blonde-haired flight attendant with a crispy high quiff fluttered over, flashing us both megawatt smiles on her expertly contoured face.

'Oh, erm, well, I think this gentleman is in my seat.' I hurriedly passed her my ticket.

She flicked her camel-length eyelashes at my boarding card and looked at the seat blocker. 'Sir, this lady is correct. Do you have your boarding card so I can check where your seat is?' she asked, filling my nose with a heavy rose-scented perfume which made my stomach flip with nausea.

He huffed once more then pinged open his seat belt to get up, acting as if it took all the effort in the world. He half stood, half bent over to rummage in his sagging jeans pocket, flashing us all a glimpse of his hairy arse crack. I glanced at the passengers waiting behind me and threw them my best apologetic face. They all glared back.

'Ah, sorry sir, you're actually in 24B, so if I could ask you to move over one?' The flight attendant took his crumpled-up boarding pass that proved me right. *Hah. In yo face, Fatso!*

'I *specifically* remember requesting the aisle seat.' He scowled at the pair of us as if we were in this together, conspiring against him and his inflight needs. 'I *can't* sit in the middle seat. I need to be able to move around frequently. Gout problems,' he replied as an afterthought.

'Madam, would you mind taking the middle seat?' The flight attendant turned to me. Her previously perky voice now had a hint of irritation at how long this was taking.

Well, yes, I did bloody mind. I hated sitting in the middle seat anyway, but trapped between Mr Rude and Mrs Chatterbox, it would make an already long flight even longer.

'Well...' I paused, trying to work out how to politely but firmly stand my ground.

'Great! Thank you,' the flight attendant said cheerfully, before I'd finished, and bundled me into my place to let the queue move on. Fatty bum-bum simply manoeuvred his legs to the side so I could squeeze past, not even bothering to say thanks.

Soon after, the pilot gave his welcome speech (that no one appeared to pay attention to) and the now flustered flight attendant told the woman next to me for the third time that she needed to end her call and put her phone in flight mode. Suddenly, I was gassed with the most noxious, eggy-fart smell coming from my right. I flung my hand up to my mouth to cover it with the sleeve of my jumper and cast a serious, pissed-off look at the man next to me. He had his eyes fixed on the small TV set in the seat back in front of him, pretending that it wasn't him with the bowels of a sewage plant. Then, as if to make matters worse, I felt something thump the top of my head.

'Ow!' I cried and glanced around, rubbing my crown. A grinning gap-toothed boy was standing on the seat behind me, holding a plastic toy train and looking pretty proud of himself. His mother in the seat next to him was too busy flicking through a magazine to apologise or even acknowledge the assault.

Great. Just great.

*

Giving up on the hope of getting my arm on the armrest under my fellow flying partner's chub, and trying to ignore the tired screams from a baby two rows up, whose exhausted parents were desperately trying to calm down, I closed my eyes and tried to prepare myself for what lay ahead.

This would be the first wedding that I'd attended since being jilted myself. I was now living a life far better than I could ever have imagined, but that didn't mean I was overjoyed at the prospect of spending the days before Ben arrived lost in the world of dress fittings, table decorations and wedding readings. I knew that I needed to help my friend out, so I'd plaster on a smile and get stuck in as best I could. Shelley wouldn't have us constantly trapped in the wedding world when there was so much of Australia that I was desperate to see, surely? I exhaled loudly and tried not to over-think it.

'Jesus, would someone shut that bloody kid up?' the fat man muttered under his breath, breaking me from my thoughts. 'These parents think it's okay to make the most of being able to fly their children for free until they're two or something. Selfish, if you ask me. All right for them, but what about the rest of us who had to fork out hundreds for the luxury of sharing this space with a screaming kid. Where's our compensation?' he rambled on, looking as if he expected me to jump in and agree with him.

I was half prepared to say that *I* should be the one to have some compensation, being trapped in this row next to him; that if I'd been in my original seat, at least I would have had a little more room and could nip in and out when I liked. A loud ding-dong sound played out, interrupting me from airing my frustrations.

'Ladies and gentlemen, we're about to enter an area of turbulence,' the suave tones of the captain spoke across the Tannoy as the seat-belt sign illuminated above our heads. 'If you can please return to your seats and fasten your seat belts.'

'Oh, just fucking great,' fat man muttered loudly as the in-flight entertainment crackled out to a blank holding screen.

I looked at him and noticed his hands were gripping the armrests, his pudgy knuckles had turned white.

'For the love of God,' he sighed even louder.

Suddenly it all made sense. It wasn't just the crying baby that was getting on his nerves; his nerves were already shot from fear. He was being such an arrogant space-hogging prick because he wanted to sit in the aisle seat so he could make a hasty escape if necessary. I bet he didn't even have gout. He was terrified of flying.

'You all right?' I asked gently, as the plane suddenly lurched downwards. The woman to my right had dozed off as soon as she'd ended her phone call, and had since been emitting nasally snores in my ear every few minutes.

He blinked open his eyes. 'Fine. Fine,' he barked and gulped loudly.

I've always been relaxed about flying, clinging on to the statistics that it's safer than travelling by car and that no plane has ever crashed from turbulence. Little comfort for someone who has a genuine phobia of being above the clouds, I know. I tried to look around for something to talk about to distract him.

'My name's Georgia, what's yours?'

'Terry,' he eventually managed to say through gritted teeth, loudly swallowing saliva that had probably rushed to his mouth in fear.

'You been to Australia before, Terry?'

Terry turned his head to face me; gone was the reddened sheen and in its place was a sickly, green shade. 'Once.'

'Oh, great. Sooo, how was it? It's my first time. I'm going to my best friend's wedding. She's having this big do in Sydney, but first we're ticking off the Great Ocean Road, something I've always wanted to experience. Should be pretty epic!'

'It's all right, just so fucking far from anywhere.' A bit of spittle stayed on his quivering bottom lip as he spoke. He gripped the armrest as we juddered again.

I flashed a friendly smile. 'Yeah, but it's got to be worth it, right?' A look passed over his features that I couldn't quite make out. 'I can't wait to see my first kangaroo, get some photos of the Opera House, chill out on Bondi Beach,' I rabbited on, hoping he wasn't noticing the air hostesses returning to their seats and strapping themselves in. Or the man in the row opposite doing the cross sign on his chest as we were again violently shaken by the bad weather. 'You got much planned when you're there?'

'Business,' he replied tartly, before absent-mindedly rubbing at his bare wedding-ring finger.

'Ah great, what do you do?'

'Develop apps, tech stuff, you probably wouldn't understand. Heading to Melbourne and then up to

Sydney to sign off on some deals. Do you think the bathrooms are still open?' He craned his neck down the empty aisle.

I shook my head, ignoring his dig. 'Doubt it, the seat-belt sign's still on. So, Terry, do you travel much for work?'

A violent lurch pulled his attention back to me. 'Yeah, too much probably. I don't know why I bother.'

'I'm sure we'll be out of the turbulence soon,' I soothed.

'No. I didn't mean that.' He shook his head. 'I'm on a work trip, one of many this year, and flying not only comes with the fear of death but the aggro I get back home for being away so much.'

He caught me looking at his wedding-ring-free finger. 'My wife and I, we're going through, err, some problems. Work taking up too much of my time and all that.'

'Ah, I know about that,' I sympathetically mused. 'Finding the balance between business and relationships is never easy.' I thought about Ben and the problems we'd had to overcome in our professional and personal life to get to where we were today.

'Harder when your wife doesn't understand that she gets to live in her five-bed house in the countryside *because* of your work,' he huffed. 'I'd like her, just once, to realise that I'm away so much to provide for the lifestyle she has come to expect.' He shifted uncomfortably in his seat. I noticed his chest had stopped heaving as quickly as it had before.

I cringed slightly; nice one, Georgia, for trying to take his mind off turbulence and on to more emotionally turbulent matters for the poor sod.

'I'm sure she does appreciate what you do; she probably just misses you when you're away,' I suggested.

He made a strange noise with his rubbery lips. 'Pfft, doubt it. Misses nagging me maybe.' He paused to collect his thoughts. 'Sorry, too much information and all that.'

I shook my head. 'It's fine.'

'So, how about you? Heading all this way by yourself?'

'Like I said, I'm going to see my friend.' I mentally kicked myself for going on about weddings to a stranger who was having such marital troubles. 'My boyfriend is flying out to meet me soon. He travels a lot too, we both do.'

'Well, you're lucky then.'

'What, with travelling?' I smiled weakly as the plane dropped sharply and other passengers let out a whooping noise.

Terry clutched his clenched pink fists to his lips.

'No.' His Adam's apple bobbed up and down as if gulping at the air. 'I mean, with making it work between the pair of you, having someone who understands that you travel a lot.'

'Yeah, I guess you're right.' I smiled. 'He's my business partner too and loves to travel as much as I do.'

It wasn't your usual relationship that Ben and I had, but we made it work. I probably should be a lot more grateful for having a supportive boyfriend who 'got' my career. I couldn't imagine running the business and dating someone who struggled with the amount of travelling I *had*, and *wanted*, to do.

'Maybe take your wife with you on your next trip?'

He thought about it for a moment as the plane wobbled aggressively once more. 'That's if we ever get off here in one piece. I love my wife. I *really* do.' He fumbled in his jeans pocket, almost taking my eye out as his elbow narrowly missed my face with the movement.

'Here, look.' He opened up his battered wallet and pulled out a faded Polaroid photo of him looking younger and slimmer, and a woman I presumed to be his wife, with highlighted blonde hair and a wide grin matching the size of the blow-up microphone she had in her hand. 'That was at our friends' wedding; they had one of these ridiculous photo booths.' Terry shook his head, remembering fondly. 'She dragged me in there as I'd moaned how cheesy the things are, but I'm glad she did. I don't know about you, but I never print off any of the photos we have together any more; everything's gone digital and all that.'

I realised that I didn't have an adorable snap of Ben and me that I could whip out to show him, and my phone was out of reach at the bottom of my bag.

'You look happy.' I smiled, pleased that this distraction seemed to be working and that he hadn't appeared to have noticed the ashen look on the air hostesses' faces further up the aisle.

'We are.' He paused, staring at the photo. 'God, we really are. When we get out of here I'm going to call her and tell her.' He firmly bobbed his head, as if making a silent vow to the woman in his trembling hands. 'This is me.' He handed me his business card from one of the leather pockets. He seemed to relax a little and ran his thumb across the photo of his wife. 'So, you and your chap been together long?'

'Yeah, actually.' I sighed happily. 'Live together, work together, travel together when we can.'

'Not married though?'

I shook my head.

'You not been giving him the signals?' Terry pressed.

I laughed. 'I'm sure he knows, one day it might happen ...'

It was Terry's turn to let out a sharp bark of a laugh. 'I know what you women are like, expecting men to pick up on these "subconscious" signals that you send out.' He raised his fingers in air quotes. I noticed that he had a large sweat patch under each armpit, but at least his hands were trembling slightly less. 'Trust me, no man *ever* reads into them. You have to literally spell it out to him, to us.'

The seat-belt sign pinged off, making us both jump. I hadn't even realised that the plane had stopped jerking violently and, by the look of relief and surprise on Terry's face, neither had he.

'Thank God.' He nodded and relaxed his hands. 'That was a bit hairy, wasn't it?'

I nodded distractedly, thinking about what he'd just said.

'Thanks for, erm, taking my mind off it,' he mumbled sheepishly.

'No problem.'

Without the fear of death hanging over us, he seemed to clam up once more.

'They still can't shut up that screaming child though,' he grumbled and put his headphones back on.

CHAPTER 7

Tepid (adj.) – Showing little enthusiasm

I woke up feeling like someone had performed a lobotomy on me as I slept. My mouth was dry and gummy, my brain felt like it had been replaced with scratchy wire wool, and my neck was too weak to hold up my head. My stomach rumbled even though I'd probably overdone it on the in-flight meals – I always got carried away with the excitement of what was hiding under each shiny foil lid. I also loved how transatlantic airlines seemed to be competing to have a mile-high Michelin star. Some of the fanciest meals I've ever eaten were on long-haul flights. Now I just felt bloated and gross.

I rubbed my tight, gritty eyes, ignored the noisy dance-off my stomach was having, and prepared to force myself to jump into the shower in the small budget hotel I'd checked into after I'd arrived. My body screeched in resistance to any movements. I felt like I had that fuzzy stage of the flu, as if my joints had been replaced with metal poles, and every single muscle ached. I hurriedly turned off the television that I'd only flicked on to check the time. I couldn't take in one thing the beaming morning television presenters were saying. Their bright and cheery smiles, along with their drawling Aussie accents, were not helping this pounding in my skull. This was not the time to get sick. I hobbled to the bathroom and hoped that a hot shower would wake me up and sort me out, except that it took all the effort in the world to stand up properly or raise my arms above my head to wash the suds from my hair. *What was going on with me?* I had to snap out of it as I needed to go and meet Shelley and her cousin pronto.

Trailing past the hotel's dining room full of tourists and business people filling up their breakfast plates made my stomach contract painfully in protest. Maybe that was what this feeling was? Maybe I'd got food poisoning from the in-flight meals? It probably was too fancy for my own good. I mean, how fresh can glazed avocado, a bed of kale, pork loins with a red wine jus, and chocolate mousse served with pomegranate and raspberry foam be at thirty-five thousand feet? Whatever it was that was causing this out-of-body experience, I had no time to analyse it as I hurriedly checked out so I wouldn't be late.

Lugging my bag through the streets of Melbourne, I felt a pang of sadness that I wouldn't have time to properly discover this city. It was going to take superwoman strength to get through the day. I had to keep stopping every couple of feet to catch my breath, blink back the autumnal, crisp air blowing at my cheeks, and crane my neck at the signs on the tall buildings around me for a hint of a street name leading me in the right direction. This arduous trip was full of hazards from trying to avoid cute, old-style trams chugging across the lines criss-crossing the busy streets, and scurrying past hip coffee shops where bearded men gripping takeaway cups spilled out onto the pavement. I narrowly avoided receiving a flat white down my front as I pushed past and weaved my way around queues of trendy people hanging around graffiti-scrawled art galleries.

'Well, look who's made it down under!' The shrill shrieks of my best friend Shelley rang across the busy bus station concourse, making me jump.

I flicked my head up from the tourist map that I'd picked up earlier and grinned at her. I couldn't shake the heavy cloud of tiredness that had settled into my bones, but I felt my spirits lift seeing her infectious smile, bright blonde pixie-cropped hair, and creased-up, freckled, button nose as she manically waved at me.

'Hello!' I sang.

'It's *so* good to see you, chick.' She pulled me into a warm embrace, filling my nose with her floral scent and making tears prick at my tired eyes. I'd forgotten just how much I'd missed her. We'd made sure we had regular FaceTime chats since she'd returned to live in her home country, but there was nothing that compared to being able to hold her and feel that familiar warmth.

'How was your journey? How did you sleep? What do you think of 'Straya so far?' She pulled back and held me at arm's length as questions rolled off her tongue.

'I got here fine, but, honestly, I feel like death warmed up.'

'Ah, jet lag. You'll get used to it and I promise it will only last a few days,' she said with a flick of her hand. Conrad's *I told you so* face suddenly loomed into my mind.

'Hmm, I hope you're right. It's like a lingering hangover but without the fun memories of a night out.'

'Yeah, it sucks. But we've got so much to see and do that you'll kick its ass in no time. I promise you.'

I stepped back to say hello to the girl standing on her right. She had the same blonde-coloured hair as Shelley, but hers was pulled into an uber-high and uber-tight bun. The severe look continued to the rest of her angular body.

Her black, skinny, ripped jeans looked expensive, her long fingers were iced with rose-gold rings and her mint-green jumper skimmed her toned frame. I couldn't take my eyes off her shoes as she towered over both of us. She was tall enough even without the extra few inches that the pair of heeled black boots gave her. I felt instantly dowdy and unfashionable in my baggy travelling outfit and scuffed trainers.

'Gawd, sorry, where are my manners? I'm just so excited to see you!' Shelley said. 'Georgia, this is Cara, my cousin, and second in charge of the wedding!'

'Hi, it's nice to finally meet you.' I smiled at the girl with impeccable pores and protruding collarbone.

Cara was a model-slash-fashion entrepreneur, had a thing for sugar daddies, and wore very few clothes for a living. I glanced at her slim frame and darted a look down at my pudgy tummy. With a figure like hers, I'd be going out in my birthday suit as much as I could too. I went to go and give Cara a friendly, if a little bony, hug, which she was either not expecting or not enjoying as, with a cursory one-second pat on the back, she pulled away and looked me up and down.

'Hey, yeah, you too,' she said in an unenthusiastic Aussie drawl. 'So, we going soon? I need to be away from these fucking buses.'

Shell nodded and turned to me. 'You ready to go? We've just endured an eleven-hour journey to get here and, as much as I love travel, there's little joy in taking the overnight Greyhound.' She shuddered. 'Poor Cara was bent in half for the whole trip.'

'Apparently extra leg room didn't occur to them to be an essential design feature.' Cara pursed her lips, which were slicked with deep berry lipstick. 'If it wasn't the lack of personal space, then it was the screaming children. Who the hell thinks it's okay to take a toddler on such a long trip? Seriously, I was so glad I'd packed a sleeping tablet and my headphones, otherwise I'd never have managed any sleep.'

I nodded as Cara strode off; with her long legs every one of her steps was three of ours. When she was out of earshot, Shelley turned to me.

'I'm sorry if she seems in a bit of a mood. Usually she's a lot chattier.' She winced. 'It's because I told her we were coming to Melbourne by bus; she presumed we'd be flying here from Sydney.'

'Ah. I gathered she wasn't enamoured with the mode of transport.'

'She hasn't really travelled before, well, not in the backpacking sense anyway, and I thought it would be fun for her, and us, to relive it a little!'

I was about to ask what exactly was planned for this trip, but I was cut off by Cara shouting at us to get a move on as she'd never needed caffeine more in her life than she did right now.

'I'm sure after a coffee or two she'll lighten up!' Shelley linked my arm and shouted back at Cara to slow down so us mere mortals could catch her up.

We'd only been walking for a few minutes before Cara stopped at an achingly cool coffee shop where Melbourne hipsters seemingly went to breed. Soothing smells of ground beans wafted in the decidedly autumnal air, tinged with pretentiousness and smugness.

'I knew Melburnians liked their coffee, but this place is ridic,' Shelley whispered, as a man with a pruned-to-perfection moustache wandered past, flashing a glimpse of hairy ankle in his loafers.

'It's *artisan*.' Cara sniffed, sipping her room-temperature, soya-milk, extra-foam, organic latte. I was struggling to get the cup of basic Americana down me as my stomach gurgled loudly.

'You say tomato, I say *tomato*,' Shelley laughed, finding us seats on rustic wooden benches and upturned oil barrels with floral cushions plonked on top.

'Oh come on, it's totally on trend.' Cara pulled her iPhone out of her handbag and took a photo of the chalkboard next to us. 'I'm so Instagramming this!' She pointed at the twee saying about how coffee drinkers make better thinkers, or some bollocks like that. 'I found this place via this new app that tells you all the hidden gems and the hottest places to go before they get too mainstream. Last week I found this café in Sydney called Midnight Munchies that's only open from midnight to 2 a.m. So freakin' cool.'

'Well, whatever it is, we can't be too long. I said I'd pick up the hire car by now.' Shelley glanced at her watch then turned to me. 'I told you that Cara can't drive so it'll be us two at the wheel, didn't I?'

'Oh, erm, no, you didn't,' I said, trying to breathe through my nose as the nauseating smells in here were making my stomach clench.

'Ah, sorry, must be this wedding brain. I'm getting so forgetful. But it's fine because we can take it in turns.'

'I just hope it all comes back to me.'

I hadn't driven for years. Living in a city meant I'd got used to public transport. I'd expected that these two would take the wheel so I could sit back and soak up the scenery. It was only now, as we eventually left the coffee shop and wandered down the streets, that I felt a sense of unease at getting behind the wheel again.

Shelley must have read my mind. 'Don't sweat it. We drive on the same side as you and, once we get out of the city, the roads will be pretty quiet. You'll see.'

A nasally employee at the car-hire place, with slicked-back hair, cement-coloured skin and sleep crusted in the corners of his dull brown eyes, led us to our car. His name tag read 'Mitch: Happy to help', but he'd kept us waiting for ages, muttering that *we* were the ones who were late, then forgot to print off some form as he was too busy ogling Cara's backside.

'Right, follow me, ladies.' He winked, taking us down a dingy dark corridor to get to the garage.

'Eurgh, what *is* that smell?' Cara asked, pulling a face. I felt like I was about to retch my coffee back up.

'Oh, sorry, I had a Mexican for dinner last night,' Mitch mumbled, nodding at the employee bathroom we hurried past. 'Anyway, here we go, here's your car.'

I'd hoped that he'd redeem himself with some easy-on-the-eye motor, but instead of a nippy runaround, we were standing in front of a beast of a vehicle. It was a four-wheel drive, but not like the classy, gleaming Range Rovers that I'd seen waiting outside the posh restaurants in Manchester. This one looked like it had had about thirteen different paint jobs over the years, and was probably as old as my dad.

'Shell, you reserved *this* one?' I gasped.

'What's wrong with it?' Mitch grunted.

'Errrm…it's a little on the large side!'

'She's a cracker, plus, we don't have anything else, well, not in your budget.' Mitch snivelled and adjusted his grubby, stripy tie. 'There's been a rush on, you see, and this is all we have left.' I couldn't tell if he was bullshitting us or not. 'Unless you want to come back in a few days when some of our fleet should have been returned, then this is all we've got.' He shrugged, trying but failing to keep down a small burp that smelt disgustingly of jalapeño peppers.

I plastered on a smile that belied my irritation at not being the one in charge of the car-hire process. This was a real test of the lessons I'd learnt on my trip to India on how to let go of the stress and the need to control everything. Easier said than done, of course.

'Thank God I failed my test after all.' Cara snorted with laughter.

'I'm wishing that I had,' I muttered under my breath.

'You'll be fine. I used to drive my dad's truck when I was younger and this isn't *that* different.' Shelley brushed off my apprehensions. 'Remember, Car?'

Cara nodded. 'Yeah, I thought we'd escaped the country-bumpkin life though.'

'Really? *You* used to drive a thing like this?' I shook my head in disbelief. The front of the truck dwarfed her, making her appear smaller than she was, even making statuesque Cara seem petite.

'Yeah, I mean it was a couple of years ago now, but they say you never forget.'

'Maybe it's not that bad. Just a little bigger than I'd been expecting.' I slapped on a fake smile. The fact we would need a hoist up to get in said it all.

Mitch had crouched to his knees, pretending he was looking at something in the undercarriage. 'What's this?' I asked him, pointing at the intimidating, rusty, steel bars welded horizontally to the front of this beast. I was sure there was a collection of bloodied feathers caught in the left headlight, which was almost hanging off.

'A bull bar,' Mitch replied, matter-of-factly, leering at Cara who was climbing up to get into the back seat.

'A what now?' How many bulls were we going to come across in Melbourne?

'It stops the car getting mangled up if you hit a 'roo on your travels.' He shrugged, as if any part of that sentence was perfectly normal. 'You'll be glad of it when it happens. Sorry, *if* it happens. You girls heading down the Great Ocean Road, yeah?' I nodded. 'Well, you're gonna see some kangaroos and cattle on your route then. Over sixty per cent of collisions involve wildlife, so you need to be as protected as you can. Well, the vehicle does.' He wafted at his mouth as he let out another chilli-scented belch.

Stop being such a worrier, Georgia. It was going to be an experience to tell the grandkids at least, I thought. I just needed to cross everything that we wouldn't be making our own kangaroo roadkill burgers any time soon.

Shelley picked up the pen he was offering to sign off on this deal.

'You'll soon get the hang, love. You Poms are all the same, feeling nervous at first, but I've had many happy customers returning their cars saying they wished they could do it all over again,' Mitch said cheerfully. 'Just remember to drop her off in Adelaide with a full tank. Here's your paperwork and there's a logbook in the dash that explains all the features.' He slapped a meaty hand against the driver's door, making it shudder. 'Well, safe travels!'

'Great. Thanks,' Shelley called out, as he wandered back to the front of the shop, itching his bum cheeks as he went.

We managed to successfully get 'The Beast' started and, with a heavy wheeze, a couple of worrying clunks and a few Hail Marys, we were off. Road-trip time!

CHAPTER 8

Pervicacious (adj.) – Stubborn; extremely wilful; obstinate

Shelley had offered to get us out of Melbourne's busy grid system of roads and do the first leg. I was in charge of reading the map and Cara had been tasked with entertainment.

'Oh God, there isn't even an aux cable for me to plug my phone in!' Cara moaned. 'I made us a road-trip playlist that was beyond amazing.'

That wasn't all that was wrong with this car. The ripped leather seats bounced, the radio was sketchy and there also wasn't a mobile phone charge point in the tatty cigarette lighter, but there was air con, although we decided to keep the windows down to try to air out the tangy smell of fumes fogging the front.

'Was there a problem with money or something?' Cara asked. 'I mean, *we* should be the ones being paid to drive around in this heap of junk.'

'What?' Shelley shouted over the engine as she changed gears.

'I mean that I transferred the cash to you that you asked; Georgia, did you?'

'Yeah, that was ages ago, did you get it, Shell?'

Shelley nodded distractedly. 'Yeah, we've all chipped in the same amount and it's all gone on this trip, why?'

'I just don't get why we couldn't have hired a modern car that actually has a sense of style.' Cara tutted, wiping a finger across the sheen of dust on the windows.

'You heard that guy, this was all they had,' Shelley said hurriedly, then peered at the windscreen. 'Anyway, it is what it is, I need to concentrate on this bit.'

Cara muttered that we'd totally been conned by Itchy Mitch and spread herself across the back seat, shutting her eyes. As sleek as this car wasn't, it just needed to get us from A to B. We were going to be travelling some distance over the next few days, but looking at the map of this enormous country, our long route only covered a speck. Bill Bryson would probably say a freckle, more like a freckle on a fly.

'It's so good to see you.' I patted Shelley's arm, which was rigidly fixed to the enormous steering wheel. 'You really gave me a fright the other day, you know!'

Shelley wiped her forehead and concentrated on changing lanes before answering. 'Ah, it's bloody great to see you too. Yeah sorry about that, I'm feeling a little more in control after we last spoke. Jimmy's been amazing since then. I've even had him superglueing fake flowers to ribbon for one of the decorations.'

'Wow! So, you must be nearly there, though, with it all?' *Surely to God.* It felt like she had been talking about this day non-stop for the past few months.

She sighed. 'You'd think so, but we've still got to decide about loads of things.'

'Really? Like what?'

'Well, the guest book for one.'

'The guest book?' I repeated. 'Oh, well, that's easy, you can just order one online, or I'm sure most stationery shops stock them, then that's another thing off your list.' I heard Cara scoff at this suggestion. 'What?'

'People don't really *do* guest books like that any more,' Shelley said softly, as Cara leant her head through the gap in the headrests to be involved in the conversation.

'She's deciding between guests signing a personalised globe, adding a fingerprint to a picture of a family tree, making a Polaroid scrapbook where everyone takes a selfie then writes a message under their photo, writing a note on some rustic driftwood, or on strips of ribbon that create a piece of art for their home afterwards,' Cara listed in one breath, ticking things off on her long, delicate fingers.

'Oh, don't forget the message-in-the-bottle idea,' Shelley added, then turned to me. 'We ask all the guests to share some marriage advice or date ideas then fold it up to pop into a big glass bottle that we smash on our first anniversary to read what people said. Doesn't that sound like such a cool thing to do!'

I was surprised she hadn't mentioned the option of adding a drop of each guest's blood to a piece of sacred linen from the underwear of a virgin.

'Oh right, well, that sounds nice. They all, err, sound nice,' I stuttered, wondering why she was making it harder for herself when she could just get an actual guest book online in about ten minutes. What was wrong with pen and paper?

'Yeah but which one to go for? I mean, you can only choose one otherwise it'll be overkill.' Cara rolled her eyes, without a hint of sarcasm.

'I guess whichever will look better on the photographs,' Shelley said decisively. 'I want the whole day to be totally Instagrammable.'

'Speaking of that, did you decide which hashtag you wanted?' Cara asked.

'There's a hashtag?' My voice went up a few levels in astonishment. When I was planning my wedding, hashtags weren't really around, but still, did a wedding need one?

Shelley mistook my shock. 'Of course. The thing is that I can't decide which I like the most.' She looked seriously flummoxed by this life-changing decision. 'Do we go with #Hitchedwithoutahitch or #MrandMrsPriors?'

She didn't give me the chance to share my idea of #OTT before she was off talking about food stations – something else that had been giving her sleepless nights.

'Food stations? I thought your wedding was being catered by the venue that you chose?' Again, Cara let out a snort of laughter at my ignorance, making me feel even more out of the loop.

'Well, yeah, they are, but it's important to offer guests some choice,' Shelley explained patiently. 'We just can't decide what to go for.'

'My friend had an ice-cream sundae station, where guests could get a cone of their favourite flavour along with all these adorable sauces and toppings like crushed-up Tim Tams in cute little jam jars,' Cara said, making Shelley's eyes light up at the thought.

'Ooh, that sounds good. I'm still trying to get Jimmy to agree to a pimp-your-Prosecco stall. It's where we have all these cool liqueurs and fruit for guests to add to their glass of fizz.'

'You could get a biscuit bar, a pie station, or even a doughnut stand!' Cara suggested excitedly.

'Is it not a bit over the top though?' I dared to ask.

I noticed Shelley huff and fidget on her seat. 'I'm only doing this once so I want it to be perfect. I mean, imagine if a few weeks later I go to someone else's wedding, wishing I'd been the one to have a tequila bar. It would ruin *everything* if I missed out on that.'

I stared at her as if she'd lost the plot. It was official – my best friend had been taken over by wedding fever and FOMO at its finest. I was waiting for her to crack into her signature throaty giggle, but there was no punchline to this joke.

I tried a different tack. 'But it must add up, all these extras, I mean.'

'God, tell me about it,' Shelley sighed. 'It's like just saying the word *wedding* makes everyone's eyes light up with the thought of the extra zeros they can add to your bill.'

'You doing all right for money? For the budget, I mean?' I asked quietly.

She paused and peered at the fuel gauge. 'Yeah. Fine, yeah.'

I thought back to when I was planning my big day. So much money I'd worked hard to save up that was spent on making it the day of my dreams. So much money that was subsequently lost as Alex left me before I got to walk down the aisle. They don't cover 'cold feet' as a valid excuse to refund you. It had been one hell of a learning curve.

'Has she told you about Lars yet?' Cara asked me.

'Lars?'

'Yeah, Lars. The wedding planner *du jour*,' Cara said in a crap French accent, making Shelley laugh. 'He's probably the campest man I've ever met; I couldn't believe it when you said he has a wife.'

Shelley had a wedding planner?

'Erm, no, she didn't say,' I said slowly.

'I thought I'd mentioned him. Lars was an early wedding present from Jimmy's mum, Johanna,' Shelley hurriedly added.

Jimmy's mum was widely known to be a bit of a diva. An Essex WAG wannabe, who swanned around spending her husband's money and who hated Shelley for taking her baby boy to live on the other side of the world.

'Well, he might be good but it still hasn't stopped you doing a lot of the wedding stuff yourself.'

'I just want it to be perfect.'

I smiled along, not really sure what to say to this. I thought it was weird that Shell hadn't told me about having this extra help, but I guess if her mother-in-law was paying, then why would you turn that down?

I rubbed at my itchy eyes, trying to shake the tiredness that was making me feel like I could sleep for a hundred years.

'So, when are Jimmy's parents flying over?' I asked, wanting to change the subject from money and wedding planning. The atmosphere was already stale enough in here with the pongy interior.

'The same day as Ben actually.'

I'd only met Jimmy's parents once, briefly, at Jimmy and Shelley's leaving do, but I hadn't been able to chat with them as Marie's waters had broken and we'd had to rush her to the hospital. I'd picked up on Johanna's snide remarks that a pregnant lady shouldn't be out of the house, let alone in a bar, and had instantly disliked her. I knew Shelley had a, let's say, tumultuous relationship with her.

'I've never met the woman and already she's got on my nerves. Seriously, Georgia, you should read some of the emails she sends Shelley. She's about to get lumbered with the mother-in-law from hell. Thank God she lives on the other side of the world, that's at least one saving grace,' Cara piped up. 'Plus, she's a Londoner.'

'What's that got to do with anything?' I asked.

'The first thing Uncle Keith, Shelley's dad, will ask you is if you're from London.'

I gave her a blank look.

'He has a thing about Londoners, thinks they're all posh numpties.'

'I bet that went down a storm when you first introduced Jimmy to him?' I laughed.

'Don't remind me.' Shelley groaned. 'I've already told him you're from Manchester, but it's Jimmy's parents that I'm more worried about him meeting.'

'What's his beef with London?'

Shelley rolled her eyes. 'Lord knows. He's never even been!'

'Pfft.' Cara made a wet noise with her lips. 'He just reckons everyone from London is preoccupied by cash. All he's heard about Jimmy's family is how tight-fisted they are, even though they're not short of it. I mean, his parents have managed to tack on a pretty nice holiday out of coming here for the big day. After spending time in Australia doing the main sights, they're taking in New Zealand and even Fiji!'

'Oh, Johanna's not *that* bad!' Shelley let out a shrill laugh.

'Come off it! She's so bloody obsessed with being part of the planning process because she doesn't have anything else going on in her life.' Cara pursed her lips.

'I'm sure that's not true.' Shelley blushed slightly and gripped the steering wheel tighter. 'Family politics, hey!'

'Well, she can't be so bad if she's sorted out this Lars dude for you,' I said.

'Ha, yeah, I guess. Right, it must be time for another coffee break. Cara, keep your eyes peeled for the next services,' Shelley called out over the tinny radio, thus cleverly changing the subject. I stole a glance at her, feeling like there was something she was keeping from us.

CHAPTER 9

*Ubiquitous (adj.) – Being or seeming to be
everywhere or in all places*

We would soon be driving along the Great Ocean
Road, a drive so scenic it made your eyes hurt – or
so all the guide books said. The rugged coastline,
thrashing waves, adorable little coastal towns and
stunning forestry made it a must-do on many
travellers' trips to Oz. I was so caught up in gazing out
of the window, taking in how quickly the landscape
had shifted from bustling city to monotonous
motorway to desolate space, that I almost missed it.

'Argh!' I screamed and caused Shelley to swerve
slightly.

'What the fuck!' she yelled, getting the car back on
track, following her gaze past my stretched-out hand.

'Jeeeeesus, what's happened!' Cara asked, flicking
her head up from her magazine, which she'd picked
up from the last service station.

'Kangaroos!' I laughed, shaking my head in disbelief.
Along the shrubby patches of earth, spindly trees and
tufted mounds of grass were two actual kangaroos
hopping alongside us. They were bloody *mahoosive*!
I couldn't stop smiling. It seemed so bizarre to see
these creatures lazily jumping around just feet away
from our car. Their long auburn tails thumped the arid
earth, causing billowing plumes of dust to rise as they
built up speed; it was as if they were racing us. Their
funny T-Rex arms seemed to be at odds with their

muscular stance, intimidating claws and all. I stared with my jaw dropped and tears misting my eyes.

'God, Georgia, you nearly gave me a heart attack then!' Cara tutted and went back to her reading material.

'Aren't you excited to see one?' I asked, unable to take my eyes from them. 'Look at them! LOOK!'

'They're like pests to us.' Shelley shook her head, not choked up in the slightest. 'My dad has a *serious* vendetta against them.'

'Oh yeah, don't get Uncle Keith started on the Spring of '93 or whenever it was,' Cara said, rolling her eyes.

'What? Why? They are magnificent,' I breathed, pressing my palms against the dirty car window and ignoring the fact I'd never called anything magnificent before.

'Well, there are more kangaroos than humans on this island. They affect livestock, eat food not meant for them and farmers bloody hate them,' she listed, matter-of-factly. 'But they do taste awesome!'

I shivered. 'Shh, they'll hear you!'

'Ha ha, we'll see when you've had a 'roo burger, you'll soon change your tune.'

My stomach flipped at the thought of it.

'Right, look at that map and tell me exactly how far we've got to go,' Shelley instructed, as the two kangaroos bounced away from us.

I pulled my eyes from the window and focused on the job in hand. 'We've got one more town to pass through, then we're there.'

'Thank God for that. I need a drink!' Cara chirped up.

'And I need another wee,' I added.

We'd been driving pretty much non-stop since leaving Melbourne, pausing briefly to take photos of the scenery, to gaze at buff surfers walking with their sand-coated surfboards down the roads in Torquay, and to pick up a quick bite to eat in the pretty seaside resort of Lorne. Everything was a novelty to me, from the food on offer in the quaint coffee shop we visited, to the rolling drawl of Australian accents. Even the road signs were different, their yellow and black diamond-shaped plates peppered the road, giving orders to be cautious and kill your speed alongside images of kangaroos. Shelley had given us a brief outline of our itinerary. We were going to stop for the night in Apollo Bay, a quiet fishing village, to get some rest in order to be up for our early start to visit the Twelve Apostles the next morning. She wanted us to get to the unusual rock towers for sunrise. I was still struggling to shake this tiredness, and the thought of an early night was exactly what the doctor ordered. The hen-do fun could start properly tomorrow.

*

We'd gotten a little lost so it was dark when we pulled up at our accomodation for the night.

'We're staying here?' Cara asked, full of disgust as she read the battered-looking sign in the car park after we'd tumbled out of The Beast. 'We're staying at a youth hostel?'

'Yeah, I thought it would be fun.'

Judging by how glamorous Cara was, this was going to be a completely alien concept for her.

'It's one of these new youth hostels,' Shell babbled, reading the sign Cara was glaring at. 'Eco-friendly and all that. It's probably as good as a five-star hotel.'

To be fair, this was unlike any hostel I'd ever stayed in before. Gleaming floor-to-ceiling glass windows at the entrance, a sloping wooden roof and wraparound balcony full of potted plants, rustic garden chairs and candles hanging from tree branches welcomed us.

Cara grabbed her bag and strode inside, muttering something under her breath.

'I knew she'd moan, but I'm sure once she's had the backpacker experience she'll be glad of it!'

'I think it's a great idea!' I smiled.

I was excited to go back to our roots of backpacking, where Shelley and I had met. It had been so long since I'd shared a dorm room, hung out in the breakaway room, and had meaningful deep chats with strangers who were passing through the same place at the same time. A lot of the places that Ben and I usually stayed in were rooms in soulless airport hotels, or accommodation laid on for us by event organisers at conference venues, so I thought this would be a laugh, if Cara ever got over sulking that she wasn't in a luxe hotel, that is.

Sadly, the excitement at the taste of five-star treatment on a one-star budget quickly faded when we wandered into the intimidating reception area. Signs listing their many strict rules and regulations were tacked all around a glass partition. Details of its eco-friendly credentials were plastered on the bare wooden wall opposite. Pretty much everything was recycled, reused and repaired here – impressive, but also fairly unnerving.

'Hello?' Shelley peered around the empty reception desk.

'Hellooooo?' Cara called out louder. 'Well, this isn't exactly a five-star welcome. They must be too busy planting mung beans to bother checking guests in.'

'It's probably because we're out of season.' I spotted Shelley clenching her jaw and was about to suggest heading somewhere else when someone called out to us.

'Yes?' The deep voice belonged to a man with a wiry beard, round spectacles and a fair few missing teeth, who seemed to appear from nowhere. He was like Lurch in *The Addams Family*, only more intimidating, and looking mighty unsure of what three weary women were doing in his establishment.

'Oh, hi, I booked a room for tonight. It should be under the name of Robinson?' Shelley smiled, trying not to be put off by his dead-eyed stare.

I felt Cara bristle next to me as he plodded around behind the reception desk.

'Here.' He thumped onto the counter a clipboard, which held a tatty form for us to fill in, and eyeballed us as we took it in turns to scribble out our details with a gnawed pencil tied on with string.

'Thanks.' I plastered on a smile, hoping to kill him with kindness, but even my fake megawatt grin did nothing to the man who clearly viewed us as outsiders. This was obviously a local hostel for local people. He took our forms and Shelley's credit card, before passing over a receipt and a key.

'Check-out is at 8 a.m.,' he grunted, before sloping off out of the back of the office.

Cara was too busy reading out the exceptionally long list of dos and don'ts to add another snarky comment about the frosty welcome. 'Check this – no pungent food to be brought into the hostel; incense burning is prohibited; don't leave your toe or fingernail cuttings on the bathroom floors; limit showers to five minutes; sleeping bags are banned; guests are not permitted to walk around naked. Animals (dogs, cats and certain smaller pets) are allowed for an extra $10 per night. Sheesh!'

'Do you reckon he's coming back?' Shelley asked, ignoring her cousin's horrified expression.

'No idea.' I shrugged.

'Eurgh, let's just go, dump our bags, then find some wine. Lord knows we need it,' Cara huffed.

'Oh well, actually, I thought the wine could be saved for tomorrow, seeing as we've got an early start in the morning and all that.'

'Great,' Cara muttered sarcastically, before lugging her bag down the dark breeze-block corridor to our room, narrowly avoiding tripping over a large basket of dirty laundry. 'Wine would have been the only thing to get us through this hellhole.'

'She's never stayed in a hostel before. Never did the whole travelling thing,' Shelley whispered to me.

'Pfft. If this is what it's like, then I don't think I've exactly been missing out,' Cara snorted.

'Here we are! Room Five!' I said brightly, pushing open our bedroom door, wanting to avoid a domestic.

'Oh,' we all chimed in disappointed unison.

'So much for luxury.'

The bedroom had two tightly made bunk beds screwed down onto a cold concrete floor; the walls were stark grey breeze blocks and a wooden rickety desk had been set up in the corner under the draughty window for guests to sit and write in their travel journals or scribble postcards to send home. Looking around the gloomy, depressing room, I guessed those notes would be more like cries for help.

'It's fine. It's for one night,' I said, trying to make light of it all, ignoring the look of fear on Cara's suddenly much paler features. 'Right, let's heat up that soup we picked up and then see what the other guests are like,' I suggested, with more enthusiasm than a tin of Heinz has ever deserved.

We wandered back down the dimly lit corridors to find some form of life in this place.

'Surely being eco they could at least have some form of light, or are we meant to be carrying candles around made from our own ear wax?' Cara muttered as we found the large and totally deserted kitchen.

With our soup on the hob, we headed to the breakout room opposite where a few backpackers sat on squishy sofas. It was surprisingly homely in here compared to the rest of the stark hostel.

'Hi!' I said excitedly, pleased to have some other form of human interaction.

No one replied or even acknowledged us. Every one of the five people already hunkered down in the room were silently on their phones, scrolling through their Facebook timeline with their thumbs, choosing filters for their Instagram updates, or watching something on a tablet with earphones firmly in.

Undeterred and wanting to help her cousin experience the real backpacking way of life, Shelley went and sat on one of the free seats. 'So, this place is a little random. I mean, that receptionist could do with some social skills for one.'

A woman who was curled up on what I presumed was her boyfriend's lap finally bothered to lift her gaze from her phone screen to give Shelley a tight smile. A smile that clearly said piss off.

'So, where you guys from?' Shelley asked, undeterred. An older man, wearing a snazzy multicoloured t-shirt, with crumbs in his bushy beard, sighed loudly at the rudeness of trying to start a conversation in a common room.

'America. You?' the girl drawled disinterestedly.

'We're from Australia and that's Georgia, she's from Manchester in England.' Shelley smiled at me.

'Hi.' I waved lamely. 'Any of you lot heading to the Twelve Apostles tomorrow?'

Two girls with platinum-blonde hair in matching cascading ponytails began giggling at some YouTube clip they were watching; everyone else ignored me. I glanced at Shelley and shrugged. This was a no-hoper. Here we were in this fairly remote part of the world, in a unique hostel, and all they could do was connect to their virtual worlds.

'Okay then, well, have a good night,' Shelley said, in a less than friendly tone, and got to her feet, purposely budging the comatose couple on her way past.

'Eurgh. Rude!' Cara said in a loud whisper as we left the zombie crowd to it. 'I thought backpackers were meant to be friendly.'

'What the hell? Is this what's happened to youth hostels now?' Shell ignored her cousin and shook her head as she angrily poured out three bowls of soup, spilling it down the sides. 'It was *never* like this when we went travelling. Back then people were chatty, fun, and you made friends for life within the space of five minutes!'

'The kids today,' I sighed, feeling as deflated as she did.

'This is why I don't travel. Imagine if I'd turned up here single and ready to mingle!' Cara spluttered. 'Add to the fact that you then have to retire to your prison cell, sorry eco-room, to get some sleep. I'd be on the next flight home telling all who would listen that this backpacking lark is a load of bullshit.'

'I thought backpacking was about getting away from things? About being independent? I mean, all those people in there couldn't care less where we're from, who was sitting next to them, or what our stories were! I can't believe we've just been ignored, standing there like utter lemons as they all chatted to their mates back home on Facebook,' Shelley seethed, as we ate our cheap dinner.

'I know. But hey, we've got each other and this is just the first stop of our trip. Don't stress it,' I said, muttering a silent prayer that tomorrow would be a lot livelier.

'I'm pretty knackered anyway,' Cara said, a yawn escaping from her mouth for good effect despite it only being 8 p.m.

We all traipsed back to our bedroom in silence. I'd tried to connect to the Wi-Fi to send Ben a message and see how he was doing, but there was zero signal in this cell. We slumped onto our beds, which were as hard as they looked, and all eventually fell asleep, dreaming of weirdo receptionists, echoing corridors and tree branches scraping the windowpanes.

CHAPTER 10

Fractious (adj.) – Easily irritated; bad tempered

We left at the crack of dawn, dropping our room key at a boarded-up reception and sneaking out without being seen or even seeing any other form of life. I never imagined I'd feel so relieved to be back in our beast of a truck and heading down the eerily silent winding roads out of this town. I still felt a little hazy from a broken sleep; surely this jet lag had to bugger off soon? Cara had braved the communal showers and had returned to our cell smelling cleaner than Shelley and me, but in a stinking mood. The five-minute-shower rule wasn't just a request. The thing turned itself off after five minutes and wouldn't go on again, so she'd had to wash the suds from her hair in the sink with only ice-cold, recycled rainwater that dribbled out of a funky-looking tap.

'So much for this eco shit. They can stick it!' she'd grumbled as we left, running her thin fingers through her damp locks. Wet-dog hair was not the look she'd been going for, though today's outfit choice was just as impractical as the one she'd worn yesterday. Patent ruby stiletto heels, black drainpipe jeans, a trendy black floppy hat and a draped maroon cape made her look like she should be some top style blogger about to cover London Fashion Week, not a backpacker preparing to soak up some culture and natural sights. 'There'd better be coffee in my hand in the next five minutes, or else.'

Her moaning increased in volume when she realised that her demands weren't going to be met any time soon, as all the small, quaint coffee shops we drove past showed no signs of life.

'How can people even live like this? I swear it's so primitive to not even have a Starbucks!' Cara spat, pulling out her phone and scrolling down the screen.

I noticed Shelley flinch but she stayed quiet.

'The guide books said there's somewhere to grab a drink when we get to the Twelve Apostles,' I offered, hoping she'd give the whining a break. Compared to Shelley's normally sunny demeanour, her cousin would make Oscar the Grouch seem high on life.

The one-hour journey took us out of the sleepy fishing village, through emerald-green forests, then down along the coast, just as the sun was trying to break through. It was only when we reached the entrance to the visitors' car park for the Twelve Apostles – taking in some pretty hair-raising bends and shutting my eyes, praying that the tyres of The Beast would stay on the narrow lanes – did I properly wake up and get excited. An excitement that even the dismal weather couldn't budge.

The blazing Australian sun that I'd imagined was here 365 days a year didn't look like it was going to make an appearance today. I'd bundled myself up in a waterproof jacket, chunky scarf and as many layers as I could find in my bag. One of the very few good things about The Beast was that it did emit a lot of heat; Cara had turned it to the max this morning to try to dry her hair. The only problem was that this toasty space made the outside even more bracing.

'Jesus, it's Baltic!' I heard Cara cry, as we clambered out into the chilly morning air. 'Right, where's this coffee you promised?'

I winced as I saw the grille on the tourist centre coffee shop pulled shut. 'I guess we're still a little early.'

'Great. Just great,' Cara huffed and pulled her coat tighter across her skinny body.

We wandered down the signposted path in silence to the main vantage point, with Cara grumbling under her breath that this was not *her* idea of a hen party.

'Is that them?' I asked, ignoring her and pointing to the bruise-coloured sea where unusual rocks stood like crumbling ruins in a messy line. According to my guide book the Twelve Apostles are imposing rock stacks out in the ocean that once were part of the rugged sandstone cliffs, and over time eroded from caves to arches to pillars. I looked again. 'Wait – I can only see eight of them?'

'What? So we've come all this way, stayed at Bates bloody Motel, forced to function without caffeine and it's not even the real deal!' Cara looked aghast at where I was pointing. 'Oh, that is just bloody typical!'

Shelley bristled next to me. 'I guess over time they've been battered by the weather and now there's only eight of them. It's still pretty impressive if you think about it…'

It was as if huge chunks of the cliff had just decided one day that they needed a break, but had only got a couple of metres out to sea before thinking, sod it, I've proved my point. I'd seen the white cliffs of Dover and the crumbling cliffs of Northern France, but the rock stacks here were more of a golden yellow – well, the photos online showed them to be that way, but in this dull light and with the froth from the churning, murky waters, we could hardly see a thing.

'Just think, when our children travel, there may not be any of them left standing,' I mused, pointing to a plastic information board glistening with sea spray.

'God, don't! I think a lot more will have changed in the world by the time we have children. Seeing those backpackers yesterday was bad enough, imagine the technology when our kids travel?' Shelley shivered, and I don't think it was just from the icy wind.

We walked higher up the coastline, more to keep moving to generate warmth than anything else, following the snaking path that a few other hardy (mad) souls had braved. There was a group of Chinese tourists with every camera and gizmo you could imagine, but none of them had brought an umbrella, and an older couple, plodding behind, shaking their heads when they nearly got a selfie stick in their eye.

'God, it is bloody freezing!' Cara unhelpfully informed us yet again.

'We'll go and see what's up here then head back to the car, shall we?' I suggested, trying to be the peacemaker. Cara grunted a 'fine', then strode off on her long legs.

I turned to Shelley. 'What's with her this morning?'

'Eurgh, Lord knows.' She seemed distracted herself, glancing over at the rocks as if looking for something. 'Do you reckon it will get sunnier?'

I shrugged and blew on my fingers for warmth. 'No idea; it would need a miracle to clear any time soon.'

Shelley nodded slowly, looking as if she was working something out in her head.

'Hurry up!' Cara bellowed at us, bouncing on the spot for some heat.

The path led us to a spectacular vantage point. Well, it would have been if the morning fog rolling over the water hadn't cast everything in a dull, milky light.

Within moments our already sketchy view was blocked off by the bad weather.

'Oh, well that's just bloody brilliant. What a fucking view,' Cara said sarcastically, stretching her arms out wide, gesturing to the thick, soupy mist.

It was almost laughable how Shelley had planned our route specifically to see these iconic Australian rocks; we'd got up before the crack of dawn to experience a spectacular sunrise, but all that lay ahead were some odd shapes peeking out of heavy clouds. We were coated in a fine sea mist, hungry, thirsty, tired and a little pissed off.

'That was such a waste of time. We could have had a lie-in and gone for a proper breakfast. I'm starving!' Cara grumbled loudly, before casting an unseen glare at one Chinese man who was now doing impressive star jumps as his companion tried to capture it on film.

'Let's think of the positives – we wouldn't have wanted to spend much longer in that hostel, we're a little closer to Adelaide, and we can say that we kind of saw the Twelve Apostles. Plus, by now it must be time for cafés to finally open for breakfast?' I said, nudging Shelley in the side gently, and casting a look to Cara. I didn't want a bad mood, tiredness, bickering or shitty weather to ruin this trip for her.

'I guess.' Cara stomped her feet.

'Right, we can head back in a minute, but first can you take my photo?' Shelley asked, handing me her phone.

'I'll take it, as there's no way *anyone* is getting a photo of me looking like this,' Cara said, taking the phone off me and pointing to her hair, which had begun to clump in the sea spray. 'Georgia, get in.'

I stepped forward when Shelley cried out. 'No! I mean, I just want one on my own if that's all right?'

'Okay...'

'It's just I'm making a wedding scrapbook for Jimmy so I need to get photos of me on my own for it,' she hurriedly explained.

'Right then, say cheese!' Cara lifted up her phone as Shelley held her engagement-ring-heavy hand in the air and grinned at the lens.

'Wait! I've got a copy of a wedding magazine in my bag...' She rummaged around, pulled out a battered copy of *Wedding Wonders* and held it up, posing like she was actually reading it. 'This might be a fun shot!'

'Err, yeah, there you go.' Cara took the photo and handed her phone back.

'Oh, excuse me. Would you mind taking our photo?' the older woman we'd seen before kindly asked and passed over a clunky camera.

'Aww, that'll be you and Jimmy soon,' I whispered.

Shelley laughed, ignoring Cara teasing that they already were like an old married couple.

'They are so cute. I just love it when you see old people so happily married after all these years.'

The woman's husband shifted from one foot to the other. 'We don't need another bloody photo,' he grunted. 'I've told her we already have more than enough photos,' he barked, as Shelley awkwardly took the camera. Judging by how loudly he was talking, I guessed he was a little deaf, or maybe it was for our benefit to make sure his negative views were heard over the crashing waves behind us.

His wife flashed a tiny smile at Shelley and shoved her arm through the gap in her husband's many layers of jackets and fleeces, pulling him closer. It was a long-suffering smile that had clearly been perfected over the many years of listening to his grumblings.

'I mean, seriously. You can't even see the rocks, and all we do with these pictures is leave them on the computer clogging up the memory!'

He was staring at Shelley like she was as much of a nutter as his wife, wanting to document this, admittedly poor, view. I was waiting for Cara to jump in and agree with him.

'Oh shush, these women don't need to hear what you have to say,' his optimistic and patient wife added brightly, nodding at Shelley to press the button and take the photo.

'Okay, err, say cheese!' Shelley said, making me stifle a giggle. The old man had his thin lips in a tight line and his wrinkled forehead creased in a frown.

'Cheese!' the woman sang. Her husband muttered something under his breath. 'Oh, thank you so much!' She gratefully took the camera from Shelley. 'You know, the weather man said it was meant to be nice today. In fact, it might still break into a lovely day.'

'Nice!' he barked incredulously. 'Look at the state of it!'

'Well, we'll let you girls get on. Thanks for the photo. Come on now, Bill, let's go for a stroll.'

His eyes almost jumped from their sockets at her suggestion. 'A stroll! Well, I've heard it all now.'

'Come on, dear.' She pulled him away and cast a grateful smile back at us as he continued to moan about the fact there was bugger all to see.

'What was it you were saying about happily married older couples?' Cara sniggered, nudging Shelley in the side as they left.

Shelley gave her a look. 'Come on. Let's go.'

'Before you know it, that'll be you and Jimmy,' Cara teased, as Shelley stomped off back to the car.

*

'Where are we?' Cara looked up from her phone a few hours later, which she had been permanently attached to for most of the morning. 'Why are we slowing down?'

Shelley flashed a sly smile and indicated to turn right. 'Oh, I just thought this would be a good place to stop and stretch our legs. Surely you want another coffee soon?'

'As long as it's not to get us to go to some crap museum or cultural site,' Cara grumbled. 'The Eight Apostles were enough of a let-down for today.'

'It's not, I promise, and the sun is coming out!' said Shelley.

Like some freak force of nature, the misty fog appeared to only be location specific. As soon as we'd pulled away from the Twelve Apostles and driven further inland, the weather had vastly improved. The town she was driving through was like something from an old classic movie. A place where everyone knew everyone. The adorable town centre was pretty much just two short streets with local businesses dotted on each side; a white latticed pavilion stood at the end. It had an air of vulnerable innocence that it had survived as a result of faithful inhabitants and sporadic passers-by.

'This is too cute,' I beamed, as a woman waved to us going past, holding a wicker basket full of colourful fresh blooms.

We drove past gas pumps with patiently waiting attendants, images of beehives hanging in the tatty-looking windows of the hairdressers, and a diner that

I imagined selling soda floats and luncheon meat fritters. Suddenly, I spotted something from the corner of my eye; hidden by a large bush was a sign tacked to a stake in the ground. 'Welcome to the home of the well-known Willie'.

'Err, Shell, what the heck is the well-known Willie?' I asked.

Cara let out a bark of a laugh and looked at her cousin. 'Have you driven us to see Willie? Finally this hen-do is picking up!'

'Is Willie a person? Who the hell is Willie?' I flicked my head between the pair of them. 'Is he related to you?' At this, the two girls burst into a fit of giggles. 'Is this some Australian humour thing, as I don't get it.'

'Well, you can't come all the way down under and not see for yourself. But first, to avoid ruining it, close your eyes and we'll take you to meet Willie.' Shelley grinned.

'Really?' They both nodded. 'Fine. But if I don't get the joke, then don't be annoyed.'

I covered my eyes with my hands as Shelley led the way. I could smell something sweet in the air, like doughnuts or candy floss.

'This is Willie. You can open your eyes now!' Cara shrieked in delight.

I slowly opened one eye. Willie wasn't a man; in fact, he wasn't a person. Willie was a giant six-metre-tall, pale pink penis.

'Oh my God! I've heard about these!' I laughed, straining my neck to look up the wrinkled sides to an impressively smooth, polished tip, covered in bird-poo stains. 'This is one of the Big Things!'

The Big Things of Australia was something Ben had told me about from his previous trips down under. Apparently nearly every Australian state had one;

they were usually man-made sculptures that seemed completely pointless but drew in crowds of tourists purely for the novelty factor. It had become a sort of challenge to see them all.

'Well, what do you think?' Shelley asked, leaning against the base of Willie. 'Pretty big, right?'

I laughed and peered up, shading the sunlight from my eyes with my hand. 'Yep, it may be the biggest Willie I ever did see.' I giggled like a schoolgirl.

'I'd only ever read about it online, never thought I'd see it with my own eyes,' Cara mused, looking much more impressed with this than the previous tourist attraction.

'As soon as I knew this was on the route, we had to make a pit stop,' Shelley laughed.

Nearby was a wooden shack serving as a gift shop selling postcards, t-shirts and even hats, all with the image of the phallic statue plastered across them. A group of tourists were posing with Willie and some children were playing in a small park area that had been built underneath the base.

'One question though – what the *hell* is the point of it?' I asked.

'Willie was this old man who lost his, ahem, little willy years and years ago. There were urban myths of exactly how he lost it – legend has it that the severed genital was found in this very spot. The most popular version was that he lost it when he single-handedly saved the town from a rabid pack of dingoes that had ransacked the place.' Her eyes widened as she retold the tale. 'Anyway, turns out he actually lost it in some farming accident when he'd been drunk one night, but he was already the town's hero by then and no one really seemed to care that he didn't save any lives as the thing had already been erected.'

Cara stifled a giggle at this. 'It is erect all right.'

'So, that's the famous Willie. The fella died a few years back and, once the truth came out that he wasn't such a legend, there was talk of taking it down, but everyone petitioned to keep Willie standing tall.'

I shook my head at the ridiculousness of it all, Australia was slowly but surely winning my heart.

'Selfie time!' Shelley said, pulling out her phone for a photo. 'Can you get one of me for the, erm, scrapbook?'

'Jimmy sure is a lucky guy!' I laughed.

She pulled out the wedding magazine from her bag once more.

'What's this? Is this trip sponsored by them or something?' Cara snorted.

'What? The last photo didn't come out very well. Cheese!' She grinned. 'Right, come on, we'd better be making a move.'

Next stop: the Grampians.

CHAPTER 11

Trepidation (n.) – A feeling of fear or agitation about
something that may or may not happen

Tonight was going to be the 'party night', to celebrate
Shelley's last night of freedom as a single woman.
I could finally bring out all the penis-shaped goodies
that I'd packed, plus the wine, Prosecco and some
fluorescent-coloured liquid called 'Intenze' to do shots
with that had been rolling around in the boot of the
car for long enough. What sort of hen do was this,
after all?

As we left Willie, Cara found some CDs that were
stuffed in one of the seat pockets. Our soundtrack so far
had been a mix of the best of ABBA and a scratched disc
of George Michael, which jumped every time we hit a
slight bump on the road. I'd taken over the driving to
give Shelley a break but also so I could tick off being
behind the wheel on the other side of the world.

'You sure you're ready for this?' Shelley had asked,
nervously chewing her bottom lip as I ungracefully
heaved myself into the driver's seat.

''Course. You've done so much driving, plus the
roads are practically dead.' I swung my arm across the
deserted lanes around us. We hadn't seen another car
for at least the last hour. 'I'll be fine.'

'Just take it slow. It's probably not like other cars
you've driven before.'

I gave her a Brownie Guide salute. It would be fine.
Shelley had made it look easy, and surely once you've

driven one car then the rest are all pretty much the same. I didn't tell her that I'd only been behind the wheel of three other cars in my lifetime.

'Oww,' Cara grumbled, rubbing her head as we aggressively lurched forward for the first fifty metres.

'Sorry!' I wiped the sweat off my forehead as I eased off the worn rubber pedals a little more slowly than before.

After a slightly jumpy start, I'd managed to get the hang of it by having my foot at a strange angle that for some reason seemed to keep us at a constant speed. Shelley announced she was going to have a nap and closed her eyes next to me. Hearing her settle into piglet-style snores and Cara humming along to the music as she pouted for Snapchat selfies, I smiled to myself.

I was driving in Australia. This may not sound like much, but a small part of me wanted my ex Alex to see. To know that the girl who he'd moaned could only drive him mad was in fact in charge of a slightly un-roadworthy four-wheel-drive vehicle and was loving it. I'd forgotten about the feeling that comes with having a steering wheel between your hands, the warmth of the rubber grasped under your fingertips and the sense of freedom this gives you. We coasted along with the breeze through the open windows bringing in smells of pine and churned-up dirt. Driving over here was nothing like battling rush hour on the M56.

The view had changed dramatically as we'd moved further inland from the coast. Gone were the crumbling cliffs, winding, thin lanes hugging the side of looming rock faces and signs for forgotten towns or sheep farms. All I could see on either side were flat plains, tumbleweed and gnarled wooden posts indicating oddly-named creeks and bogs. Not a building, house or sign of life anywhere. If we broke down now we would literally be up shit creek without a paddle. I felt myself shiver at the thought and glanced at the petrol gauge. It was three-quarters full still; apparently this thing was fairly economical after all.

'Looks like someone needed that break.' Cara jolted her head towards Shelley who was catching flies.

'She must have been exhausted. I wish she'd told me, I could have taken over ages ago,' I said quietly.

'That's Shelley though.' Cara shrugged, fanning her face with an old road map.

'What do you mean? She loves to drive?'

'No, well I don't think she's that bothered by it. I mean that she'll never ask for help. She wants to do *everything*, even if it means exhausting herself. She doesn't like to put people out. That's why she's been so on top of this wedding as she wants all the control.'

'How's it going with them living with you? It must be difficult sharing your space with soon-to-be newly-weds?'

'Nah, it's cool,' Cara mused and began picking at a hangnail. 'I'm still figuring out the whole living by myself thing, so having noise in the house again makes me happy. I'll actually be a bit gutted when they do get their own pad, to be honest. It's been so great having her back; she's been travelling for so long that I'm just happy to spend any time with her in one place.'

'You never fancy doing the travelling thing?'

'I get to see enough of the world with work. I mean, modelling is one of those jobs where you never know where you'll be sent for a shoot, but I've never fancied backpacking. I'm more comfortable with luxury than slumming it and would never imagine going solo like you did.' She shuddered, as if thinking about the weird hostel last night. 'To be honest, I don't really like living by myself, never have. I only moved there because it was too good an offer to turn down. I'd been used to living with my ex, but that ended so...' She trailed off, lost in some painful memory.

'What happened?' I asked softly. I didn't want her to think I was prying, but we also had a fair few hours to fill and it wasn't like the view provided much distraction.

'He was shagging his personal trainer. How fucking cliché can you get?' She rolled her eyes, trying to hide how hurt she obviously still felt. 'I don't want to go into it, but it's hard when you think you have everything lined up to go a certain way and then – BAM! – it all comes crashing down.'

I nodded. I knew this better than most people. 'But being dumped can also be just the beginning. You not on the lookout for love then?'

'Pfft, no.' Cara made a noise that was between a snort and a cough.

I took my eyes off the road, glistening in the hazy sun, to look at her face in the rear-view mirror. She was bloody gorgeous, willowy, sinewy, or whatever other weird terms they use for girls who lucked out on the model genes, with impeccable bone structure and a body made for showing off clothes. 'I doubt you'd struggle to find a fella!' I blurted.

'I get by. But the men I meet aren't exactly marriage material.' She rolled her eyes. 'Plus, you saw that old couple.' She shivered. *'That's* not exactly something to aspire to. I'm single and loving it! Seriously, Georgia, it's so much effort having a man all the time.

The worry, the trust issues, the way they make you feel like you're losing your mind at the smallest of things,' she listed.

'Mnrrpmmm.' Shelley woke up with a start, interrupting her cousin's man-bashing sesh. She wiped the dribble from the side of her lips and grabbed the bottle of water at her feet. 'God, I needed that! What have I missed?'

'Nothing much: saw some kangaroos, tried to get the radio to work as we are officially ABBA and George Michael-ed out.' Cara shrugged, looking down at her phone screen.

'Ah cool. So, where are we?' Shelley asked between gulps.

'We've just been going straight on this road like you said,' I replied, stifling a yawn.

Shelley rubbed her eyes and picked up the map, looking around for a marker to indicate where we were. 'Boggy Waters Creek. We're not too much further. The Grampians should be coming into view soon,' she said excitedly.

'Thank God. I need to stretch my legs,' Cara chimed.

I nodded. 'Me too and I need a wee.' My neck was aching, my wrists felt sore and my bum had gone numb long ago as I bounced around on the springy seats.

'Well, ladies, I reckon, according to this, we'll shortly be in Halls Gap!'

Halls Gap was the largest town in the Grampians and was where we'd be spending the night. The guide book said it was a small, pretty town, but with enough going on to keep you occupied. I daydreamed about cute coffee shops lining sun-dappled streets, cheerful hikers waving good day as they set off with their day packs full of sandwiches and flasks of coffee.

'How we doing for petrol?' Shelley asked, stretching her arms in the air as another yawn escaped her mouth.

I glanced at the dial. 'Fine. We've still got three-quarters of a tank.' I shook my head. This Beast was amazingly efficient on fuel.

'Err, Georgia, are you sure?' Shelley narrowed her eyes. 'Three-quarters left?'

'Yep.' I nodded.

Her eyes grew wide. 'But that's as much as it had when I was driving. And that was a few hours ago now,' she said slowly.

I heard Cara's sharp intake of breath.

'Oh, erm, well, I did think it was a bit weird how it hasn't moved.'

'What? It hasn't moved at all?' Shelley leaned over to have a look at the dials in the dashboard herself. 'Fuck!' she cried.

'What?' Cara and I asked in unison.

'The dial must be broken. Lord knows how much gas we've got left.' The sandstone ridges of the national park were slowly coming into sight but they still looked a hell of a way off. Between us and them were only open plains, straggly trees and the odd rusting road sign. 'Did you not think there may have been a problem?' she asked, in a tone that was a lot sharper than I'd ever heard her use with me before.

'I...I just thought this was surprisingly economical,' I mumbled, realising how ridiculous that sounded. I mean, one look at it was enough to realise the only hybrid that this car could be described as was a cross between a dinosaur and a monster truck.

Despite the sun beaming through the open windows, the atmosphere had suddenly grown very frosty. I felt awful for not questioning the fuel gauge earlier, especially as we'd passed a petrol station a while back.

'Shit. We need to turn everything off to save as much fuel as we can. If we break down here then I don't fancy our chances walking all that way to town, if there's even a petrol station there,' Shelley ordered. 'Turn off the radio, any dials that might be the air con and close the windows. Are the lights definitely off? Georgia, you need to keep your speed as constant as you can. If we go too fast then what little we have left will burn faster.'

I nodded, feeling a bit like Keanu Reeves in *Speed* and a bit like a giant numpty. Shelley's mouth was set in a straight line, her arms tightly folded and her face sporting a pretty pissed-off expression.

'Crap!' Cara cried.

'What?'

'My phone battery has just died.'

'I think we're kind of dealing with other more important things here,' Shelley snarled through gritted teeth, keeping her eyes on the fuel gauge.

'That is important! No Google Maps, no Siri to ask for help. Fuck, if we break down we're going to be vulture food!' Cara pouted and scowled out of the window.

'I'm sorry, I just didn't think to check. I'm sure we'll be fine. It's managed to get us this far so I'm sure we'll make it to—'

Just as the end of that sentence was forming, The Beast let out a loud wheeze and juddered beneath my tight grip on the steering wheel.

'What the hell!' I was losing control of the bastard car. We were slowing down even though my foot was still pressed to the ground on the gas pedal.

'Shit!' Cara and Shelley cried in unison.

The Beast jerked forward as if still moving, but then glided to a complete standstill. We'd run out of petrol, going as far as the fumes would take us. We'd reached the end of the tank. I turned to look at them both. 'I think we've reached the end of the tank.'

'Try the ignition again, maybe we've just stalled?' Shelley ordered, her pale cheeks beading with sweat, as without the cool breeze coming in it was like a sauna in here.

I did as she said and forced the key to turn but it was pointless. Nothing was coming to life. I flicked on the hazard lights and slumped back into my seat. Now what? I'd never broken down before and between the three of us we didn't exactly know our way around a car bonnet.

'Get out and grab that map,' Shelley snapped at Cara, who was flicking her head between the two of us, hoping this was some sort of wind-up. 'We need to work out exactly where we are and how the hell we're going to get out of here.'

CHAPTER 12

Apoplectic (adj.) – Overcome with anger

We piled out into the warm sun – the old woman from the Twelve Apostles was right, it had finally cleared up. I immediately had to take off a few layers that I'd piled on this morning – our cold start felt a world away now we were cooking on the side of a road. The heat was dancing on the surface of the dusty tarmac and licking at our legs.

'I'm no expert but they must be the Grampians.' I pointed my arm to the tumbling and slightly hazy-looking green mountains in the distance.

'No shit,' Shelley said through gritted teeth. 'I don't know about you but that looks one hell of a walk away.'

I glanced at my feet, hurt that she was being so sarky. It was a complete accident we were in this situation. And not entirely my fault either. She was co-driver on this trip too.

'It's bloody miles away! What are we going to do? Oh God, do we have enough water?' Cara asked, clasping her hand to her throat and widening her eyes in shock.

'We've got two choices – either we head to the nearest town, which, by the look of it, is a good few kilometres' trek, or we wait and hope someone passes to give us a lift,' Shelley said, glancing up from the map spread out on the bonnet to the looming mountains that appeared closer than they actually were.

'I can't bloody walk all that way in these!' Cara pointed to her completely impractical footwear.

'You didn't bring any other shoes with you?'

She looked at me like I was stupid.

''Course I did.' She tutted and pulled open her bag to bring out three other pairs of high heels, just as pretty but equally as impractical. 'What? I thought we'd be hanging out in wine bars and nice restaurants, not trekking to get petrol in the middle of the bloody outback!'

'My size threes won't even fit one of your size eight toes,' Shelley muttered.

I shook my head. 'None of mine would either.'

'Right, well that sorts it. You can't walk because you'll break a bloody ankle so you're going to have to stay here with the car and mind our things,' Shelley said decisively, before wiping the sheen from her forehead.

'What! You're leaving me here! I'll get my neck snapped by murderers if you do that!' Cara stepped back in shock.

'You can wait in the shade of that tree over there; we've still got some food left over from dinner last night and there's enough water.' Shelley glanced at me to see if I was on board with this plan. I didn't know what our other options were. We couldn't all just wait here hoping a friendly driver would pass by. We hadn't seen any other cars for the last hour, and heading off to find a town was something more than one of us should do in case we got lost.

'I think she's right. You can work on your tan?' I offered.

'This is bullshit,' Cara huffed. 'It's not even my fault we're in this situation. I thought you two drivers knew how cars worked!'

'You should have been better prepared with your fucking wardrobe, Georgia should have checked the petrol more closely and we probably should have just sacked this trip off and headed straight to Adelaide for the sample dress sale—' Shelley flew her hands in the air.

'What dress sale?' I asked slowly, flicking my head to her pissed-off grimace.

She sighed loudly, as if explaining was a huge inconvenience. 'To get my wedding dress.'

'You haven't got your wedding dress yet?' Cara sharply inhaled. 'But you said it was all under control, that Lars was on the case.' She looked as confused as I felt. What was Shelley thinking, leaving the most important item until the very last minute, and why hadn't she told us that this was the reason for our road trip earlier?

'He is,' she snapped. 'He told me about this sale. Anyway, it's my issue not yours, but now that plan may be ruined and the wedding may as well be called off seeing as we don't know how long we'll be out here!'

No one spoke for a minute.

'Hang on, so this girly road trip was just an excuse to get from A to B and pick up your dress.' I clenched my fist. Things were starting to make sense; it had seemed too out of character for her not to make this journey more wedding central. 'God forbid we miss out on getting you to the dress sale in time; forget the fact we're roasting in the flipping Australian outback, oh no, got to get the *perfect* dress for your *perfect* day!' She glared back at me. 'If Cara hadn't spent ages in Melbourne faffing about, then we would have got to the hire-car place on time to get an actual car that has a reliable fuel gauge!' My legs were shaking and my head was pounding in the exposed heat we were all standing in.

'Err, don't blame me!' Cara swung around to face me, her lips pursed and stance quite aggressive, given the height difference she had on me.

'Fine. I'll go by myself.' Shelley balled up the map in her hands and began stomping up the gravelly road ahead.

I forced myself to calm down and catch my breath, realising that arguing wasn't helping the situation. I turned to Cara. 'Stay in the shade and only flag down a car if the driver looks trustworthy. We'll be as quick as we can.'

I couldn't believe Shelley's first thought was not about our safety but about her precious wedding dress, or the fact she'd planned this whole trip just to go to a dress sale rather than hang out with her besties. I was pissed off at her and didn't want to be spending the next few hours alone with her, but I couldn't let her walk off on her own, not in this foul mood. I picked up my pace to catch up with her, ignoring Cara whining that we were a pair of bitches as she stomped over to the cluster of trees opposite the car.

I muttered under my breath with each heavy step I took. Shelley had stalked off and was busy muttering profanities under her breath too. What had happened to the girl I'd met on that dreamy beach in Thailand? She'd be cracking jokes at how inept we all were, making it a fun story that we'd all remember fondly years later, not causing tension so thick in this oppressive heat that I felt like I couldn't breathe. We still hadn't seen or heard another car since setting off. I was glad that we hadn't chosen to wait on the roadside for a prince to rescue us – at least every step was a step closer to civilisation, petrol, and for this hen-do trip to be over. I was quickly drenched in sweat as I plodded on behind Shelley. It was more of a slog than I had imagined – that or I was ridiculously out of shape. High leafy trees surrounding the road blocked out most of the sunlight and the fresh air, making it feel as muggy as a greenhouse, not helped by the weight of unspoken words. In the distance was a smattering of huge granite rocks, seemingly piled haphazardly on top of each other, like some natural game of Jenga. As much as I was struggling to catch my breath, slicked in sweat and desperate for a cold, refreshing drink, I had to admit that the view from here was sensational. Heavy woods stretched out like a mossy blanket as far as the eye could see, gently shaded from pea greens, to rich auburns to mustard yellows. Out from the cover of the trees that rolled to the horizon like billowing sheets on a washing line, the sky was as piercing as denim blue jeans. Leaves the colours of an autumnal rainbow danced around us. Smells of perfumed plants floated up to greet us, and the faint cry of a kookaburra singing from the top of a nearby eucalyptus tree was just about audible.

Being surrounded by such natural beauty made me realise that bickering over silly problems was not worth it. I didn't want this moment ruined by foul moods and sharp tongues; this was her hen do, despite the hidden motives, and, as a bridesmaid, it was my duty to put any issues to one side and smooth things over. I was going to be the bigger person.

'Sorry about before, Shell,' I said, gently taking her warm arm and pulling her to a stop for a second.

'I should have been more observant and less snappy with you.'

She resisted initially then dropped her hunched-up shoulders to face me. Her cheeks were flushed, mascara was puddling under her tired eyes and her cropped hair was tufted up at the front.

'Me too. I just know how dangerous it can be breaking down in the middle of nowhere. I mean, I was probably overreacting, considering it's the middle of the day, but still, once you've lived here, you know that these horror stories can and do happen.' She scuffed her feet in the dirt. 'It has been quite nice to stretch my legs; it is pretty spectacular here to be fair.'

We silently called a truce and stood in awe of the crumbling and peaceful vantage point. Neither of us spoke or moved for a minute or two as we caught our breath, seemingly forgetting we were on a mission to get petrol, just letting our argument float away on the autumnal breeze trailing past.

'I still can't believe you've not got your dress sorted, hun. Are you not cacking yourself about leaving it to the last minute?'

'Sometimes you've got to take risks, I guess.' She shrugged. 'Come on, we'd better get a move on. We don't want Cara to be attacked by a bunch of dingoes.' She paused and gave me a look. 'Well…'

'Wait, you don't think that would happen, do you?' My knowledge of the Australian wildlife amounted to knowing that most things here could kill you.

'Pfft.' Shelley shook her head as we started walking again. 'If they did bother to sniff around her they'd regret it. She's tougher than she looks, plus the town isn't actually too far away.' She pointed to a sign I hadn't spotted up ahead, partly tucked behind overflowing thorn bushes.

I didn't want to push the dress thing, seeing as we'd only just made up, but it felt like she wasn't telling the whole truth. The control freak Shelley, who I'd seen emerge over the last couple of months, obsessing over every small wedding detail, would not be so blasé about leaving her dress to chance. My gut told me that something else was going on here, something she obviously didn't want to discuss.

CHAPTER 13

Enervate (adj.) – Lacking physical, mental or moral vigour

Eddie, our saviour and petrol pump attendant, had filled up a jerry can and driven us back to The Beast, where Cara, who looked a picture of calm, was sitting idly flicking through her magazines under the shade of a tree. Thanks to this knight in grubby overalls, we'd made it to the hostel, which was mercifully nothing like the place we'd stayed the night before. Tonight's accommodation was like a large wooden ski chalet full of homely charm – from the soft tartan blankets lying on the squishy sofas of the common room to the admittedly basic but clean and welcoming bedrooms. Cara hadn't even been able to grumble about the communal showers, as they were newly refurbished *and* there was even free shampoo and conditioner on offer. No five-minute rule here.

She'd been playing her 'get ready' playlist that she'd pre-prepared for the night, and both she and Shelley had been on a walk down memory lane as they reminisced over some obscure Australian pop songs from the late nineties blasting out of the travel speakers.

'So, to get us all in the mood, I've bought some things with me!' I smiled and delved into my backpack.

'Oh, that reminds me!' Cara jumped to her bare feet, almost knocking over the mini bottle of Prosecco she'd given each of us as we got ready. 'I've got some gifts too!'

Shelley placed her eyeliner lid back on and turned around smiling at the pair of us. 'Girls, you didn't have to do that.'

'Me first,' Cara said, ignoring Shelley's protestations that us just being here was a gift in itself. I was still trying to reach into the bottom of my bag. 'This one is for you.' She passed Shelley a white vest top and handed me a pale peach-coloured one. 'Georgia, we've got the same. I thought we could all wear these when we go out tonight.'

I pulled my hand out of my bag. 'Oh, I bought a top for us all to wear too,' I mumbled, but was overshadowed by Shelley falling into a fit of giggles as she opened up the top and read aloud.

'"Soon-to-be Mrs Priors!" I love it!'

I glanced up at the vest top that Cara was holding for me. It read 'Bride Tribe' in gorgeous swirly glittery rose-gold font. Suddenly, my cheap fluorescent pink t-shirts, which that I'd picked up in Primark and on which a lady at the indoor market had ironed a crispy 'Girls on tour' logo in garish neon yellow, seemed even more naff next to these classy-looking tops.

'Erm, wow. Thanks.' I forced a smile, feeling the expensive, cashmere-like material.

'I've also got us one of these hen-do bags each.' She pulled out three perfectly wrapped brown paper packages and handed them out. Inside was chewing gum, plasters, posh make-up wipes, bottles of FIJI water, hair bobbles with a note that said 'to have and to hold your hair back', and some aspirin.

'I thought we could do with a hangover kit tomorrow.' Cara nonchalantly shrugged, but inside I could see how chuffed she was with Shelley's reaction.

'This is perfect! Isn't this a great idea, Georgia?'

'Yeah, erm, great.'

'Wait – what's this!' Shelley burst into a fit of giggles as she pulled out a pregnancy kit, hidden in amongst the other items. 'A preggo test?'

Cara blushed slightly. 'Well, you never know how wild this night will be!'

I glanced down at the pink box. 'I don't want to be a party pooper, but I'm not sure how crazy it's going to get. Did you not see how small this town is!'

'Meh, whatever, we may be in the back end of nowhere but that won't stop us bringing a touch of city glamour to the place.'

'If this is glamour then I'm not sure I want to see what you get up to on a normal night out!' I laughed.

'Did you say you had some stuff too?' Cara asked me.

I shook my head, shoving the pregnancy sticks back in the bag. 'I must have left them at home.' I decided against pulling out the hen-do stash that I'd brought with me, the collection of hilarious willie games and penis-shaped sweets suddenly felt very cheap, tacky and naff.

We decided to have some pre-drinks in the hostel common room and wandered in, clutching a carrier bag of booze and wearing our matching vest tops, Cara and Shelley's both fitting like a second skin, whereas I looked and felt like doner meat wrapped in cling film.

Already well established in the room, sprawled on the royal blue sofas, were three lads huddled over a tablet watching what sounded like a football game, and two girls swiping their phone screens in silence. My heart fell. It was like the hostel common room from last night all over again.

I caught Shelley's eye.

'Hey, guys! How you all doing?' she asked, going into over-the-top friendly traveller mode. The booze had clearly started to kick in.

The three lads looked up and immediately rearranged themselves to appear interested now they'd clocked Cara sauntering in.

'All right?' one of them said, muting the game. 'What you up to?'

'We, my friends, are here to celebrate this one getting married!' I said, spotting the two girls put their phones down as they heard the rustle of plastic bag in my hands. 'Fancy a drink?'

Within seconds, technology was forgotten, plastic glasses were found and large slugs of alcohol were poured out. Turned out the three lads in their late twenties were from Newcastle and had been working on a nearby farm picking oranges for months to extend their working visas. They'd taken a holiday to come and hike the Grampians. All three were single and Cara soon found herself seated between them as they asked her about life in Sydney, the next place on their travel itinerary. The two girls were friends from Sweden who were also driving the Great Ocean Road but going in the opposite direction; we made sure they knew not to stay at the strange hostel from last night.

'Oh God,' one of the guys groaned under his breath as the door to the common room swung open and in plodded a woman who I guessed was in her mid-thirties. She was as short as she was round and seemed to be sweating under her thick tortoiseshell glasses as she cast an inquisitive glance around the room.

'What, do you mean "oh God"?' Cara asked the lads, who'd picked up their tablet once more.

'You'll see,' one of them replied, and hurriedly turned the volume back on the football match.

The late arrival came and sat in the gap next to me, plonking her wide butt down with a shove, then rearranged her baggy t-shirt, which had a cartoon dog on the front, its nose squished into the folds underneath her large bust.

'I'm Sarah-Jane.' She offered me a small, warm hand.

'Hey, Georgia.' I smiled.

'So, what are you guys drinking?' She leant forward and peered into our cups, sticking her nose so deeply into the glass I thought she was going to snort the liquid up.

'Oh, erm, wine. Do you want some?' I offered politely. I could see the guys behind Cara making a hand gesture as if they were slicing at their necks.

Sarah-Jane pondered for a moment and tucked her brown hair behind her ears. 'Oh, okay then. I guess I will.'

She didn't wait for me to hand her the bottle on the table, instead she grabbed a glass and poured a very generous serving and smacked her lips together as she slugged it down in one.

'So, what are you celebrating?' she asked, wiping red wine that was dripping down her stubby chin.

'Shelley here is getting married next week.' Shelley waved and flashed her engagement ring. Sarah-Jane just looked her up and down, rocking a confused expression, as if trying to work out why we were all wearing matching vest tops.

'Pfft.' She tutted and refilled her glass without asking. Shelley's face was a picture; most people she told at least *acted* like they were interested. 'Married?

Why would you want to do that?' She didn't pause long enough to let Shelley answer before she was off again. I would soon learn that Sarah-Jane liked the sound of her own nasally voice. 'I was married once. BIG mistake.' The lads let out a whooping cough to hide their sniggers of surprise that someone had wanted to take Sarah-Jane up the aisle.

She ignored them and continued. 'Never again. Seriously. You should think long and hard about this decision. It's not too late to back out. My sister tried to tell me not to marry him, but I ignored her. And do you know what she said to me afterwards?' She turned to face Shelley.

'Erm…'

'She said, *I told you so*. And do you know what I'll say to you?'

'Let me guess…'

'*I told you so*.' She took off her glasses, let out a short sharp puff of air to fog up each lens and used the edge of her t-shirt to wipe them clean, inadvertently flashing her doughy white stomach as she did.

'Oh, right, well, we have a little more hope for Shelley and Jimmy,' I said politely, trying to ignore the three lads almost pissing themselves in the corner that we'd been stuck with the hostel guest it seemed no one wanted.

'Hmm, you'll see.' Sarah-Jane pushed her glasses back up her stubby nose with her index finger and stared at me. 'Never again. So, how did you get here? Is that your truck out front?'

I nodded.

'I thought so. I said to myself, *Sarah-Jane, that looks like a new truck, I bet there's new people staying here*. I've been here a few days now. Always come and stay here. It's my third time doing the Grampians; done all the big trekking routes around here.' If she noticed everyone's eyes widen at her plump frame in disbelief, she didn't let on. 'You come in by the west or east?' she continued, deciding that I was going to be her buddy for the evening, whether I liked it or not.

'Oh, I really don't kn—'

'See, the east is the best as you get the views, but if you come from the west it's an easier drive.' She interrupted me again. 'I said to myself that next time I'd try a different route, but I like what I know, you know? It's better to stick with what you know. That's what I've learnt over the years. Much easier that way.'

She eventually paused to take another swig of her, sorry, *our* wine. I glanced at Cara and Shelley for some help, but they were deep in conversation with each other. The pair of bitches.

'Hmm,' I mused politely.

'Now, let me tell you, the road that's just off by the big petrol station, you know the one that passes over by the campsite? You should *never* use that one.' She sucked air through her yellowing teeth. 'Big mistake. I always tell myself that. I say, Sarah-Jane, *don't even think about going that route*. I've been here three times now, did I tell you that?'

Oh God, kill me now.

'Well, we all made it here safely, I guess that's the main thing.' I smiled brightly, trying to do that typically British thing of nodding my head and pressing my lips together as if about to say something else, but staying silent, hoping the conversation would dry up so I could escape.

Sarah-Jane took off her glasses and breathed heavily on each lens again. 'You say that, but actually did you know that…'

And so it continued, and, before I knew it, I was being lectured on the Australian road network.

'Right, let's finish these then head out before she gets back!' Cara cried a few minutes after Sarah-Jane had gone to get a pen and paper to draw out a map for me to fully understand its intricacies.

I got to my feet, realising that Sarah-Jane had nicked my drink and I was all out. I'd not even managed to finish one glass since we'd arrived.

'Who's with us?' Shelley asked.

As much as the footy-loving lads had enjoyed an impromptu drink, they passed when we said we were heading out. Apparently they had an early start tomorrow to get back to their work and the boss had no problems with docking wages or kicking them out altogether. I suspected that was utter bullshit and they wanted to escape from Sarah-Jane and her never-ending mindless chatter. The two girls were going to cook some dinner at the hostel and then join us later, but they said this without much conviction.

'I'm in!' Sarah-Jane strode back in at the precise moment we were heading out.

So we were unable to shake off the most boring woman in the world. Maybe she'd lose interest once we got to the bar and find some other backpackers to hang out with instead. Maybe.

CHAPTER 14

*Lugubrious (adj.) – Looking or sounding sad
and dismal; mournful*

'Apparently Big Al's bar is *the* place to go,' I said to Shelley, linking her arm.

'Big mistake.' Sarah-Jane made that irritating teeth-sucking noise once again. 'That place is full of teens. You want to try and find Dingoes, it's just up by the laundrette.'

We bowed down to her local knowledge, which it soon transpired was pointless. For all her bluster about her experience of this town, considering she'd been here three times before, Sarah-Jane didn't appear to have the faintest idea of where anything was.

'Oh, well, it used to be around here.' She had her hands clasped on each hip, frowning up and down the quiet street that we'd walked along for the second time in fifteen minutes. Her eyes squinted through her glasses, as if the bar was playing a trick on us and would suddenly appear by the patch of trees opposite. We were all a little pissed off, thirsty, and bored of being sent on a wild-goose chase with Sarah-Jane as our inept guide.

'Right, this is ridiculous. It's Shelley's hen do and we need to get booze in us fast.' Cara raised a hand in the air. 'Let's just go to Big Al's. It's got to be better than traipsing around going nowhere. These shoes were not made for walking.' She pointed at her killer heels, the soles darkened with what could have been kangaroo poo.

'You're right,' I said, turning to Sarah-Jane. 'Let's head there. Maybe someone in there will know where this Dingoes place is?'

Sarah-Jane muttered that she was certain it used to be down here but followed us as we headed back up the street to the first bar. I couldn't help but feel sorry for her. I knew both Shelley and Cara were giving me looks to get rid of her, but for all the worries I had that she would start slagging off marriage once more, I didn't know how to nicely tell her to F off. Yes, she was annoying thinking she knew it all, but she was harmless enough. So, we ended up in Big Al's bar with Sarah-Jane trailing behind, moaning that this was going to be One Big Mistake.

I hated to admit it but, glancing around the place, she had a point. Everyone in here looked at least fifteen years younger than us. Since when had we become the oldest backpackers at a backpacker bar? Big Al's was an indie electro club that played classic tunes butchered by a heavy bass. My head started pounding the moment we set foot in the dingy and dim room.

'I'll get the drinks in!' Cara shouted over the awful music, and hurriedly barged through the crowd using her sharp elbows.

'I'll come with you,' Shelley offered, leaving me and Sarah-Jane surveying the scene. I was sure I'd just seen a girl, who couldn't have been older than sixteen, stagger past holding a bottle of alcopop, wearing a tiny, bright blue playsuit with images of the Teletubbies plastered over it.

'I'm going to the loo.' I turned to Sarah-Jane who was gawping unsubtly. Her small mouth was set in a perfect 'o' as she took it all in. To be fair, in her naff animal t-shirt, she probably fitted in more than the rest of us; at least she could pass her look off as retro hipster with an ironic twist. In my black jeans and sparkly skintight hen-do top, I felt like I'd raided my mum's wardrobe to hang out with the 'yoof' of today.

I didn't let her answer before I zipped off to the ladies'. It was even worse in here. Three girls in near-matching neon-pink, lace-bra tops were leaning over the filthy sinks, trying to perfect their eyeliner or adding a swipe of bright lipstick. I'd expected the bar to be dead, judging by how remote this place was, but it seemed that everyone under the age of twenty-three had rocked up from nearby towns and villages to be here tonight. Posters advertised two-for-one on chips and burgers served until 1 a.m. The floors were sticky, the music awful, and the smell in here was horrific. The heavy clouds of powdery perfume couldn't mask the fumes of vomit and piss. I nipped into the last free cubicle and hovered over the toilet seat, which was peppered with droplets of the previous user's bladder.

You're here for Shelley, her last night of freedom and all that. So maybe she was hoping for more of a classy cocktail bar than a scuzzy dive club, but she has Cara and me here. We can have fun anywhere, I told myself, as I gave up hope of finding any usable loo roll. It wasn't just the dodgy place we were in that made me feel anxious, Shelley hadn't seemed herself since I'd arrived. Yes, the old Shelley wouldn't care that her feet stuck to the floor or that we had to wear a naff neon wristband to get in. But this new Shelley, the stressed-out and frazzled one, had failed to hide her look of disgust as soon as we'd paid our five dollars entry fee. I sighed and hoped that Cara had got the round of drinks in and that this would be one of those stories we would tell in years to come of how we had the best night ever in the middle of nowhere. Even with Sarah-Jane hanging on.

Another girl barged past me to get into my cubicle before I was even half out of it, and proceeded to decorate it with the lining of her flat stomach. I hurriedly washed my hands and shook them dry.

'I'm telling you, he's flirting with you, he's totally up for it!' one girl with blonde, curled hair said to her mate, who was rubbing lipstick off her slightly protruding front teeth.

'But he's been with that bitch Lauren all last week and there's no way I'm going to be a rebound,' her friend replied, slicking on more lipstick with a swaying arm.

I wanted to wrap the girls up into something less revealing, read them bedtime stories and basically mother them.

'You all right there?' Blonde curls turned to me. I didn't realise I'd been staring at them so intently.

'Fine, sorry,' I mumbled, and pushed past the growing queue of girls to get out into the loud club.

I hurriedly weaved my way past spotty lads bouncing to the music with their arms around their friends' shoulders. Something cold dribbled down my back as I pushed through the boisterous group.

'Hey, guys!' I plastered on a smile at Shelley, Cara and Sarah-Jane, who'd managed to find a free booth to sit in. Their faces gave it away. They were hating this too.

'I just got asked if I was the mother of the bride!' Shelley moaned, having to shout in my ear to be heard over the music. 'I've sat in chewing gum and Cara has already had her bum pinched three times.'

'The last one was lucky not to have got a punch in return,' Cara growled in the direction of a man who was unsuccessfully lying on the floor nearby, attempting to do the worm.

'Since when did we get so old? Or everyone else get so young!' Shelley grimaced as a group of three skinny girls strutted past wearing tea towels as dresses.

'I don't want to say it but…' Sarah Jane paused. *Don't say it, don't say it.* 'I told you so.'

She said it.

I thought Cara was going to use that punch she'd been saving up for Sarah-Jane's face.

'I'm psychic, you see.' Sarah-Jane shrugged, sipping her drink.

'You couldn't bloody see the future to find that other bar, could you?' Cara bitched under her breath, taking a big gulp of whatever she was drinking.

'Why don't we play a game?' I suggested, ignoring Cara's sly dig. I rummaged in my handbag for the only hen-do-related prop I hadn't hastily buried in my bag, after deciding they were tacky compared to what Cara had brought. It was a funny game that I'd printed off from the internet. No one seemed excited apart from Sarah-Jane, who raised her pudgy arm in the air.

'I do! Ha ha, get it? *I do!*'

'Okaaaaay then.' I wished she would put her hand back down and hoped that a light-hearted game would get us all in the mood for fun. 'Although, I'm not sure how well you'll do as it's about Shelley and Jimmy. A *Mr and Mrs* game,' I explained.

'Oh. Well, I can give it a good shot. I always used to win games like this in college. In fact, I was the champion of the Scrabble club, the pub quiz team and Cluedo class.' She stuck her chest out proudly.

'I bet you didn't win any popularity contests,' Cara mumbled loudly.

I began reading out the first question, focusing my attention on Shelley, who looked bored rigid. 'So if you get it right we drink and if you get it wrong you drink.' The three girls nodded along. 'Question one, how many times did Jimmy take his driving test?'

Shelley chewed her bottom lip, thinking about this one. I heard Sarah-Jane tut that she had an unfair advantage. 'Erm, twice?'

I shook my head. 'Ben told me it was five times.'

'Five!' Shelley gasped.

'Bloody hell. No wonder you don't own a car over here,' Cara laughed.

'Wow, erm, I didn't know that.'

'Next up, what age did he lose his virginity?'

Shelley raised her hand, ignoring Sarah-Jane doing the same thing. 'I know this. He was eighteen but told everyone he'd already lost it aged sixteen.'

'I would have said seventeen,' Sarah-Jane piped up.

'The answer is…' I paused, turning over the sheet of paper that I'd asked Ben to help me with. 'Nineteen.' I winced.

'Oh, right, yeah, well, it was one of the two,' Shelley mumbled and gulped her drink. I was beginning to regret this game.

'The next one is, what was the name of his first pet?' I asked tentatively.

Shelley nodded confidently. 'I *definitely* know this. It was a hamster called George Best.'

'What?' Sarah-Jane asked, flicking her head between us.

'Sorry, wrong again,' I mumbled, catching a look that Cara was giving me. I hurriedly tucked the piece of paper back into my handbag and picked up my drink.

'Really?' Shelley asked in surprise. 'What was it?'

'A ferret called Mr Kimble. But, it doesn't matter. It's just a silly game.'

'So, when are you and Ben going to be tying the knot?' Cara asked, picking up on the stale atmosphere and quickly changing the subject.

I scrunched up my nose. 'I don't know. I mean, not that long ago I was convinced he was going to propose, but it wasn't the right time, for either of us. Who knows what will happen in the future?'

I couldn't admit that seeing Shelley stress so much about her big day had raised concerns in my mind about whether I wanted to get thrust into the crazy world of weddings again. I wasn't sure I could stomach the downsides that came with organising such a big party and everything that came with this circus. I took a sip of my drink. The alcohol tasted strong and difficult to swallow.

'You know what I think about weddings,' Sarah-Jane piped up.

'Well, you know what they say about the engagement domino effect?' Cara said, now acting as if Sarah-Jane was invisible.

'What's that?' I asked.

'That once one guy in a group of friends pops the question, you can guarantee it won't be long until the others follow suit, hence why so many summers are filled with weddings within friendship groups. It's like they think they're missing out, or it's something that they *should* do regardless of whether they're *ready* to do it,' Cara explained.

'And who said romance was dead?' I laughed. I wasn't pushing Ben to get down on bended knee any time soon; it would happen when it would happen. Organically rather than forced.

'You're not thinking he might whisk you off to the Opera House whilst you're both here and use that as a backdrop?' Cara winked.

I felt Shelley tense beside me.

'No.' I paused. 'You don't think he will, do you?'

Shelley shrugged. 'Well, I mean he *could* do it. Jimmy hasn't said anything to me about it though. But then, as we've learnt tonight, Jimmy doesn't tell me much about himself.'

As soon as she dismissed the idea, I felt my stomach flip a little – strange when I wasn't even waiting for a proposal, although that would be a pretty great story to tell the grandchildren.

'Oh my God!' Cara squawked. We all turned to face her. 'What if he proposes to you at their wedding?'

Shelley's face dropped, Cara began clapping her hands and Sarah-Jane joined in, not really knowing what she was applauding.

'No, he wouldn't do that.' I laughed awkwardly.

'He'd better bloody not!' Shelley said, gripping her glass so tight her knuckles turned white.

'Oh come on, it would be nice!' Cara teased her cousin, who looked like she could think of another four-letter word to describe Ben stealing her thunder and proposing to me at her wedding.

'Anyway, you can't get engaged this year. It's my year!' Shelley slapped the palm of her hand on the sticky table, making our glasses judder. She was not joking. This only made Cara burst out laughing.

'What? Shell, you can't have a whole year. You get one day, remember?'

Shelley muttered something into her drink as Sarah-Jane patted her on her hunched-over shoulders.

'Shell, don't worry. Ben wouldn't dream of doing it then; he'd know I would hate that!' I said, slightly shocked at how seriously she was taking this silly idea of Cara's.

'Yes, but it *might* happen.' She turned to me, her glassy eyes narrowed, as if I'd suggested that we may as well have a joint wedding.

'It won't happen,' I said more forcefully.

'You *thought* he was going to propose to you in Chile. Excuse me if I don't think you have the best judgement when it comes to matters like this.'

I sat back in my seat. I knew she was pissed off that she'd fucked up on the *Mr and Mrs* game, that this was not her idea of a rocking hen do and that Sarah-Jane still had a chubby hand clasped on her shoulder, but there was no need for that.

'Shelley. He won't propose to me at your wedding, you're being ridiculous.'

Cara had stopped laughing and was now leaning out of her seat, trying to catch the eye of one of the group of lads at the next booth, who were flicking up soggy beer mats, looking for an escape route.

'Shelley, when were you born?' Sarah-Jane asked, ignoring the stale atmosphere that had settled over the booth.

'What?' she snapped.

'What time were you born?' Sarah-Jane repeated, not put off by the look Shelley was giving her. She clearly wasn't in the mood for playing any more games.

'Dunno. The morning sometime.'

'And when was your soon-to-be husband born?' Sarah-Jane asked.

Shelley let out a deep sigh. 'I couldn't tell you.'

'Oh!' Sarah-Jane's squinty eyes popped open a fraction. 'Well, that's not a good omen to begin with. Right, well, unless you have that information then I can't help you.' She folded her arms, squishing the face on her t-shirt, which now had a reddish stain on the shoulder. 'I really can't believe that you don't know this sort of information.'

'What's that supposed to mean?' Shelley sat up a bit straighter. I wished Sarah-Jane would shut up – had she not seen what a mess I'd made of playing games earlier?

'Well…' Sarah-Jane paused, pleased to finally have all of us as an audience. It was either listen to her or watch two lads down a line of shots and howl like wolves at the table next to us. 'Georgia, do you know when Ben was born?'

I cautiously nodded. 'He was born in a thunderstorm, at midnight, and they weren't exactly sure if his birthday was the day before or after as there was a power cut,' I said, then quickly added, 'But I only remember that because he jokes that technically he could have two birthdays.' I spotted Shelley's face fall, as if she'd failed another sort of bride-to-be test. 'Right, anyone for another?' I asked, getting to my feet, hoping to change the conversation.

'Yeah. Sarah-Jane, it's your shout.' Cara nodded at the bar, finishing the dregs of her glass.

Sarah-Jane ignored her and let out a bellowing sneeze before wiping her nose on her bare arm. 'Excuse me. Actually, I think I have to be making a move. All the dust in here is making my allergies flare up.' Without a moment's hesitation, she got to her feet and waddled off out of sight, leaving us staring at the empty space with matching expressions of *What the hell just happened?*

'Is she for real?' Cara shrieked. 'I know I've been called a freeloader in the past but that girl is ridiculous. Seriously though, drinking our wine, taking us on a wild-goose chase, then moaning constantly about this place, no wonder she's travelling by herself – no one else could put up with her.'

'I should know Jimmy's time of birth though,' Shelley mused sadly. 'And all the other questions.'

I turned my head to look at her. 'No, that's not a normal thing to know. I wouldn't know what time my other boyfriends were born, or even what some woman in a dog print t-shirt would make of that, and I don't care. Don't let it ruin your night.'

Shelley shrugged and finished her drink, looking as if the night had been ruined long before this moment. Without Sarah-Jane's non-stop chatter, it felt like the atmosphere was as flat as a deflated balloon. All around us was a teenage apocalypse and we were out of place, pretty much sober, and seriously jaded.

'Let's just call it a night?' Shelley yawned.

'What? No! It's still early and this is your hen do!'

'My feet are killing me,' Cara admitted, pulling her gaze up from a stain on the table.

Shelley nodded and stood up. 'Mine too. I'm too old to party like I used to.'

'But, but, it's your last night of freedom!'

She'd made her mind up that the night was over, and no matter how many times I offered to get us a drink, have a dance or talk about the wedding, she still wanted to leave.

'I also need to go and swot up on my soon-to-be husband,' she added without a hint of sarcasm, as we made our way outside and started the walk back to the hostel.

We'd only got as far as the end of the street when Cara pointed, breaking the dejected silence we'd found ourselves in.

'Is that Sarah-Jane?'

We followed Cara's gaze over the road where, sitting on a bench, swinging her chubby little legs, with a polystyrene takeaway box on her lap, lost in the ecstasy that a post-booze kebab gives you, was Sarah-Jane.

I shook my head in disbelief. 'She managed to find the kebab shop all right then.'

'Yeah, maybe she is psychic after all,' Shelley muttered sadly. 'What does that say to you about my luck?'

CHAPTER 15

Machinate (v.) – Engage in plots or intrigues; to scheme

The journey to Adelaide was our quietest one yet. I wasn't sure if it was because we'd been in each other's company for too long, were slightly hungover, or just wanting to be back in civilisation, but it felt like something had changed. We'd left, thankfully not bumping into Sarah-Jane as we checked out, and made sure to fill up a little at each petrol station we passed. Fool us once and all that.

It was strange returning to civilisation. Swapping dusty barren plains for sprawling motorways, wide pavements, busy roads, and lush green parks plonked between it all. Adelaide is the fifth biggest city in Australia; everything appeared to be stretched out. It felt as though you had the whole street to yourself but also needed to walk the length of it just to get to the next tall and wide building.

'Shell, is the sample sale, like, an evening late-night shopping thing?' I asked, glancing at the setting sun highlighting the dust motes and sticky fingerprints on the dusty dashboard.

'No,' she replied, shifting in the driving seat.

'Are we staying in another hostel tonight then, to be there for first thing tomorrow morning?' Cara asked, trying with all her might not to let out a moan at the thought of another hostel.

'No.' Shelley fixed her eyes on the road signs.

'A hotel?' Cara's voice lifted three decibels in anticipation. This was clearly a woman in desperate need of room service, feathery soft duvets and tasteful soft furnishings.

'Not quite,' Shelley wouldn't give any more away and told us to look out for the Serenity Bridal Store. Cara and I passed looks of confusion between ourselves.

'Ah, there it is!' Shelley shouted, and veered The Beast into a parking space.

'I don't see any hotels.' Cara peered outside the window at the quiet street; the sky was darkening with every second. 'I don't see this shop either. You sure we're in the right place? Where's the hotel you've booked?'

'You can't see one because we're not staying in one,' Shelley said, cutting the engine and turning to face both of us. 'We're staying here.'

'Here?' Cara and I said in confused unison.

'Like, in the truck?'

'No!' Shelley laughed as if we were idiots, 'Out there…' Opposite us was a large, red-brick shop with two enormous flouncy bridal dresses in the window. Signs announcing the sample sale of the year were hung haphazardly in the softly lit glass, but the most worrying part about all of this was that trailing off, just to the left of the wide double doors, were rows of tents pitched up for the night.

'You cannot be serious!' Cara quickly caught up to speed with what Shelley had planned for us. 'I thought you were joking when you said you were packing a tent!' The colour had drained from her face, even in the bright street lamp that had just flickered on outside.

'If we expect to stand any chance with finding the dress I want, then we have to get the best spot in the queue, and that means spending the night in line. It'll be fun!' Shelley dismissed our open mouths and flung her door open.

'It's official. She's lost the plot,' Cara gasped.

I just stared in disbelief at the impromptu campsite, unable to string a sentence together.

Shelley poked her head in the door as she began heaving our things out of the boot. 'Come on, hurry up. The queue is already building!'

She raced off with bags under her arms, leaving Cara and me to shake our heads in disbelief.

This was surely taking bridesmaid duties to the extreme?

*

'You girls packed your thermals?' The woman from the next tent along asked, after we'd managed to put up the blasted thing. 'It's set to be a cold one tonight.'

'Screw this!' Cara huffed. 'I'm sleeping in the car.'

Shelley didn't say a word as she watched her storm off to take shelter.

'You want me to go and talk to her?' I asked.

'Nah, to be honest, I could do with a break from her moaning.' She sighed and plumped up a pillow that was peeking out of her sleeping bag, then passed me a sandwich and bottle of water she'd picked up at our last petrol stop for our dinner.

'Thanks for staying here with me,' she said quietly, picking out some tomato and flicking it on the pavement outside.

'It's an experience. I don't think I'll ever go on another hen do like this one,' I said honestly. 'I still can't believe that you've left your dress to the last minute.'

'I hadn't planned to!' She sighed. 'It's been crazy. I mean, the first time I went into a wedding dress shop, I was expecting it to be like you see in the films. But, actually, it's just row upon row of extra decisions that you have to make. I never knew it would be so tricky. What fabric do you want: lace, satin, taffeta, tulle, silk?' She pulled a face as she ticked things off her fingers. 'Then what shape: A-line, princess, Grecian, drop waist, tea dress, full skirt with or without ruffles, mermaid? And that's not all!' She paused for breath. 'Then you need to know what you want on the top half: strapless, sweetheart neckline, spaghetti straps, halter-neck, one-shouldered, full sleeves, cap sleeves, high neck. Honestly, Georgia, I'll never look at a wedding dress the same way again. I feel like I've passed some sort of exam to get where I am now. That's before you decide if you want a train, a veil, a tiara, or matching accessories. In one shop I went to with Cara, some woman was trying to get me to wear white gloves as apparently they're making a comeback.'

I smiled, imagining Shelley rocking a Michael Jackson-inspired solo glove on her big day.

'I told my mum about it all and she said that in her day she made her own dress, but that's probably because she couldn't find exactly what she wanted. Now we're spoilt for choice and it's so hard to be decisive.'

'But you do know *exactly* what dress you want?'

Shelley nodded. 'Yep. I tried it on and I just knew.' She had this dreamy look on her face, as if she'd just been whisked off to somewhere other than this chilly nylon den we were huddled in. 'But then Lars told me about this sample sale that he'd heard about. I just knew I had to give it a go; even if it doesn't fit, Lars has got an amazing seamstress lined up for me, so all we need is the dress!'

Here was a small spark of the free-spirited Shelley I knew and loved.

'Once we get back to Sydney, it's going to be pretty full on,' Shelley said, scrunching up the wrapper of a cereal bar that passed as our dessert.

'You've got me to help with whatever needs sorting.'

'I need to check that Jimmy has taken care of Cara's place since we've been away – knowing him he'll say he's cleaned it, but actually it'll be a man's clean rather than a proper clean. Then we have loads of wedding stuff to finalise before everyone arrives. I'm still waiting to hear back from some of our suppliers, but we'll be seeing Lars so I can chase that up with him.' She didn't pause for breath, reeling off the list from her mind and tapping her fingers as she spoke. 'I'm terrified I'm going to forget something,' she admitted, lowering her voice. 'You don't really think Ben will propose to you at my wedding, do you?'

I wanted to laugh at how seriously she was taking this ridiculous idea. 'No. I'm sure of it.'

She was silent for a moment. 'Okay then. Well, that's good. Right, we should probably try and get some sleep. It's going to be an early start tomorrow.' She shuffled further into her sleeping bag and turned off the torch light on her phone.

*

As soon as the sun rose, movement rippled among the tents around us. It was almost time. Cara had eventually rejoined us, complaining that she was tired and hungry. I bit my tongue. I'd spent a cold and uncomfortable night with a numb arse, fingers aching from possible frostbite, and had to suffer through constant snorts emanating from the lady in the next tent along.

'Right, we all need to get our heads in the game, ladies,' Shelley said after packing everything up. She had this steely glint of determination in her tired-looking eyes as she prepared for battle. 'Our plan of attack is that we hunt for the Cerise Coco "Heavenly" gown, in a size ten.'

I half expected her to pull out the swatches of fabric she wanted, strips of colours in the exact shade, or cuttings from a bridal magazine with the different variety of dresses we may find. Instead, she pulled out her phone and swiped through a full photo album of identical-looking wedding dresses.

'This is the *exact one* we want to get. Memorise it.' She thrust the screen at both of our faces. 'A-line, tulle skirt with illusion neckline, covered in beaded lace.' I wasn't about to ask what the hell an illusion neckline was, I just nodded and hoped Cara would find it first. 'If that isn't there, then just grab any size ten dresses, preferably from Cerise Coco, and we'll go from there!'

'Fine by me,' Cara said, rubbing her hands together. 'Be warned, Georgia, the competitive streak is genetic in our family and I expect you to join us. There's no way we're leaving this shop without Shell's dream dress, even if I have to take some bitches down in the process.'

'God, remind me never to get on the wrong side of you two!'

'Right, by my reckoning, the shop will be opening in twenty minutes. Have you seen the length of this queue now?' She looked so pleased with herself as I craned my neck to take in the snaking line of hungry, savvy brides who'd emerged sometime during the night. 'All the good stuff will be gone by the time they get in!' she said smugly.

I hadn't anticipated quite what an 'up to seventy per cent off' sign would do to the women of Adelaide. This place was packed. Police had even turned up to try to direct traffic from rubbernecking at the stationary line to see what the fuss was about. We hadn't stepped a foot in the door and it was already bedlam. Guys wearing fluorescent jackets were blowing whistles and shouting at everyone to move over on the pavement to let other shoppers past. Rumours had been spreading that the sale was going to get cancelled for health and safety reasons. Shelley looked like she might faint.

'You girls missed it all kicking off at the store in Brisbane,' a lady in front of us said, breathing pickled onion crisps as she spoke. 'One of my cousins lives there and told me it was a complete nightmare.'

'What happened?' Cara leaned in.

'Well, three sheilas pushed in. Big girls they were; decided they didn't need to wait patiently like the rest of us and marched straight to the front. Chaos it was. She thought the store assistants were going to come out and tell everyone to go home. The police had to be called in and they even had the local TV station there filming it all. My cousin got interviewed and everything.'

Her mate, wearing an unflattering crinkly pink bomber jacket, groaned. 'Pfft. Purlease, this ain't no different than any other busy shop with a sale on.'

'Yeah, I hope so. To be honest, they'll have to open soon or it will be bloody murder if all these ladies get sent home having waited all night for nothing.'

'Wow,' I mused, shaking my head. All this for a cheap wedding dress. 'Is there even enough stock in there for everyone?'

The trio of women in front started laughing at me. 'Lovey, those at the back probably won't even get a look in. The website said there would be over a thousand dresses here, but I also heard that there are dress touts who sneak through the back to get in first,' she whispered, making the others suck air through their teeth.

'A what now?' I asked, thinking I'd heard her incorrectly.

'A dress tout.' Shelley shivered. 'Like at a pop concert, they're the people who go in and buy all the best tickets – or in this case dresses – to sell on the black market for triple the price.'

'There's a black market for wedding dresses?' I asked in amazement. This was getting weirder by the second. 'I bet they hang out in alleyways in the dead of night offering to do you a deal if you follow them to their mate's truck for a dress that "fell off a lorry",' I joked, making air quotes with my fingers.

The women nodded solemnly. 'Exactly.'

'They can't do that, surely! There must be, like, a limit on the number of gowns you can buy?'

'Didn't you hear what I told you earlier about fights breaking out?' the first lady asked, getting sick of my protestations that she was bullshitting us. 'There ain't going to be nothing or nobody who will stop these women getting what they want, you mark my words.'

I saw Cara gulp.

'Oh you'll be fine, lovey. You can just peer over all of their heads and spot your way out. In fact...' She paused and flashed her friend a look. 'With you being so tall and all that, you wouldn't mind looking out for this dress, would you?' Her mate passed over a photo of an ivory strapless gown with big ruffles at the bottom and material folded to make a couple of roses dotted under the corset-style top.

'Hey!' Shelley pulled herself taller and cast a look at the lady with gross crisp-breath. '*She's* with us.'

The woman glanced at the floor, hurriedly put the paper away and turned back round.

'Don't be fraternising with the enemy.' Shelley narrowed her eyes at the back of the woman's head as she spoke in hushed whispers to Cara.

Just then there was a loud, high-pitched shriek further down the queue. Half expecting to witness handbags at dawn and fisticuffs on the pavement, Cara leant forwards. 'Oh my God.'

'What?' we all turned to ask her.

'The doors have opened.'

At that, the line nudged forward a fraction before we all pushed and shoved to get in as soon as possible. Operation wedding dress was on.

*

The noise was insane. Women of all ages and backgrounds were squawking like ravenous baby pigeons.

'Oi, I had that one first!'

'You want to take this outside?'

'Back off biatch!'

I felt like I'd stumbled into some female wrestling match with every competitor experiencing raging PMT as women eyeballed each other, clutching different halves of the same dress. The shop assistants cowered behind the long line of tills set against the far wall. Three security guards were swamped by wall-to-wall racks of wedding dresses. It was every woman for herself in here.

'I'll go left, Cara, you go right, and, Georgia, hit the central aisles. Get as many size tens as you can!' Shelley screamed, and was quickly lost in a throng of women lurching towards a fresh rail that was being dragged out by a wide-eyed, spotty lad who dumped the rack and legged it back to the safety of the storeroom.

I was being pushed and shoved by faceless arms, elbows and handbags as I tried to get over to the central section. The shop was enormous, but because of the frantic brides and their entourages it felt like we were trapped in a phone box. So much for letting people in one at a time. Racing my trembling hands over the coat hangers, stepping over dresses that had been pulled to the floor and almost tripping on abandoned bags and shoes as women raced to try the dress on in the centre of this bedlam, I spied the section for size ten and made a beeline over to it. I didn't even get the chance to check the price tags, I just scooped up four dresses that were within arm's distance and awkwardly bundled them up.

With my selection in hand, I barged my way over to the suit section of the shop to catch my breath. There were three bemused-looking men gawping at the madness playing out in front of them. I felt like I'd reached base camp. I held up the dresses that I'd safeguarded for Shelley – thankfully three of them were slimline gowns and looked pretty similar to the one she liked. Now I just had to wait.

I didn't know if it was the noise, the heat, or the suffocating air of hysterical energy but suddenly I felt like I couldn't breathe. It hit me like a punch to the stomach that the last time I'd held a wedding dress in my hand it had been my own.

Gripping the soft fabric of these dresses in my clammy hands made my own dress-buying experience come rushing back. The anticipation of what would suit me, the desperation to be wearing something that made me look the best version of myself, the need to please Alex and his traditional mum...The fact that I never got to wear *my* dress.

Tears sprang to my tired eyes, my heart was pounding, and it felt like I couldn't get enough air into my heaving chest. *For fuck's sake, get it together, Georgia.* Except, I wasn't doing this on purpose. It was as if I'd taken leave of my senses and all these emotions that I thought I'd had a handle on came spurting out, like a pipe that had been repaired with tape that wasn't strong enough to hold against the blast of water.

I didn't even know why I was crying, or why I felt like I'd been punched in the gut. I certainly didn't have any feelings for Alex any more, that part I knew to be true. I just couldn't stop this crushing, invisible weight of lost chances and broken promises pushing down heavily on my shoulders as I ran the fabric of Shelley's potential dresses through my trembling hands.

When I thought Ben was going to propose to me in Chile, I'd tried to get my head around the prospect

of being someone's fiancée again. However, when
the proposal never happened, I'd placed 'weddings'
in the *maybe some day* category, along with buying
a dog, getting a tattoo and learning how to ski, and
I was totally okay with that. I knew he loved me and
I loved him, but we had our hands full with work
and relocating so there wasn't a spare minute to
think properly about going up the aisle. At this very
moment, I missed Ben more than I had during any
of my other trips away. It was as if my body ached to
see him, and for him to see me wearing one of these
dresses.

'You all right, darl?' A man with a severe buzz cut
and faded anchors inked on each forearm hesitated
before coming over to me. 'My daughter's out there at
the moment.' He nodded to the carnage. 'Didn't you
find the one you wanted?' He was awkwardly holding
a fuchsia-pink handbag – his daughter's, I presumed –
and looked like he wanted a distraction from waiting
in the men's zone.

I sniffed loudly and wiped my eyes with the back of
my hand. 'Yeah, well no I…' I trailed out, trying to
find the breath that had been knocked out of me. I was
about to blurt out what had happened, how I'd never
got to have *my* moment and wear a dress like the ones
around me. How I didn't know if I ever would have
my moment. Looking at his kind face, his dark eyes
knotted in concern for this English woman dripping
tears on rental suits, I knew I didn't need, or want, to
spill my guts about my past.

My past had to stay there. It had no place in my
future. I'd realised a long time ago that Alex wasn't
the man of my dreams. He was just a man who I'd
loved once, but who hadn't loved me enough in

return. Ben, on the other hand, was everything I wanted. I wasn't going to let Alex ruin all weddings for me. I would get to have my moment, one day, however and whenever that may be.

I cleared my throat. 'Sorry, I think I just got a bit too excited,' I lied, wiping my cheeks.

'No dramas. I bet you're not the only one.' He smiled and cast his eyes over the crowd. 'I've been waiting here for ages for my daughter. She's got her heart set on this *one* dress. We've driven a couple of hours to be here so I hope to God she finds it. Otherwise she'll be sobbing like you, and I can't be consoling two upset women today,' he chuckled.

'What style did she want?' I asked him in a wobbly voice, wanting to get out of my head and brush off that bubble of emotion threatening to spill over again if I stayed locked in my own thoughts.

He pulled out his phone from his jeans pocket and swiped through to the photo albums. 'This one – she sent me the photo of it to look for, but there's no way I'm getting involved out there. Ain't no place for a man.'

I glanced at the screen. It showed a halter-neck lace gown with intricate beading along the plunging neckline and a fishtail bottom; it was stunning and surprisingly similar to one I thought I'd seen.

'They all look the same to me, but this was *the* dress, apparently.' He shook his head, as if trying to understand the fascination women had for white dresses.

'Wait,' I said, handing back the phone and looking down at the selection of dresses I'd swiped. 'She's not a size ten, is she?'

He nodded slowly. 'Yeah, think she is. I only know that because her mum used to be the same size and had been grumbling that the older she got, the less likely it was she'd ever be a size ten again.' He looked surprised, as if this piece of knowledge had been locked away in his mind somewhere.

'Is this the dress?' I cautiously held up one of the ones in my stash. I'd picked it up not knowing if Shelley would want such a low-cut one, but I'd thought it was too pretty to leave on the rails in case someone else took it.

'Blimey, yeah. I reckon that's it.' The man flicked his head between the dress in my arms and the picture on his phone screen.

'Here.' I passed it over to him.

'What? This not the one you want?' He almost stepped back in shock.

I shook my head. 'I'm not getting married. I'm just here to help a friend.'

'Isn't your friend going to be annoyed that you're handing out her dress to strangers?'

I laughed, for the first time since coming here. 'No, she has a different dress in her sights. This lot was just backup choices for her.' I waved my arms over my stash.

'Jeez, wow. Good on ya.' He looked like he didn't know what to do or say. My heart lifted immeasurably.

'No problem. I hope she loves it and has the day of her dreams,' I said, without a hint of sarcasm.

He placed a warm hand on my shoulder and looked me deep in my eyes. 'Thank you, darl, you too.'

I shifted uncomfortably under his gaze and mumbled that it was fine. For God's sake, why did I want to cry again? What was going on with me and my emotions? Realising that he might set off the waterworks once more, he made a speedy path to the tills before any of the vulture-like women could snatch it out of his arms once he'd crossed the threshold from the safety of the man-zone back into the melee of the shop. As soon as he'd gone I said a silent prayer that Shelley didn't have a secret lust for the dress that I'd just given away.

'Georgia!'

I felt exhausted. Flicking my head over to where the sound came from, I saw Shelley with her own large carrier bag in hand and the biggest grin I'd ever seen her wear.

'I found it!' she sang, pushing past three women stuffing their feet into delicate, diamanté, strappy heels.

'You did?' I asked in amazement. 'So, I can put these back then?' I gathered up the other size ten dresses as she nodded.

'Cara played a blinder,' Shelley said, as I placed my backup stash on the rails, only to see them immediately seized by eagle-eyed brides. 'I swear she nearly started World War Three in the process, *but* she managed to get it for me without killing anyone!'

'All's fair in love and sample sale wedding dress shops, apparently.' Cara let out a weary laugh, as we tried to push our way to the exit. 'Now, come on, let's get the hell out of here before it really does all kick off!'

CHAPTER 16

Peevish (adj.) – Easily irritated, particularly by unimportant things

I was like a kid on its first visit to the big city, the way I was craning my neck to peer out of the taxi windows. Everything was so tall in Sydney, the gleaming skyscrapers we passed on our way to Cara's flat could rival the skyline in New York. It made Adelaide seem like a small village compared to the bustle and energy here.

We'd left the sample sale and driven to the airport to return The Beast to the car-hire place. Shelley had got misty eyed saying goodbye to the rusting heap, but Cara and I were glad to see the back of it. Now we'd landed after the short flight to Sydney and I couldn't wait to get out and explore.

'Right, this is us,' Cara said, getting out of the taxi and nodding her head up to the stone-clad building looming over us. I helped get our bags out and traipsed into the plush lobby, trying my hardest not to gawp.

'Wow, Cara, this place is insane!' I breathed, as I walked from room to room in her flat. 'Flat' seemed the wrong word to use; it was more like a flashy penthouse slash three-bed house slash *Grand Designs* dream.

'It's all right for now.' She shrugged without a hint of sarcasm. I turned to Shelley, who shook her head at her cousin's blasé attitude about living in such a dreamy place.

'It's amazing, isn't it?' Shelley said, giving my arm a little squeeze.

'Epic, is the word I'd use. Epic.'

Shelley walked off to the kitchen laughing, as Cara went through her mail. I trailed around the bright and airy lounge, enjoying the rustle of the warm breeze that made the sheer white drapes swish slightly. There were two large chenille sofas that looked like they would eat you up if you sat down. A flat-screen TV hung on the opposite wall over an exposed brick fireplace. The brickwork had been whitewashed to complement the cool, dusky grey walls. The kitchen was to the right through a coved doorway and every surface shone under the halogen ceiling lights. The black marble and chrome fittings looked like they'd never been used, not a fingerprint or coffee stain in sight. No wonder Jimmy and Shelley weren't in a hurry to move out of here. I'd never want to leave either.

'You want to see your room?' Shelley asked, as I absent-mindedly traced my hand over the cool, smooth surface, never having been so enamoured with fixtures and fittings before.

'Erm, yeah!'

There were three bedrooms, the largest for Cara, the second that Jimmy and Shelley shared, and the third was for guests. My room had a king-size bed in its centre facing the small balcony. It was decorated in soft, blush-apricot hues, and, with the sun streaming through the toile drapes, it looked like I was going to be sleeping in the middle of a giant fuzzy peach. I padded over to the balcony doors, hearing Shelley and Cara excitedly talking about the hand-painted cake toppers that had arrived from some Etsy seller that were 'better than she'd dreamt about'. I held back the drapes and inhaled sharply at what I saw.

Cara hadn't said anything about having the best bloody view in all of Sydney. The glinting white sails of the Opera House lay to my right, and across the glistening harbour stood the imposing steel lattice of the famous bridge. Small steam boats and white ferries bobbed along the waterways, with tourists leaning from the railings to get the best shot of the iconic scenes around them.

'Pretty good, hey.' Jimmy's deep tones made me jump as I stepped back, tried to pick my jaw from the floor and gave him a hug.

'Good? More like incredible!' I smiled, shaking my head at having a room with such a view. 'How are you, apart from being so jammy in getting to live here?'

He hadn't changed, apart from a deeper tan, his blond spiky hair a shade lighter from the sun, and a tight tank top showing off his gym-instructor sculptured arms – he still had that boyish grin I knew and loved.

'Ah, not so bad.' He smiled, revealing white teeth that shone against his stubble. 'It's good to see you, Georgia. How was your wild hen-do trip?'

I was just about to explain that his wife-to-be hadn't been tempted by any outback Australian men when Shelley burst into the room.

'Jimmy, why is there a message on the answerphone about the cake?' she barked, hands on her hips and a fierce expression on her scowling face.

Jimmy seemed to shrink back into himself.

'You did go and sort that while we were away, didn't you?' she demanded.

Under her piercing stare I felt like I wanted to wrap the drapes around myself and be at one with the view, not in the middle of a boiling domestic row.

'Ah, shit.' Jimmy ran a hand through his hair and shuffled his large feet against the fluffy beige carpet.

'Oh great. I gave you one job to do. One!' she shouted. 'Well, you'd better go and get it sorted right now before we have to go and see Lars.'

Jimmy nodded. 'Okay, okay, I will.' He leapt into action then paused. 'Where is it again?'

At this Shelley sighed overdramatically. 'Do you know what, I'll go. I'll just do *everything*, shall I?' It was less of a question and more in order to bait him into an argument. 'Also, Cara is fuming at the state you've left the bathroom in. She's gone to the gym to calm down. That had better be sorted when I get back.'

'I don't mind helping out,' I offered, my voice not sounding like my own against her high-pitched tirade.

'No, I'll go. You'd better stay and watch that he actually does something around here for once.' With that, she slammed the bedroom door, making a picture frame dance against the shuddering wall.

Jimmy sank onto the bed and rubbed his face. 'She's still as uptight as ever then.'

I stared at the door, the view seeming less important than what I'd just witnessed. I'd never seen Shelley speak to anyone like that before, but judging from Jimmy's reaction, it was not the first time.

'You okay?' I asked him softly.

'Yeah,' he said in a low groan. 'Just hoping that once this is all over, I'll get my Shelley back.'

I winced. This wedding was really getting to her, to the pair of them.

'Come on, let's go and clean the bathroom. You don't want to be in the doghouse any longer.'

He wearily got to his feet and plodded behind me. 'Ben can't bloody get here soon enough, if you ask me. To be honest it will be nice to have a break from it all and hang out with him.'

'You been finding it hard?'

Jimmy nodded. 'Yeah, I mean you saw what she was like just then. We haven't had as many rows in all the time we've been together as we have had in the last few weeks.' He looked like he needed to vent, and before Ben made his way here I was the one to lend a sympathetic ear.

'This stupid crash diet she's been on is making her even crankier. The stress of my parents coming – but without my grandma – has fucked up her seating plan; she's full of ideas of how to make it "original", but seems to forget that there's a limited budget, which makes me feel shit that I can't afford to throw more cash at the damn thing to keep her happy. I'm terrified that after all this she's going to be so disappointed that none of it matched up to the ridiculously perfect vision she has in her head.'

His eyes looked like they were about to well up. I could see that the past few weeks of full-on wedding planning had put him on edge.

'She cares too much about what others will think, and she can't step back and see that it only matters what *we* think. I just want to marry the girl and call her my wife; I can't be doing with all the drama that comes with it.' He paused, catching his breath and letting out a deep sigh. 'I mean, the other night we got into yet another sodding row because she told me that my mate Neil from the gym wasn't allowed to bring his missus. Apparently, her tattoos would look crap on the wedding photos.' I wished I thought that he was joking, but judging by how uptight Shelley had been about it all, I could easily imagine this bridezilla version of herself saying that. 'So, did you have a nice trip or was it wedding talk non-stop?' He changed the conversation and passed me a pair of Marigolds.

I shook my head. 'It wasn't too bad, she's just keen that everything goes to plan. You can't blame her. I mean, every woman wants their wedding day to be amazing.' I began squirting bleach into the toilet pan.

'Yeah, I get that. But, at the same time, it's like she's lost all perspective on everything. All she talks about, her and Cara, is bridal this and bridal that, and whenever I try and show an interest my ideas get shot down. Then she moans that I'm not doing enough to help.' He huffed, aggressively scouring the taps. 'It's my wedding too, but apparently anything I suggest is ridiculous.'

He was a braver man than I thought to even offer suggestions when Shelley seemed to have such a tight image in her mind of what she wanted. He had a point though. This was about the two of them.

'What ideas did you have?' I squeezed out the soap suds as I began on the scuzz lining the sink.

His eyes lit up. 'Well, I've seen this thing where you can hire a fella and his bird of prey to come to the ceremony, and the bird has our wedding rings clasped in its talons. Now that would be epic. Imagine me at the front with Shell, each of us with a bird on our shoulder and a ring on our finger.'

I almost dropped the scouring pad as he was speaking. 'Oh, erm, that's interesting,' I said, not able to look at him without wanting to laugh at the image he was conjuring. No wonder Shelley and Cara knocked him down if his ideas were like that.

'Don't you reckon that would be really cool?' he asked without a hint of sarcasm.

'Well, it would be *different*,' I managed to say. 'I guess the only problem is that what if one of the birds shat on you. I doubt bird poo would be the easiest thing to get out of a wedding dress or your suit.'

'Ah.' He paused. 'Yeah, hadn't thought of that.'

'Any other ideas?'

'Oh, there is one thing I wanted your help with.' He glanced behind him, even though we were the only ones in the flat.

'Mmm,' I mused, hoping that he wouldn't suggest swapping birds of prey with any other feathered species.

'I wanted to surprise her.'

Oh gawd. 'Oh?'

'Yeah, well, kind of to show her that I do have some good ideas and also that she doesn't need to control every part of the day.'

I nodded along, wondering if he had a death wish. Surprises and Shelley were not something I would imagine would go down too well, given her current control-freak status over every wedding-related detail. 'What do you have in mind?'

He took a deep breath and flicked a small bath towel over one shoulder. 'I've been taking singing lessons in secret.'

I turned to look at him, wondering if he was having me on. Jimmy had a worse voice than I did, and that was saying something. When they'd lived in Manchester we'd once had a night out to an open-mic evening, where Jimmy had got booed off the stage as it sounded like he was murdering a cat.

'Now you can't tell anyone, not even Ben.' Jimmy shook his head as a slight blush developed on his cheeks. 'He'd never believe me and would probably make me chicken out. I'm already starting to shit myself about getting up there to perform.'

'Wow, I mean, that will be lovely.' I hoped to God that he'd chosen a decent singing teacher. 'What do you want me to do though?'

'I need you to keep it a secret and distract her when I get up on stage to sing. I've also had to send an email to the DJ asking him to add it to the set list without telling her.'

'I think that will certainly be memorable. You still got many rehearsals to do?'

'Yeah, one more tonight. I've told her that I'm working late so hopefully she won't twig. Cheers, Georgia. I'm so pleased you're here to help her out.'

'Yeah, me too,' I said, watching the dirty water pour down the drain, not one hundred per cent sure if I meant it or not.

CHAPTER 17

Canard (n.) – A false or unfounded rumour or story

'Now if you hate it, you have to tell me,' Shelley ordered for the forty-ninth time, holding her sample sale wedding dress wrapped up carefully in its bag for the seamstress to work her magic on. We were on our way to meet Lars, the wedding planner extraordinaire, to try on the bridesmaid dresses that Shelley had picked out for both of us.

'I'm sure I'm going to love it,' I said, linking my arm with hers and picking up our pace through the busy streets. There was also no way I'd wake the beast and kick up a fuss, even if it did look hideous.

'I hope so!' She squeezed my arm and pushed open the door to the wedding dress shop.

She went to speak to the girls at the counter, leaving me to check out some of the dresses hanging up. Flicking open their price tags made my eyes water. I was shaking my head at another extortionate price when I heard someone call my name.

'Georgia!' I turned around to see a man who was in his late fifties, wearing a well-fitted three-piece suit, and who appeared to have styled his hair to resemble a polished conker.

'Lars?' I guessed, as he took my hand.

'That's me! The one and only. Ah, now I can see this is going to work effortlessly!' He grinned, still holding my hand in his, but now making me do a twirl, which was harder said than done seeing as he was almost a foot shorter than me.

'What's going to work effortlessly?' I blinked. Shelley was trying not to laugh at my reaction to this funny little man who was now pulling out a tape measure and making me hold my arms out like I was going through airport security.

'Your dress! From your colouring and complexion, the gown that Shelley and I have picked out is going to work wonders on your sallow skin, giving it the lift it certainly needs, darling,' he whispered behind his wrinkled hand, ignoring my look of shock. Maybe I was looking a little peaky and I wasn't wearing much make-up, but still that seemed a little harsh.

'And the future Mrs Priors, you're looking as radiant as ever.' He twirled Shelley around. 'Is Lars to be mistaken or is this…' He placed a hand to his chest and paused dramatically, before whispering loudly, 'Is this *the* dress?'

Shelley hung up the bag containing her gown and nodded excitedly. 'Sure is!'

'Oh wonderful. The Cecile Coco in Heavenly?' Lars dared to ask, and then shrieked as Shelley nodded. 'I don't know how she did it or who is looking out for her up there.' Lars flicked his eyes up to the ceiling. 'She is one lucky lady getting *this* gown.'

'Mmm.' I glanced at Shelley, who was unzipping a bag that was hanging from a long silver rail, trying to catch her eye to check if this man was actually a real person and we weren't unsuspecting fools on a hidden camera show.

'So, Georgia. What do you think?' she asked expectantly, as the bag she was messing about with opened to reveal a champagne-coloured silk dress tumbling out of it. Lars was clapping his hands together in excitement before taking it out from its casing as gently and carefully as if handling a butterfly with a broken wing.

'Wow, Shelley.' I grinned.

The fabric seemed to flow through my fingers. The floor-length dress in a soft, almost buttery satin was the colour of pale fudge and it glimmered under the chandelier lights in the dress shop. Intricate lace panels at the top acted as capped sleeves, and a cinched-in waist was finished off with a spectacular diamanté brooch on the hip. It was stunning.

'Do you like it?' She had her hands to her mouth, trying to hide her excitement as she flicked her wide eyes between me and the dress. It was something a Hollywood film star would wear.

'Like it? I love it!' Suddenly all worries of me flouncing around in some awful, puffy-sleeved gown with over-the-top Little Bo Peep frills melted away.

'And do you know the best bit?' she teased.

'Oh my God, what?'

'It has pockets!!' She shrilled. Every girl knows that there is nothing better than a dress with pockets. Nothing.

Lars dabbed at his eyes with a spotted handkerchief that he'd pulled from his top pocket. 'Stunning, stunning. Don't forget the *pièce de résistance*.' He whipped out a blinking great floral crown from behind his back. A member of staff I hadn't spotted earlier began clapping like a child watching a Punch and Judy performance.

'Oh. Wow,' I stuttered, with less enthusiasm than everyone else in this room. It was enormous. Huge, blousy, peach blooms were wrapped around a crown dripping with ivy; it looked like the ginormous Snapchat filter that Kelli had once made me pose with.

'Don't you just love it!' Lars shrieked, plonking the creation on my head. I winced at the weight of it.

'You and Cara have matching ones!' Shelley added, admiring the flower mess. Great, I bet Cara styled hers like a bloody woodland nymph, whereas I looked like some overgrown May Day flower girl.

'Now you need to try it all on.' Lars ushered me behind a heavy velvet curtain at the back of the shop, commanding the sales assistants to make way for us. They all gave him bitchy looks as we passed. Shelley was told to wait in the seating area for the big reveal as she tried to phone Cara to see where she was so she could try on her matching dress.

'Erm, do you mind, just…' I bent down to take off my shoes and smiled awkwardly at Lars to leave so I could get undressed.

'Oh, okay. I'll be right outside.' He gave the dress one last lingering look and swiftly glanced at my hands, as if to check I was clean enough to hold such beautiful fabric. I must have passed, as he flounced off and closed the curtains to wait for me to get changed. I gazed up at the dress and hurried to get down to my underwear. I couldn't wait to feel the soft silk against my skin. Apart from the wedding dress that I had been going to wear, I don't think I'd ever tried on anything as fancy as this before.

'Ready, darling?' Lars barged back into the changing room. I was still standing in my mismatching bra and knickers.

'Oh, I…' I clasped my hands over my almost naked body to protect my modesty.

'Shush. Don't worry. Lars has seen everything before. Now, let me help you get into the dress. If you turn around...' He placed his hands on my waist and steered me into position, not feeling the slightest bit embarrassed at invading my personal space like this.

'I'm sure I can manage myself,' I tried to protest, but it went unheard as he flicked the gown off the hanger and had it outstretched for me to step into.

'Come on now, chop, chop,' he said.

'I can pull it up myself,' I said firmly, getting hot and flustered at sharing this space with a man I'd only just met, who was currently tugging at the dress to ease it over my hips. The material that I had thought was billowing suddenly seemed to have shrunk in size. I sucked in my stomach to get it to inch up a little further, but it was as if there was a button or a fastening still done up that was blocking its path. There was no way it would go up and over my hips.

'Oh my, oh no.' Lars stepped back dramatically, leaving me to grab the dress before it fell to the floor.

'What? What do you mean "oh no"?' I asked, feeling extremely self-conscious as he looked my body up and down. I wished I'd at least been wearing matching underwear.

'Right. not to worry.' He clapped his hands together and fixed his eyebrows into a determined knot. 'We'll try going from the other way. Step out of it and we'll go over your head.'

As before, he took control and almost made me stumble backwards into the ornate full-length mirror that was propped against the wall behind me. The dress was bunched between his expert hands as he ordered me to hoist my arms in the air and then carefully place one through each sleeve. I did as was told, feeling like a giant twat being dressed by this perfect stranger. I'd managed to get my arms through each armhole and he'd been able to pull the material down over my squashed breasts. But there was not a chance that the dress would get over the rest of my lady lumps.

'Oh my God, it doesn't fit!' I squealed in a hushed whisper. Shelley would be furious. I felt like one of Cinderella's ugly stepsisters, shoving my nasty feet into the delicate glass slipper. My bridesmaid dress didn't fit! 'What size is it? Maybe you've picked up the wrong one, the smaller one meant for Cara?' I was clutching at straws and I knew it.

Lars clasped his hand to his chest, looking mighty pissed off that I had suggested he would make such a mistake. 'This is the size that Miss Shelley ordered. It is *you* that is wrong, not the *dress*.'

'Do you have a larger size in stock?' I hissed, ignoring his sly dig.

I really didn't want Shelley to freak out about this. I knew I'd been eating larger portions since moving in with Ben and my clothes had felt a little tighter, but I'd never expected that I wouldn't be able to fit into the damn dress. I couldn't have changed *that* much since giving her my measurements a few months ago. Lars took the dress and hung it back on the hanger in silence. I braced myself for him to give me a lecture about my diet or how I'd ruined the wedding. Instead, he took a step back and pulled my hand into his.

'Georgia.' He looked into my eyes, his voice a soft and measured whisper. 'How long have you known about *this*?' He nodded his head up and down my body as he emphasised the last word.

'This? What do you mean *this*?' I stuttered, trying to get my hand out of his grip so I could put some clothes back on. I needed to face the music with Shelley and see if we could find a good seamstress, and pronto.

Lars sighed, closed his eyes – was he wearing mascara? – and gently shook his head at my denial. 'Darling, like I said, Lars has seen it *all*.'

'Okaaaaay,' I said slowly, trying to follow along with whatever he was getting at. I already felt like a heifer. I didn't need his judgy looks or mean-girl comments on how I could try a colonic or maybe do a three-day juice cleanse. Although both of those things might help with the dress being slightly less snug – there was no way they would make it fit.

'All okay in there, guys?' Shelley's worried voice floated through the curtain. 'Cara says she's on her way. I can't wait much longer though!' she sang. 'Georgia, do you love it?'

'Mmm,' I replied. 'Just give us a minute!' My voice didn't sound like my own. Lars was still holding my hand, his eyes fixed on mine. 'You need to find a bigger size; she'll be crushed if I can't wear this!'

'Georgia.' He was starting to freak me out by how calm he was being. Thankfully he'd dropped my hand so I could at least try and put my jeans back on. 'Answer Lars, how long?'

'What the hell are you on about "how long"? I don't know what you mean! How long have I been fat? Is that what you're trying to say? I'm sorry but that's not a very nice question to ask a woman!' I was struggling to get my right leg into my jeans under his fixed gaze.

My eyes filled with tears; I felt like a dumpy meat pasty crossed with a bloated beached whale and I just wanted to get out of here. The changing room was too small and hot, never mind this weird man staring at me in this uncomfortable way. I then had to go out and tell Shelley that she needed to find another dress and quickly.

'Georgia. The baby?' Lars said.

'What baby?' I replied, louder than I meant to.

'*Baby*? What are you talking about in there?' Shelley called. 'Cara's just arrived so we need to get a move on so she can get in there and put her dress on.'

'Why, you're pregnant!' Lars clapped his hands together just at the moment Shelley pulled back the curtain and saw me still in my bra with one leg in my jeans and the stunning dress back on its hanger.

'What?' we both asked in high-pitched unison. Cara's mouth dropped wide open as she peered around to see what was going on.

'Georgia, you're...you're pregnant?' Shelley's face dropped as her eyes immediately flew to my doughy stomach. I self-consciously used an arm to cover myself and tried to get into the sodding jeans properly. 'Why are you not in the dress? Wait – you're pregnant?' It was as if she couldn't work out which part of this new information to deal with first.

Lars was dancing about and clapping his hands together like a demented seal.

'I'm not pregnant!' I shouted, wishing that he would stop that. 'I'm just fat!' I wailed.

'But, wait, why did you say that?' Shelley twisted her head to Lars, allowing me to finally get my jeans up.

'Because look at her! Of course she is pregnant. Her breasts do not stay in her bra—'

'That's because it's a cheap Primark one,' I replied. Wait, why was I defending myself to this odd little guy?

Lars ignored me and carried on. 'Her stomach is pronounced and she has this aroma. Lars has smelt it many times before and I just knew. Pregnant!' He made a motion with his hands as if a light bulb had gone off over his head.

'A pregnant aroma? Oh purlease,' I snorted in indignation. I'd never met a ruder man in my life. I turned to Shelley, who was still looking at me as if I was hiding something from her.

'I thought you looked different!' she squealed before clocking my horrified expression.

'I knew it!' Cara matched Shelley's high-pitched noises. 'I thought you looked bigger than the photos Shell has shown me of you! I told you, didn't I, Shell?'

'What? Different how? And no, I'm not pregnant!' My cheeks flamed with embarrassment.

'Oh. Sorry. No, not different, just happy...' It was Shelley's turn to fade out sheepishly. Cara mumbled something about good lighting and photo angles.

'Shelley, I'm sorry, but I've got a bit fatter since going out with Ben and well, the thing is, I can't fit into the dress. It's just too tight. I am *SO* sorry! But I'm sure there's time to find a bigger size or get it altered somehow?'

'Wait – you're not pregnant?' Shelley stuttered.

I shook my head forcefully. 'No. I've just piled on the pounds.'

'Seriously?'

'Seriously.'

She let out a breath I hadn't realised she'd been holding, then broke into a slightly hysterical laugh. 'Thank God, because that would *really* ruin the wedding day!'

'Lars is always right!' Lars piped up, feeling left out that the conversation wasn't involving him.

I glared at him and his preposterous suggestions that I might be 'with child'. I'd just put on a little bit of weight – okay, judging from how tight that dress was and how they'd looked at me in my underwear, maybe it was *slightly* more than just a few pounds – but apart from that everything was normal.

'Erm, so the other thing.' Shelley had stopped laughing and was holding the price tag between her fingers. 'Are you all right to pay for this? Cara has covered hers and I just figured that with you running your own business you wouldn't mind chipping in?' she hurriedly added.

'Oh, erm, yeah sure,' I blustered. God, this was awkward, but I would have paid any amount of money to be out of this changing room.

A grateful smile broke over her face. 'Thanks, Georgia. Cara's seen these amazing shoes she thought you could both get too.'

'Cool.' Oh, great.

'Alterations are extra,' Lars unhelpfully piped up. 'It will cost more because of how late you've left it to get the first fitting too.'

'Fine,' I said through gritted teeth, handing over my credit card.

CHAPTER 18

Haughty (adj.) – condescending; behaving in a superior or arrogant way

'They're here! They're here!' I called excitedly as the doorbell to Cara's apartment chimed. I raced across the wooden floors and skidded to a halt by the front door. Flinging it open, I was greeted with Ben, Jimmy, and Jimmy's parents, who were ushered in and began the round of kisses, hugs and formal handshakes as introductions were made. I couldn't wait to wrap my arms around my Ben, standing on tiptoe to kiss him and breathe in his smell that I'd missed so much.

'Hey there,' he whispered into my ear, as I closed my eyes, forgetting the bustle of bodies around us.

'I've missed you.'

'Me too.' He placed a heavy kiss on the top of my head as I forced myself to peel away from him and be sociable. It just felt so great that he was finally here; it had been slightly strained with Shelley at times, so to have a distraction from all the wedding planning and get to hang out with my boyfriend in a non-work-related sense, in Sydney of all places, was going to be wonderful. It still made me smile that despite how much time we usually spent together I missed him so bloody much when we were apart.

'Georgia, these are my parents, Mike and Johanna.' Jimmy grinned.

I'd heard so much about Jimmy's parents and, turning around to face the couple, I felt as if I already knew them.

'Hi! So nice to properly meet you.' I smiled, extending a hand. His dad shook it warmly and creased his eyes into a wide smile, saying how it was nice to put a face to the name for him too. His mum, Johanna, just nodded her head of expensive-looking blow-dried hair.

'How was your flight?' Shelley asked them, as Jimmy moved the bags inside.

'Fine, fine,' Johanna said with a tight smile, casting her eyes around the apartment as she spoke. 'You've had your hair cut shorter.'

Shelley self-consciously brought her fingers to her pixie crop. 'Erm, no, well, a slight trim...'

Johanna nodded her head but said no more.

'So, I thought I'd give my parents a tour of the city, then take them to the hotel so they can check in and freshen up,' Jimmy said, stepping between the two women. 'What time are your parents here, babe?'

'The table's booked for 7 p.m.,' Shelley mumbled, patting the back of her hair down.

'Seven p.m.?' Johanna repeated with a shrill cry. 'Heavens, that's early!'

'Oh, well, I thought you may be tired and, well, my parents don't really like eating too late.'

'Maybe seven is a little early, babe. How about I give the place a call and push it back half an hour or so?' Jimmy suggested.

I could sense Shelley bristling that he was siding with his mum over her already and they'd only been here five minutes.

'Well, it's that fancy place in Surry Hills, so I'm not sure how easy it will be changing the time at this late notice.'

'It'll be fine, trust me.' Jimmy kissed her on the cheek and then led his parents into the kitchen to make them a drink.

Shelley set her lips into a tight line. 'I'll let my parents know then.'

I was about to ask Ben what he fancied doing when Shelley pulled at my sleeve.

'Can I have a word?' She jabbed her head towards the closed bedroom door.

Ben nodded. 'I'll grab a coffee, don't mind me.'

'What's up?' I asked, as Shelley smiled politely at Ben and pulled me into Cara's bedroom.

'You *have* to come for dinner with us!' she breathed, her eyes wide and hands clasped in front of her.

'Well, we were going to do our own thing tonight, hun, you know, I haven't seen Ben for a while and—'

'Please, Georgia! You've seen what Jimmy's like in front of his mum. I can't be the referee between them and my parents on my own! Please!'

I sighed. She looked desperate but she had to understand I wanted some alone time with my boyfriend.

'Can Cara not go with you?'

'She's working. Please, I promise I won't ask anything from you again,' she whined, dropping to her knees. 'I've booked, like, the fanciest restaurant in town just to impress them, which I already know my parents are going to hate!' I went to protest once more but was cut off. 'Call it your duty as maid of honour.'

I rolled my eyes. 'Fine, but don't be pulling that card again.'

*

The meal was a disaster.

The restaurant was what I'd describe as urban slash industrial meets trendy and up its own arse.

You know the type, where it's all exposed brick, steel and uncomfortable chairs around distressed wooden tables. People walking, sorry gliding, around as if they've pulled one of the pointless iron bars lining the walls to stick up their arses. Everyone pausing from their conversations to turn and see if the latest diners were worth their attention or not. A place that specialises in a mix of Asian-fusion served with a side of intimidation. It was not a place I'd choose to eat but Johanna seemed in her element. It was possibly the first time I'd seen a smile crack on her smooth Botoxed cheeks as she took in the soft, plinky-plonky music, the ridiculously handsome bar staff and the supermodel-sized waitresses who looked like they could do with a good meal themselves. I felt Shelley's mum, Patty, stiffen beside me as she wound her scarf from her neck and seemed to shrivel in on herself. She was the complete opposite of perfectly groomed Johanna. When we'd been introduced, she'd effortlessly pulled me into a warm hug, smelling of gingerbread, unlike the frosty welcome from Jimmy's mum.

Patty was a shorter, pear-shaped version of Shelley, with wiry greys peppering her blonde bob; she looked like a kindly dinner lady in her crocheted cardigan and the type of beige trousers that can only be referred to as slacks. Shelley's dad, Keith, was seen before he was heard. Easily over six foot tall, broad and bearded, he could pass as Father Christmas on his day off in his paint-splattered jeans and checked shirt with the sleeves rolled up. I guessed that was where Cara's height came from. The room suddenly seemed to shrink as he entered.

'Georgia!' he boomed in thick Aussie tones. His previously narrowed eyes creased into a smile and he opened his wide arms to embrace me. I cautiously accepted the strong hug, though it almost knocked the wind from my chest, as he let out a bark of a laugh which instantly put me at ease.

'You don't mind us being here, do you?' I asked Ben, as we took our places at the table.

'As long as I get you all to myself tomorrow.'

'Deal.' I grinned. 'Although, you're going to be hit with jet lag.' I shuddered, remembering how ill I'd felt when I first arrived.

'Nah, I'll be fine.' I pulled a "we'll see" face. 'Well, how about we sack off doing the Coogee to Bondi walk, or the Harbour Bridge climb? I'm sure lunch near the Opera House won't be too taxing.' He winked.

'That sounds perfect!'

'So, Shelley, tell me how the plans are going?' Johanna asked once we were all seated with large menus spread out in front of us and had finished ordering a round of drinks.

'Oh yep, all fine, it's all coming together,' Shelley said, rubbing Jimmy's arm.

'I thought you might need some help; planning a wedding can be overwhelming.'

'Well, that's what Lars is for I guess.' I smiled, noticing Shelley's jaw tense.

'Lars?' Johanna flicked her hair and looked at me.

'Yeah, you know, the guy you—'

'Anyone know what they're having for a starter?' Shelley interrupted me and wafted a menu in my face. *What the?* She wouldn't meet my eye but I could see her firmly shaking her head. Was there something I was missing here?

'We have done quite a lot ourselves, haven't we, love?' Patty piped up, running her white linen napkin between her fingers for something to do with her hands before the drinks arrived.

'Oh, really?' Johanna raised an HD brow.

'We wanted to make it personal,' Patty explained, trying not to squirm under Johanna's cold stare. 'You know how it is, we just wanted to put our own touch on things, so we've been busy making a few crafts and decorations to help add a certain *something*.'

You could tell that Johanna imagined the certain *something* was bound to be distasteful. She was not the type of woman who would know what to do with a glue gun.

'So, Johanna, Shelley tells us you're both heading off to Fiji after here?' Ben said, moving the conversation away from weddings, much to the relief of everyone.

Johanna smiled tightly at the waitress, who placed our drinks down, and took a long, slow sip of her vodka and slimline tonic before answering. 'Yes, well, we thought as we've come all this way we may as well make the most of it,' she purred. 'You're both so lucky being able to go there all the time, what with it being practically on your doorstep,' Johanna said to Keith and Patty.

Patty paused and flicked a look at Shelley. 'Well, we've never been. Not really big ones for travel. I think that's why our Shell makes up for it.'

Johanna looked confused that someone wouldn't want to jet off to Fiji every weekend when it was so close. 'Oh, right.'

'I'm sure it will be lovely though,' Patty mused, as she pulled her reading glasses from her battered-looking handbag to peer at the confusing menu.

'Well, this is a bit bloody fancy.' Keith sat back in his chair, staring at the menu with trepidation. 'Needs its own translator if you ask me. I don't understand what's wrong with places telling you what the dishes actually are, rather than requiring you to guess or keep your mouth shut in case of embarrassing yourself. I mean, what the hell is soil doing on a menu?'

Michael laughed in solidarity. 'I think that's the new term for dried-up scraps made to look like soil; don't worry, it's edible.'

'You mean we are paying to eat dirt?' Keith grunted, shaking his head at such a preposterous idea. I spotted Patty dab her napkin to her flushed cheeks.

'I had it once at this place in Copenhagen; it's not actually as bad as you might expect,' Michael said.

Johanna was looking longingly at the table next to us with two couples, the women in expensive evening dresses and the men in smart suits, as if she wished she could pull up a chair with them instead.

'So, how was your journey?' Patty asked Jimmy's parents, cutting off her husband from grumbling that they'd be serving up compost and calling it haute cuisine next.

Johanna rolled her eyes. 'Long. It's such a long way from anywhere around here, isn't it? I mean, not only do you lose a day of your life travelling, you then have to switch your body clock. I just don't see why anyone would bother doing that all the time.'

I heard Keith mutter under his breath that that may explain why her son had chosen to live on the other side of the world from his mother.

'Flying business is really the only way to make it bearable,' Johanna added.

Keith's eyes grew wide at this; I could almost see him working out the cost of two return business-class flights from London.

'Oh, very nice,' Patty mused. 'I once got to go into the VIP lounge at the airport.'

Shelley laughed gently. 'That's only because you got lost and then swiped all the free cakes into your handbag before they kicked you out!'

Patty let out a tinkle of a laugh at the memory. 'Oh, it was mortifying really. I had jam from the mini doughnuts leaking in my handbag for the whole flight!'

'I'd do exactly the same,' Michael said kindly, as Johanna looked horrified at the thought of cream scones ruining the lining of her Louis Vuitton. 'May as well make the most out of every opportunity you get, right?'

'So, Georgia, what do you think of our great land?' Keith boomed over the table. 'You work in the travel industry, don't you?' he asked, confusing me with the change of topic.

'Erm, yep, I do, well, Ben and I both do...'

'Well then, here's a thought for you.' He paused; Shelley and Patty both groaned in unison. 'Now, don't be like that, Georgia here might understand that this is a fantastic idea.' Keith turned to me. 'Why don't you set up a tour that allows people to come to Australia and see all of the Big Things in one journey. It would be quite a long trip, the logistics would need working out...' He trailed off, rubbing his bushy moustache, thinking hard. 'I guess the only issue would be that there are over one hundred and fifty to see, and they're spread all over the country...'

'Plus, once you've seen one big poo, you've seen them all,' Jimmy teased.

'There's a big poo?' I repeated, quickly apologising as Johanna tutted, making Shelley and her dad laugh. 'Sorry.'

'Yeah, we're not so sure about that one either.' Keith rubbed at his beard.

'Can we stop talking about the Big Things? I want to hear all about what you've got planned with your parents whilst they're here!' Patty smiled at Jimmy expectantly.

'Hopefully a bit of sightseeing, well, if we can fit it in.' He glanced at Shelley. 'We've got a lot to get through during the next few days but hopefully we can schedule in some downtime.'

'Oh, you've got your bucks' night coming up too, haven't you?' Patty asked Ben and Jimmy, whose faces lit up at the thought of Jimmy's last night of freedom.

'Yes, but he's promised me that he won't be too hungover to help get the flowers the next day,' Shelley chided.

'Already under the thumb, eh, lad!' Michael chuckled, and caught the waitress's attention for another drink. 'Good for you, I say. Enjoy it all before you become a father and have real responsibilities.'

Jimmy laughed. 'We'll see.'

'Ben, you got any plans for the pitter-patter of tiny feet any time soon?' Johanna asked, leaning over the table, flashing my boyfriend the full view of her crêpey breasts.

Ben choked on the bite of bread he had just taken and let out a dramatic cough, quickly picking up his glass of water to wash it down.

'I'll take that as a no!' Keith chortled.

Ben smiled and cleared his throat, giving my leg a squeeze next to him. 'I don't think children are exactly on our list of priorities. There's just too much going on with the business for one.'

'But one day you'll want to have children?' Johanna pushed. 'No?'

'I guess if it did happen it would be way, way, waaaaaay in the future.'

I fixed on a smile, feeling the eyes of the other diners turn to me. I didn't want them to see that I was shocked that starting a family had been taken off the agenda so firmly. I always knew that it would be tough managing parenthood with growing our business, but I hadn't realised just how against the idea he was.

'Well, you don't want to be putting your career over kids for too long,' Patty chimed, giving Shelley a loving glance. 'You either, love.'

'Yes, but they'll be back in England when that happens, won't you?' Johanna said.

'England?' Keith piped up. 'There's no way my first-born grandchild is growing up over there.'

Patty patted his clenched fist. Shelley took a big gulp of her wine and Jimmy fiddled with his linen napkin.

'Well, as soon as they come back home they're bound to find a nice place to live and start making a family.' Johanna had Keith's eye in a tight stare as she spoke.

Keith slapped a thick hand on the table, making everything shudder. 'They're not going back to England,' he growled. '*This* is their home.'

'The thing is, Mum...' Jimmy tried to act as peacemaker.

'James Arnold Priors, you promised me that you would get married and then come home.' Johanna was starting to shake with the effort of controlling her emotions.

Patty had welled up, Keith was leaning forward almost menacingly over the table and Shelley was shredding the menu into tiny pieces.

Jimmy took a deep breath. 'Well, this is our home now, Mum. Here, in Australia.'

'It's not a bad place to raise a family.' Ben jumped in to save his best friend and try to lighten the tone.

'You don't even want children,' Johanna snapped at him and turned pleadingly towards her daughter-in-law. 'Shelley, you can't do this to me.'

'Well, she won't be taking her children away from us either!' Keith barked, forcing Michael to finally look up from the wine list he was staring at intently. 'Bloody Londoners,' he muttered. His eyes narrowed at Johanna and Michael as he raised his wine glass to his lips, leaving a dark drop of liquid on the white hairs of his chin.

'Dad, don't start,' Shelley mumbled.

'Start what?' He turned to his daughter with an innocent look.

'That'll do, dear,' Patty squeaked.

Keith grumbled something under his breath.

Shelley's cheeks were flushed and the vein on her temple was throbbing under the dim light. 'Let's all just calm down. I'm not even pregnant or planning on being pregnant any time soon,' she said, her voice wobbling. 'I just wanted us to have a nice meal out altogether.' She threw her chair back and raced off to the ladies' toilet, almost knocking over a waiter who was bringing out our starters. 'I need to get some air.'

'Oh goodness.' Patty sniffed, whilst rummaging in her handbag for a tissue, hopefully one that didn't have the remnants of stolen airport cake on it.

'I'll go and check on her,' I said, getting to my feet.

'See what you've done now,' Michael chastised his wife, who was muttering under her breath about how stupid this country was and how it had ruined everything. Everything!

'I wish they hadn't even boarded that flight,' Shelley said, blowing her nose into crumpled toilet paper as I pushed the door into the even dimmer light of the industrial-style toilets. 'Sorry, I just needed a second to myself. You saw how pissed off his mum was, finding out that we're not moving back to England once the wedding is over.'

'I'm amazed she even managed to frown judging by the amount of Botox she's had.' That made Shelley flash a small smile. 'It's probably a shock to her, but she'll come around. This is your life, not theirs, remember?'

'I guess.' She shrugged.

'Come on, let's go back out there. God knows if anyone will be talking to each other and, if they are, then I'm not sure how Ben will cope being grilled about children any more.' I was slightly worried that we'd return to find the table on its side, Keith and Michael in a headlock and Johanna sobbing into her pricy glass of Pinot Noir.

'Yeah, he seemed pretty adamant that they're not on the cards for a long time.' Shelley winced.

'I know!' I shook my head. 'I mean, I'm not planning them for a while either, but still it was a little awkward hearing him dismiss them so hurriedly.' I paused, 'What was the Lars thing about? Johanna looked like she didn't have a clue what I was going on about?'

She rubbed at the flakes of mascara under her eyes. 'She probably got confused, but actually it's for the best if you keep it to yourself. I haven't told my parents about Lars as my mum would be crushed if she thought her help wasn't needed.'

'Ah.' I nodded, peering at my own reflection and thinking I probably should have done something about my eyebrows before the wedding. 'But it might help break the ice and show your dad that his parents are financially helping towards the big day?'

'No!' Shelley cried. 'I mean, no, better not to mention money. I think we need to steer any more conversations away from the wedding.'

'And babies,' I grumbled as we walked back out to the table. I felt utterly exhausted and a little confused that maybe I didn't know Ben as well as I thought I did.

CHAPTER 19

Histrionic (adj.) – Overly theatrical or dramatic

So much for spending the day exploring Sydney with my boyfriend. Instead, I'd been traipsing around florists, haberdashery shops and nail salons all day. By the time we eventually made it home, Ben had already moved into the hotel ahead of the stag night. I was exhausted and grateful that Cara had organised a quiet evening in with girly films, face packs and a ton of ice cream as Jimmy enjoyed his last night of freedom with his mates. Well, that's what I thought was going to happen, but Shelley was using it as a chance to rope in some of her friends to have a craft night making last-minute wedding decorations.

I was currently surrounded by church candles and bags of eucalyptus leaves that I was in charge of artfully sticking around the base. I was not doing such a great job of it.

'So, what do you reckon the boys are up to right now?' Cara asked, bending down to pick up a reel of laced ribbon.

'Oh God, I have no idea. To be honest, I reckon it's probably better it stays that way,' Shelley laughed.

I took a sip from my luminous, pink drink. Shelley had tried to ban booze as she was on an alcohol detox before the wedding, but Cara had thankfully ignored her and created this 'Shell on the beach' cocktail which was slipping down a little too easily.

'You need to add more glue; they won't stick as well otherwise,' a woman with badly applied blue eyeliner piped up next to me.

I squeezed the tube harder and a whoosh of glue squirted out.

'Careful!' Shelley cried.

'Sorry!'

Shelley tutted, but was pulled from assigning me to another task by one of her friends, a woman wearing an extremely tight vest top who smelt of cigarettes, who shouted across the room, 'You starting to get nervous about it all yet, Shell?'

'Well, I'm worried I'm going to have to restock the diarrhoea tablets if that's what you mean.'

'I was like that before my big day. Always stressing that I'd made the wrong choice, worrying about the last-minute things I was sure I'd missed off my list,' one of the women chirped up as she picked chalk paint from her fingertips.

'Yeah, but you've got Lars to make sure everything has been taken care of,' Cara added, making the other women coo that she was so lucky to have a wedding planner.

'To be fair, he has been a godsend,' Shelley chimed. More like a gobshite, I thought, remembering that awful dress fitting. 'Although I kccp reading these articles on Pinterest about all the things I'm supposed to have done and I swear I haven't done them all. I'm terrified I've left something off my to-do list.'

'You'd be planning a wedding for the next year if you tried to do everything you see on there!' The women laughed.

'How are you going to cope with the post-wedding blues?' one of her friends piped up. 'I was *so* depressed after my big day; it was like there was a huge hole in my life.' I tried not to scoff at the dramatic face she was pulling. 'I even thought about going into wedding planning myself.'

'I hadn't even thought of that!' Shelley's eyes lit up as she explained how she could do with a career change.

I picked up the nearest wedding magazine to occupy myself with.

'Check this one out,' I said loudly, breaking up the chat about nightmare caterers and pervy Masters of Ceremonies that one of the women in the room was going on about. The article was 'Fifteen Things You *Must Have* for the Perfect Wedding'. '"To add a personal touch, why not monogram drinking straws, arrange a chill-out area complete with Balinese handcrafted throws, or ask your guests to start an impromptu sing-along of your favourite songs." Jesus.' I shook my head, laughing.

'What's wrong with it?' Shelley looked up from painting the base of a jam jar. 'I think that sounds lovely. Maybe we should nip out to get some straws; I'm sure I can find something online we could print off and decorate them with.'

I let out a bark of a laugh. 'Oh, come on, you don't seriously believe that without these things – things that most people won't even remember – you won't have the perfect day?'

If I hadn't been so glued to the next article on the 'Ten Ultimate Tear-Jerking First Dance Songs', most of them naff classics, or been on my third 'Shell on the beach', I might have noticed the atmosphere in the room cool.

'You do? Really?' I said to her silence, stifling a giggle at how serious she was being. One of the women already had her coat on to head off on the straw-buying mission.

'Well, why not?' Shelley folded her arms.

'Oh, excuse me for being such a sceptic, but I thought you had more brains than that.'

The others looked up at me as if I was the Grinch who stole weddings.

'I mean, enough with the ridiculous wedding rituals. Actually, if you think about it –' I raised my finger to make my next valid point and put on this ridiculous clipped English accent – 'the whole institution is just so antiquated and extremely anti-feminist.' I paused, hoping for one of the women to take her bra off and wave it in the air in solidarity with me. They all continued to look at me as if I'd lost the plot. 'I mean, you have your father literally give you away, like you're some flipping cow or prize bull, then you have to honour and obey this man. I mean, come on – obey!'

'If you think all this wedding stuff is just a load of shite, then why did you bother to fly over and help me?' Shelley asked, putting her hands on her hips.

'Shell, come on, I didn't mean it like that!' I said, slowly picking up on the fact she wasn't finding this funny in the slightest.

'Do you know what I think?' She was baiting me to answer. 'You're jealous,' she said, pursing her lips. I swear I legit heard someone gasp.

'What?' I scrunched up my face at such a ridiculous suggestion. Where had this come from?

'Yep. You're jealous because I'm getting to go up the aisle and you never made it that far.'

'Pfft. Whatever. I think you need to wake up and realise that spending three months deciding what to have as a wedding hashtag is complete bullshit.' She looked as if I'd slapped her. 'Fancy table decorations, quirky centrepieces and an unusual font on your invites doesn't make a bit of difference. No one in this room will remember.'

'So, why were you going to marry Alex then, if you think weddings are so pointless?' she barked.

'Because I didn't know any better,' I answered back, with a little too much sass.

'Well, if you're not jealous then you're scared.' She angrily screwed the lid of the paint pot back on and got to her feet.

'Scared of what?' I laughed, standing up to face her, possibly swaying slightly.

'Hiding your true feelings means you *pretend* that you don't want this. You're a coward, Georgia Green. You're convinced that it will all go wrong as it has done with every other relationship you've had, so what's the point?'

I wasn't scared, I was being realistic. Shelley didn't know what she was talking about. I wasn't jealous. It was all just a giant ego-parade.

'Oh, so you've remembered what happened to me then? Because you've not once thought to check that this would be hard for me. Or bothered to see if I was okay giving up my holiday and reliving this wedding stress after what I went through?!' I knocked some of the candles over as I stretched out my arm clumsily. 'You haven't *once* thought about me to see if I was fine being surrounded by your chaotic wedding planning twenty-four-seven, if it would be a little difficult to deal with for a previously jilted bride. I mean, where has my friend Shelley gone? The girl who would lighten up about fucking candles and place settings! The one who is sympathetic and kind and would realise that her wedding might be the most life-changing event to ever happen to her, but for everyone else in this room it's not such a big deal.'

She gritted her teeth and stared back at me. The others in the room were silent, trying to breathe through this tense atmosphere. I was on a roll. It was as if the past few months of stress with work, house-buying, losing out on the investment cash, hearing about this bloody wedding, and biting my tongue on the hen-do road trip suddenly began spilling out.

'Even Jimmy thinks it too! The poor fella is sick of having a bridezilla stomping around. If you're not careful, there will be no fucking wedding!'

I was fuming. My head pounded as I finally let her in on some home truths. I didn't care that I looked deranged in front of her friends, I just wanted *my* old friend back.

She reeled from that last comment. 'You're just bitter, Georgia. You don't know anything about what Jimmy thinks.'

'Fine,' I spat. 'If you're going to be like that, lost in this superficial wedding crap, then I won't stay here for a moment longer!'

I stomped off to my bedroom and hurriedly stuffed my things into my bag. Luckily, as Cara had way nicer stuff and beauty products than me, most of my things were still packed up in my case, so it didn't take long. I was desperate to be away from her and her warped views on everything. I could hear hushed whispers once I'd left the room. No one attempted to come and speak to me, which only made me bang around even more loudly.

Fuck this! I'd come all this way to help Shelley out, to support her, putting my own issues and feelings to one side, even slept on a sodding street, and this was how she repaid me? I tried to control my rapid breathing that was leaving me light-headed, and stomped back into the lounge, unable to even look Shelley in the eye, banging my shin on the edge of the shiny coffee table as I did.

'Thanks for a *lovely* evening,' I said spitefully to Cara. The other girls were picking at the carrot sticks and dips that Shelley had laid out, loving every minute of the real-life drama playing out in front of them.

'Georgia, don't go, come on, we can sort this out,' Cara said quietly, stretching out her long yoga-pant-clad legs.

'No, I think everything has been said. I'll leave you to it.' I flicked my nose in the air, managing to only look at Shelley through the corner of my eye. She'd slumped onto the sofa and was picking at the cushion and stubbornly refusing to look at me or say a thing. I had the door handle in my hand and was about to step foot outside when I finally heard Shelley pipe up.

'Wait!'

I turned to look at her, hoping for an apology, or at least for her to admit she had lost her mind in bridal bedlam. Instead, she got to her feet and stood tall. 'You are no longer welcome in the bridal party; in fact, I don't want you to come to the wedding at all!'

One of her friends gasped loudly. I know that just a few minutes earlier we'd been screaming at each other, but I never expected to be expelled from Team Wedding. I went to speak, but nothing came out of my mouth. My whole body felt tense and I was willing the tears not to show. I flung the front door open.

'Georgia, wait—' Cara called.

This time I didn't wait. I slammed the door behind me as dramatically as I could and pulled my bag down the thick padded carpets of the hallway to the lifts. My breathing was all over the place, my mouth tasted metallic and my head was banging. How had tonight ended up like this? After calling the lift to the ground floor, I walked out into the cool evening air. Standing in the cobbled courtyard, in a place I hardly knew, with every shape and noise sounding ominous, I shivered. Now what?

I pulled out my phone, half expecting to see WhatsApp messages from Shelley or Cara begging me to go back, apologising for overreacting, but the phone screen remained empty. I kicked my foot against the wall, chipping off a piece of concrete with it, glanced around the courtyard and looked back up at the window of Cara's flat. I don't know what I imagined to see, maybe the group of them pressed against the windowpane, but it was empty.

I spun on my heel and walked out into the street, pulling my jacket closer and trying to hold back the sniffs of tears. *What now, Georgia?*

CHAPTER 20

Fortuitous (adj.) – Happening by chance or accident

It took me a moment to work out where I was, why I was alone, still fully dressed, on top of a crisp, white hotel bed, with bright morning sunlight piercing my tired eyes. I rolled my head off my pillow, feeling the pull of an aching neck as it came back to me. The fight with Shelley, me storming out and booking myself into a nearby hotel, falling asleep almost immediately after my dramatic departure. I'd never felt this exhausted before. I must have had a solid twelve hours' sleep but I desperately felt like I needed more. This surely couldn't still be jet lag clinging on to my brain; those cocktails had been strong but this wasn't like a normal hangover. I pulled my phone towards me, which had been on charge overnight, feeling the sink in the pit of my stomach as I realised that there were no new messages. Not a single text, tweet or Facebook notification lay waiting for me, from either Ben or Shelley.

My stomach turned as I thought about what Shelley had said to me. Was I jealous? At the time I'd dismissed the idea as ludicrous, but maybe I did feel a little left out. I mean, plenty of divorced people remarry, so why was I finding the wedding world so tough to stomach? Originally when I thought Ben was going to propose, it had taken me some time to get my head around it, but I had actually been excited by the prospect of being able to call him my husband.

I thought I'd put it all to bed during my unplanned freak-out at the wedding dress sale in Adelaide. But I guess since being here and having weddings shoved in my face every single bloody day of this trip, I'd been given a wake-up call that left a bitter taste in my mouth. And I couldn't work out why. I was happy for Jimmy and Shelley, and in no way did I want to take away from their happiness, but something still niggled in my stomach that the froth and frills of the big show were totally pointless.

Maybe I'd said some things last night that I didn't mean. Truth be told, I couldn't remember exactly what it was I'd spouted off about. I wasn't going to apologise though. I'd had enough of pussyfooting around Shelley for fear of awakening the bridezilla beast. I knew that weddings were stressful, emotionally draining and expensive, but that didn't mean you treated your friends like shit.

I felt like I'd gone over and above in my bridesmaid duties. From breaking down in the outback to playing referee between her family and Jimmy's, camping on a cold street so she could get her dream dress, and even being humiliated by that cockwomble Lars because I'd put on a bit of weight, sorry, *baby* weight. Pfft. Thinking back to that embarrassing bridesmaid-dress fitting, a thought rushed into my head out of nowhere. When *was* my last period?

I sat up quickly, feeling a burn of sick in my chest as I mentally raced through the last month. I usually came on like clockwork, but the last time had been when we'd been holding a travel meet-up in London. I remembered because I'd been so stressed about the event going well that I'd been furious with myself for forgetting to pack some tampons when I realised mother nature had visited midway through the party. But that was almost two months ago now and I hadn't had one since. Shit.

Okay, maybe you've got the dates wrong, Georgia; or the stress of moving house, the investment pitch with the bank, planning this trip, have all affected you? That happened, didn't it? You always heard tales of women missing periods due to stress. Plus, my body clock had been so messed up with the long journey here, and the jet lag, maybe that just meant my cycle was slightly off course too.

I jumped out of bed faster than I was prepared for and gave myself a head rush in the process. I remembered the pregnancy tests Cara had added into our hen-do kits as a joke. This better had be a bloody joke, I thought, as my fingers found the box in my messy bag. It wouldn't hurt to take it, would it? With the sound of Lars's observations that I had the pregnancy aroma ringing in my ears, I headed to the bathroom. It would be one way to explain my unusual dramatics last night, which were so out of character for me; they say hormones can make you say and do crazy things. *No, you're overthinking this. There's no way you're pregnant.*

I would know if I was knocked up; it was ridiculous even entertaining the thought. I mean, surely you *know* when you are with child? Your body changes, you get morning sickness and you start having cravings, and none of those things had happened. Yes, I'd put on weight, but that was because I was comfortable in my relationship, and had been eating a lot of fast food because of all my business trips. Try as I might to talk myself out of it, something in my subconscious pressed me to carry on and take the test. Hurriedly reading the instructions, I weed on the stick and tapped the timer on my phone as I made myself keep busy and brush my teeth, waiting for the negative result.

Positive.

No, that can't be true! I picked up the box and reread the instructions. This was probably a joke from Cara. They weren't real pregnancy tests, they were fake ones designed to give everyone a good laugh when you all did them on a hen do. Ha bloody ha. I needed proper, pharmacy-supplied ones to tell me my fate before I even thought about freaking out.

I quickly got dressed and raced out of my hotel, remembering seeing a chemist on the next block before I'd checked in last night. At the time, I'd made a mental note to visit for some more plasters as my feet were still in a bad way from that long hike to the petrol station at Halls Gap. Glancing up and down the street, I made my way into the empty shop and spotted the aisle I needed. I plonked four pregnancy tests on the counter and prayed that no one I knew would wander in.

'Oh! Are these all for you?' a woman with half-moon glasses on the tip of her neat nose asked as I dropped my stash at her till. I was convincing myself that it was a waste of time and, blinking back the eye-watering tears at how expensive pregnancy sticks were, money.

'Yes,' I said, checking behind my back that Cara or Patty hadn't popped up behind me to pick up some prescription.

'Well, I do hope that you get the news you're after!' She winked.

I just nodded and gave her a tight smile. *You and me both, love. I couldn't be pregnant. We'd been careful. I would know if I was pregnant.*

'Is there anything else I can tempt you with today?'

'Oh no, just tho—'

'We've got a lovely selection of bath salts currently on two-for-one,' she rabbited on, stopping to scan each individual pregnancy kit and wave a wrinkled arm at a small cosmetics stand on her right.

'No, no, just these.' I smiled tightly. *Hurry up, hurry up!* I wanted to scream over every agonising second she was taking.

'Well, if that's not to your fancy then can I suggest some men's fragrances that are also on offer.' I gritted my teeth as she left the counter to open a glass cupboard behind her. She slowly pulled out some naff-looking bottles of aftershave and showed them to me. 'My nephew is a real fan of this one.'

'Just this, thanks!' I said, my voice sounding high-pitched and overly polite, even though I wanted to throttle her with the pearl chain keeping her glasses attached to her.

'Not a problem, darl'. Now then…' She rested a liver-spotted hand on my purchases. 'Oh, this one's not going through right. Just give me a second and I'll get Janine on the case.' She tutted at one of the kits, ignoring me taking a deep breath at how long this charade was taking. 'Janine to the tills, please. That's Janine to the tills.' She spoke through the store's intercom system, even though it would have been quicker to raise her voice to call for her colleague to do a price check across the empty shop.

'I can just take the other ones if there's a problem,' I said, pleadingly.

'Oh no, don't worry. Janine will be on the case.' She winked and spoke back into the mic. 'Janine, this lady needs a pregnancy test. Please can you come to the tills.'

Please, ground, swallow me up now.

Sure enough, Janine headed over, holding a box full of athlete's foot cream, and they both got into a detailed conversation about the scanner playing up.

'You need to try it again, Diana,' Janine said, holding the rogue pregnancy kit right up to her eye and peering intensely at it. 'We've just had new scanners installed,' Janine explained as Diana tried again. 'It's been causing us all sorts of headaches. Last week I had a gentleman buying two bottles of shampoo, you know, that special sort they have now for hair regrowth.'

'A load of nonsense if you ask me!' Diana piped up.

'Well, yes.' Janine put down the box on the counter and placed a warm hand on my arm. 'Anyway, I scanned them through and it came up on the system as tampons! Well, you can imagine just how embarrassing that was for us all!' She let out a chuckle at the memory.

'Oh, right,' I mused politely, secretly working out which one of them I would punch first. 'Actually, do you know what, I'm in a bit of a rush so I'll just leave that one. I think I've got enough.' I picked up the other three kits and prepared to put them into my handbag.

'Oh, no, well, if you do that then I'll need to start again, sorry. Don't worry, it won't take a moment,' Diana said, gently prising the kits from my clammy hands. 'Janine, we do need to do something about it though. I'll mention it to Richard when he gets in.'

Janine's face lit up as if that was the most wonderful suggestion. 'Yes, *he'll* know what to do.' She turned to me. 'Richard is the new area manager, lovely bloke and very handsome too.' She raised a thin, pencilled-on eyebrow, as if suggesting that Richard and I would make a lovely couple. 'Oh, excuse me!' She clasped a hand to cover her mouth as she chuckled. 'I think with these you probably don't need a new man at the moment!'

'Hmm,' I mused. *Kill me now.*

Before Janine could matchmake me with Richard the area manager, Diana had thankfully and successfully scanned all of the items. I paid, grabbed my stash and shoved them into my bag before hurrying out of there.

'Come back soon!' I heard Janine call as I flashed her a tight smile and raced out.

Back in the safety of my hotel room, I chugged a bottle of mineral water and waited for the need to wee to kick in. I ripped open the first packet, rustled the instructions out of the box and read what to do. Open stick, pee on the tab, close it up, lie it on a flat surface and leave it for two minutes. After that the small window on the side of the stick will show a pink cross for a positive test or a single pink dash for a negative test. I got my phone out to set up the timer for two minutes, did a wee and followed the instructions.

They were the longest two minutes of my life, even longer than the awkward show in the pharmacy. I forced myself to leave the bathroom to stop myself sneaking a look at the small window in the plastic stick. The window that would tell me my fate. A window that would be negative.

I paced over the wiry carpet, sank onto the bed and flicked open Instagram, swiped down Twitter, and scrolled through my Facebook wall. None of the information went in, as all I could think about was the fact that in the next room was the news that could change my life for ever. The shriek of my alarm telling me my two minutes were up shocked me like a slap around my face. After rushing back into the bathroom, I stood over the stick, carefully placed on the side of the sink. I closed my eyes and took a deep breath. *God, stop being ridiculous you're not preg—*

'I'm pregnant!' I breathed out, the stick dropping through my fingers and hitting the bathroom tiles.

A bubble of manic laughter came from my mouth. No, no. That must be a mistake. I hurriedly grabbed the other three testers and ripped them open, not bothering to read the instructions. I guessed once you've done one test you've done them all. I guzzled some more water and forced myself to wee. All of them came back with thick, definitive, undeniably, one hundred per cent concrete, big, fat positives.

I was pregnant.

CHAPTER 21

Veracity (n.) – Conformity to facts, accuracy

I held the pee sticks in my trembling hands and gave them a shake, as if like an Etch A Sketch they would fade the truth from my unbelieving eyes. The positive crosses on all of them remained. I slid to the floor, the cold tiles adding to the shock I was in. The air had been punched from my gut and my mouth had gone surprisingly dry considering the amount of water I'd just necked. I felt like I was gripping on to my emotions with my fingernails, trying to make sense of what this meant. Was this a normal reaction? Shouldn't I be jumping for joy or bursting into tears at this miracle Ben and I had performed? Shouldn't my maternal instinct kick in the moment I saw the bright pink cross in the small window? I just felt numb. No tears of joy or shock. No overriding emotion other than one of disbelief, as if these sticks I was holding were meant for someone else.

As my mind eventually woke up, it started to come together. It wasn't just jet lag or alcohol making me grumpy and argue with Shelley. It must have been pregnancy hormones causing me to act so unstably.

I'm pregnant, I'm pregnant, I'm pregnant.

I needed to speak to someone. I couldn't call my parents, not when my head was in this much of a state. Ben would no doubt still be fast asleep and half-cut from Jimmy's stag do last night. How was I even going to break this to him? He'd been so adamant that children were off the table. I'd fallen out with Shelley so I couldn't ring her for advice. The only other person who would understand this situation was Marie. I picked up my phone and willed my shaking fingers to tap open the FaceTime button. Thankfully, she answered within seconds. Her face filled my phone screen and made me smile sadly at seeing her sitting on her sofa in her house, thousands of miles away.

'Hey!' She beamed, adjusting the volume and propping her phone up against a mug. 'How are you? I was wondering how you were all getting on. There's not as many photos online for me to stalk you all for my liking.' She smiled. 'Georgia … what's the matter?' Her grin faded as she realised I'd started crying.

'I'm … I'm …' The words refused to budge from my chest as gasps of tears fell.

She shifted her position and grew more concerned that this wasn't a friendly catch-up call.

'Take a deep breath. What's happened? Is it Ben? Is it Shelley?' She knotted her eyebrows together.

I shook my head, burping down the acidic sting of bile hitting the back of my dry throat.

'Erm, has anything happened to Jimmy?' she guessed again.

Another shake of my head as I choked on the tears storming my eyes.

'Are you sick?'

It was beginning to feel like she was trying to communicate with Lassie to find out whether little Jimmy-Bob had fallen down the mineshaft.

'Georgia, just take a breath, you need to give me a clue at least …'

'I'm pregnant,' I eventually managed to spit out. The alien-sounding words tasted bitter on my tongue. I felt numb; it was as if someone else was saying them.

Marie's eyes widened. 'Seriously?'

I nodded, wiped the snot tickling the tip of my nose and leant over to show her the five positive pregnancy tests.

'Oh my God! How do you feel?'

'Like an idiot,' I said, shaking my head, trying to get some control over my emotions.

'What do you mean?' she asked softly.

I sighed. 'I mean that I should have been more prepared with keeping an eye on my periods, that I should have used titanium-strength condoms, that I shouldn't be in a situation feeling such intense shock at finding out I'm going to have a baby at my age. I feel like the girls on *Teen Mom* have a better handle on things than I do right now.'

Marie smiled. 'Of course it's a shock, but that's totally normal, Georgia! Do you not remember when I found out about Cole?' She shuddered as I thought back to her surprise discovery after a one-night stand with his dad, Mike. 'Wait. It is Ben's, isn't it?' She narrowed her eyes.

'Of course it's Ben's!'

Marie let out a dramatic sigh and wiped her forehead. 'Well, that's one less thing to worry about then. So, what's he said about it all?'

I chewed on my fingernail. 'I haven't told him yet,' I said quietly.

'Is he not with you?' She leaned forward as if trying to see around the camera lens.

I shook my head. 'He went out on the stag do and stayed over with Jimmy. I was meant to be having a girls' night in with Shelley but we sort of had a fight.'

'A fight? You and Shelley? Why?' Marie looked as if she wished she'd got some popcorn ready for this call.

'I don't really know.' I sniffed loudly. 'Weddings bring out the worst in people, I guess.'

'Does she know about your news? Has she gone mental that you've sabotaged her big day with this announcement?'

'No!' I looked horrified. 'One, I would never steal her thunder and two, I only did the test a few moments ago and I've not seen her since.' Oh God, now I had that to add to my list of worries.

'Well, you can't tell her until after her big day, especially if she's off with you at the moment.'

I nodded. 'I know. Don't worry. I'm not going to say a word. I still need to get my own head around the idea first.'

'Do you need me to run through your options with you?'

I stared at her. 'Options?'

'Well,' she sighed. 'There are three...'

'Three options?'

'You abort it, you have it and give it up for adoption, or you keep it,' she said calmly.

I stared at her. 'I can't even think about two of those; they are not options in the slightest.'

She breathed a sigh of relief. 'Okay, good. I just needed to see where you were at with it...' It hadn't even crossed my muddled mind that I would abort it or give it up. 'Well there's so much to do!' She sat upright and counted things out on her fingers. 'Folic acid! You need to start taking that as soon as possible. I'm sure you can get that in the pharmacies over there. You need to watch what you eat. No raw fish, no pâté, no caffeine, no soft cheese, no fresh mayonnaise. Oil!' She seemed to jump each time a new thought came to her.

'I can't eat oil?' Not that I regularly poured myself a shot of olive oil, but it just seemed tricky to police this one.

'No, you need to *use* oil. Every. Single. Day. All over, and I mean *all* over your body if you want to minimise stretch marks. My stomach looks like a wild wolf has clawed at it since having Lily, and that was because I was slack on using the oil.' She shook her head, berating herself. 'Everyone also says you're eating for two now but that's bollocks. Ignore those people as they just want you to get fat. Obviously you know about not drinking.'

My stomach flipped so violently at the thought of having a glass of wine I thought I might need to end the call and throw up. 'I don't think that will be a problem,' I said, hoping I wasn't turning green.

'Oh, you say that now. That is *classic* first trimester. As soon as those nauseous months pass, you'll be craving a bottle of rosé like never before. Luckily, nine months go much faster than you can imagine.' She focused her eyes to check I was taking all of this in. I wasn't, but tried to pretend I was. My attention was still with rosé wine and how I never wanted to see a glass of that ever again.

'But I've been drinking since coming over here. What if I've done some awful damage?'

Marie wafted her hand. 'Don't worry. Unless you've been doing hard-core drugs and raving every night, you'll be fine. I was hardly the picture of good health when I found out about Cole either, remember?' I nodded. 'Apps,' she said matter-of-factly.

'Apps?'

'Yes, you can get all these pregnancy apps that give you loads of info about the things you should and shouldn't do, depending on what stage you're at.'

'Oh, okay.' I really should be making notes of all this.

'Then you've got loads of other stuff to think about, and that's before you even work out how to afford it. Babies may be tiny but they're not cheap. There is *so* much to buy. I mean, I can share a lot of my things with you but there are certain items you'll want to get new. The big stuff like the crib, the pram, the car seat, all need to be budgeted for. You'll need to think about if you're going to do breast or bottle or both. You'll also need to think about the birth; whether you're at home or the hospital, if you want a special type of labour.'

'A pain-free one?' I laughed weakly.

'In your dreams.' She snorted. 'Now it's in there, there's only one way it's coming out. Well, two ways, and neither is pleasant.'

This was all making my head swim. I knew she was trying to be supportive and share her wisdom from having two children, but it felt like I was being drowned with information I'd never even thought about before.

'Names!' She half screamed, raising her finger in the air. She was getting excited now. 'You need to start thinking of what to call him or her, something unusual but not too strange. When we had Cole, no one had ever heard of that name before; now there are loads at the baby classes that I take Lily to. Ooh, you should think of how you want to announce it. You should get booked in for a maternity photo shoot, or you can set up this app to take a photo of your stomach every day from the same place and at the end of the nine months you get a video of how your body has changed. Or you could throw a party! I wish I'd been able to do this, as it's all the rage over in America for women to hold gender parties where they reveal the baby's sex. You are going to find out the gender, aren't you?'

'Jesus, I haven't—'

She cut me off. 'It's up to you, of course, but some women say it helps with the bonding process. Oh, I nearly forgot – perineum cream! That's essential. Your body is going to change so much and you need to do all you can to try and keep it as tight for as long as possible. Kegel exercises are going to be as intuitive as breathing from now on. Are you doing them now?'

I felt like I was being interrogated by the vagina police and quickly nodded, pulling over-the-top facial expressions to show how I was strengthening the inner walls of my lady bits. Was this actually happening?

'I'm not joking, Georgia. You'll thank me when it's born and you can still wee and have sex like a normal person. I know this one woman who had an awful time because she never did her exercises and guess what…?' She paused, dramatically widening her eyes.

'What?' I asked slowly.

'She had to get a designer vagina done at the plastic surgeon's. Couldn't feel a thing when she, you know . . .' Marie held up her pinkie finger as a hook and raised one eyebrow. 'You'll also have to deal with strangers coming up and touching your stomach.' She rolled her eyes. 'It's fucking annoying, but then you do get some perks out of being up the duff, like cutting in line, getting seats on public transport and being treated like royalty. Apparently, you can even get upgraded on some flights! That would be perfect for you!'

Flying. Travel. Fuck. I hadn't even thought about how having a baby was going to affect my career.

No more last-minute trips, long-haul flights or spur-of-the-moment holidays. I was about to lose all the freedom and independence that I felt I'd only just started to make the most of. I felt an ache for the things I hadn't yet achieved, the things I had but would never get to do again, the end of my world as I knew it.

'Oh my God, how am I going to still do my job! How am I going to tell Conrad and Kelli, let alone break this to Ben?' I felt like I was on the verge of hyperventilating.

Marie clocked my anxiety levels rocketing dangerously high. 'Georgia, take a deep breath. You will figure it all out. Right now, it's probably really scary, but, I promise, you and Ben will work out how to manage. Every new parent feels exactly the same.' She paused. 'So, when are you telling him?'

My stomach dropped. 'I have no idea.' I could feel myself welling up again at how overwhelming this all was.

'I know it feels like there is so much to take in, but every day you're a day closer to meeting him or her, which means there isn't a moment to waste.'

I swallowed back the bile in my throat. 'I need to go. I think I might be sick.'

Before she could say another word, I hung up and vomited into the toilet.

CHAPTER 22

Benevolent (adj.) – Showing kindness or goodwill

Wiping my mouth clean, I staggered to my feet, quickly sent Marie a text explaining I'd call her later and flopped on the unmade bed. I went online and typed in 'unexpected pregnancy'. A whole host of mummy blogs, health websites, medical sites and abortion clinics pinged up on my screen. One site had a handy chart explaining what size your offspring was each week, apparently thought up by some bored greengrocer. Week seven, your baby is the size of a blueberry. Week nine, it is the size of a grape. Week fifteen, you have an avocado growing in your nether regions.

After clicking an online forum called 'Welcome to the club', I felt the room tilt as I read what these women had shared about their birth stories. Ripping and tearing, pooing during labour and basically describing what it was like to be tortured. Each of these harrowing tales ended with 'but it was all worth it'. I felt as though I was reading information meant for someone else. I mean, I'd thought I had a fairly decent understanding of babies and pregnancy from helping Marie through hers, but this was like reading a foreign language.

Marie had kept repeating that it was normal to feel scared about all of this. I didn't feel fear – well, it was fear mixed with confusion, mixed with awe, mixed with grief, mixed with a hint of excitement. Was it selfish that my immediate reaction was to run through all the things I was going to lose and give up? All the things I currently took for granted, like taking a hot bath in peace, flinging things into a backpack and roaming around India or Chile at a moment's notice, living without care and doing exciting, adrenaline-pumping activities such as sand boarding or scuba diving – basically, just being me. My mum's voice rang in my cluttered mind: 'No matter how much adventure you have, it never seems enough.' I loved my life and had worked so bloody hard to get to where I was, but now I was going to dismantle it piece by piece. I closed my eyes and pushed my phone away. I'd already shown how incompetent I was at this whole motherly instinct from the chaos of looking after Marie's children.

I decided that the sooner I faced the music with Ben, the better. I needed to know if I was going to raise this child as a single mother, or if he might have had a change of heart and be on board with being a dad once faced with the news. I decided that it would probably be better to tell him that he was going to be a daddy in a public place. I was hoping that he would scoop me up, tell me I was wonderful and that everything would be all right. I sent him a quick text asking him to meet me on the steps of the Opera House in two hours.

Luckily, Ben was keen to meet up as long as there was coffee. A strong one. I decided to reserve my hotel room for another night; tonight Ben could stay with me and we could actually have a nice evening just the two of us, talking things over and getting our heads around the news. If he was on board with it. If Shelley didn't want or need my help any more, then I would actually get to enjoy some time in Australia with my man. I kept going to type her a message, but I couldn't find the right words. I was hurt that she had said those things to me and kicked me out of her big day, but I had a much bigger issue to sort out first.

I still felt terrible; I swear the cup of tea I'd made with the small hotel room kettle and fiddly cartons of milk almost came back up in the toilet bowl as I took a shower, dried my hair and did my make-up whilst still feeling dizzy. I applied a ton of foundation to my face, which was decidedly greyish in colour, and went to leave. Thankfully, as I breathed in the fresh air and hit the streets, I instantly felt a lot better.

Sydney has this energy about it; everyone looks so happy and those endorphins seem to travel through the air like pollen in the summer time. I swear every person I passed was fit, both in the sporty and good-looking sense, or smiling from being in one of the most incredible cities in the world. Women in tight yoga pants walking tiny dogs on leads and holding Starbucks cups seemed to breeze past, joggers with their phones in holders strapped to their muscular upper arms skipped around me, and couples pushing sleeping babies cocooned in their three-wheeled pushchairs sauntered along, stopping occasionally to glance in shop windows. Seeing their child wrapped up against the autumn breeze, I felt my chest tighten. I picked up my pace, wanting to hurry and meet Ben.

I didn't feel how I imagined I would after finding out that I was pregnant. In those daydreams I'd had before, I was living in a stunning house that I owned with my husband, having reached all my career and personal life goals before actively trying for a child together. I self-consciously rubbed my stomach. According to the pregnancy app I'd hurriedly downloaded, I was carrying something the size of a kidney bean. Do you know how minute those things are! Of course I wasn't showing yet, my stomach was just bloated from the carb overload, but it felt different placing my hand there. Psychological maybe, but things had changed big time.

I'd got a little lost as I wandered around and soon found myself cutting through the Botanic Gardens to get to the Opera House. The vast, lush green space was filled with every type of exotic plant, flower and stunning water feature you could imagine. I followed a gravel path that wound through a small children's playground. I hurried up my pace past the families playing on the funky-coloured equipment, not wanting to be late for Ben but also not wanting to be surrounded by my future just yet. But finding out my news on an empty stomach and rushing in the clammy heat meant I was struck with a wave of nausea and dizziness. I quickly spotted a bench and forced myself to get my breath back before moving on.

'Mummy!' a little girl called as she ungracefully climbed to the top of the steps of a small slide. 'Look at meeeeeee!' she sang, then pushed herself off on her bum down the metal to land in a heap at the bottom, giggling to herself. I glanced up to see her mum on her phone, oblivious to her daughter now with wood chips in her frilly white socks.

There were so many mummies in this world but only one of me: Georgia Green. I had to prepare myself for losing my identity and just being another 'mum' in a sea of other mums. The mums with their years of knowledge and know-how. The ones who said they were born to do this job, whose lives had been enriched by having sex and keeping the by-product. I bet they never lost their shit when they found out they were pregnant. I bet the instant they saw the pee stick turn pink they wept with joy that their true purpose for being on this earth had finally been realised. I knew how to be Georgia – I'd been her for three decades – but I didn't know how to be a mum.

'You all right, love? You've gone a little pale?' the woman who'd previously been engrossed in her phone, turned around to ask me.

'I've just found out I'm pregnant,' I admitted without meaning to.

'Ah, a "surprise" one eh?' She made quotation marks with her fingers and gave a knowing nod. 'That's what you call them nowadays, not a mistake or an accident, they're surprises.' She smiled at me. 'I'm Christie, mum of Bella over there.' She nodded at the little girl who was heaving herself through a bright red tunnel.

'Georgia.' I pointed to my chest.

'Well, Georgia, have some of this.' She pulled out a bottle of water from her bag, which was chock-full of small coloured plastic pots, soft toys, nappies and God knows what else. 'I'm afraid I just finished off the gin from the hip flask earlier.' I gawped at her. 'Joking.' She placed her hands in the air defensively and laughed, then pressed one against her mouth. 'Well, I did *use* to have a hip flask, but that was for emergencies only. You can't go around saying that to strangers, and not to other mums unless you know them, if you know what I mean?'

I just stared at her and took a tentative sip of the water she'd offered me.

'So, I'm guessing this is your first?'

I nodded.

'I was exactly like you when I found out about Bella. I wore the same pale and shocked look on my face that you have now for days, trying to get my head around it and working out what it would mean in terms of my current life.' I self-consciously pressed a hand against my cheeks. 'You'll mourn the days you spent hungover, napping on the sofa on Sundays, flicking through your favourite TV soaps, as they'll become a long-lost dream. You think you will stay the same.' She cast a look at the small handbag resting on my knees. 'But you don't. I mean, you can't. *Everything* has changed.'

This was the thing. The phrase that freaked me out the most. *Everything is going to change.* Everything. I didn't want everything to change, I loved my life how it was now; how happy Ben and I were, how well my career was going, how I'd come to peace with my body, how we were on the cusp of starting a new life in London.

'You don't think you can keep your identity?'

She thought for a moment and cast a look at her daughter, playing with another toddler who had a string of snot so long it almost touched the collar of his t-shirt. 'Yeah, you can still be *you*, but it's a totally different you.' She looked at me to see whether that made any sense at all. 'I really don't want to put you off as there are so many positives; if I listed them to you now you'd think I was making them up. I used to feel the same before Bella, when new parents would give me advice. That's another thing: everyone will want to share some piece of advice with you, and all of it will be contradictory.'

'The way I feel now, I think I *need* to hear the good bits, as all my brain is computing are the negatives, the things I'm about to lose.'

'The good bits are things like when they smile at you for the first time, when they do or say something super cute and your heart just melts, when they make you appreciate the smallest things that pass you by, like staring at butterflies or aeroplanes with complete wonderment. You'll become more patient, compassionate, understanding and, although you won't stress less because your reasons for worrying just increased tenfold, the things that you used to freak out about will seem so insignificant. You discover things about yourself you never knew possible.'

I cast my mind back to how I had felt going backpacking, how travel had shown me the person I never thought I could be, the one who bartered for tuk-tuks or stood her ground when being offered a bad deal, the Georgia who had more patience than she thought she was capable of when waiting for cancelled flights.

'But,' Christie sighed, 'kids can be a bit boring, especially as toddlers, when everything is on a repetitive loop; you can feel like you're losing your mind some days. Bella, come and have a drink.' Her daughter ignored her and continued to whizz down the battered slide. Christie turned to me. 'Do you work?'

I nodded. 'I actually own my own business.'

Her eyes widened in a look of respect before she made some strange sound through her teeth. 'Eeesh, then this is going to be even harder. I worked in advertising, you see; wanted to be Don Draper with a vagina. Thought I could handle anything – I mean, once you've been in the boardroom with thirteen men all competing in a willie-waving competition over budgets and bonuses, then you think you've dealt with enough immature toddlers, but that's until you actually have a toddler. One that throws things at your

head, tells you they hate you because you make them
put on shoes to go to the park, one that loves apple
juice until one day when she decides she hates apple
juice for no reason other than you gave it to her in a
different cup.' She sighed and pushed back her hair.
Glancing at her daughter Bella, I couldn't imagine this
was the same child she was describing.

'And then you get the health workers, or any
busybody, who constantly refers to you as *Mum* –
"How's Mum doing? Is Mum getting enough sleep?
And Baby, is Baby feeling okay? When did Baby last
get a feed?" She rolled her eyes. 'By *Mum*, you mean
Christie and by *Baby*, you mean Bella; both Christie
and Bella are doing amazingly, thank you.' She laughed
and shook her head. 'Seriously, Georgia, you'll begin
to feel like you've swapped lives with someone else,
someone who you barely recognise when you look in
the mirror, especially during the newborn stage when
you turn into a giant milk machine.' She pulled herself
together, taking a look at my gawping expression. 'Oh,
God. I've just realised that you're a total stranger, just
found out you're pregnant and here I am spouting off
about everything that's soon to be coming your way.'
She gingerly patted my hand.

'It's fine!' I breathed.

'I'm sorry for ranting a little.' Christie glanced up
to see if the other mums on the opposite bench, who
seemed to be responsible for the kid with the long,
stringy snot, were listening to any of this conversation.
'People will think you have post-natal depression
if you discuss the negatives of it all, which I know
I haven't. I just think it's important to stress that it's
not all baking fairy cakes and cuddles. Sometimes
when reality hits, it does get really monotonous, boring

and mundane. That's not to mean you're depressed, but more that you're adjusting to this new world that you've found yourself in.' Christie sighed. 'You do what you can but then there's always this guilt that you're not doing enough. That being at work means you're neglecting your child and being with your child means you're neglecting yourself and your own dreams and ambitions, something I certainly promised myself I wouldn't lose when I became a mum.'

'So, how did you do it?' I asked. She wasn't lost in some magical world of motherhood bleating that everything was perfect. It was actually really refreshing, if a little terrifying, to hear.

'Well.' She smiled kindly. 'I have a great husband and supportive parents who help me out. I also realised that the Christie before had spent thirty years being selfish. I am still fiercely protective about the time when I do my own things. I take an evening gym class once a week, come hell or high water. I just think of it this way: the child will benefit more from having such a strong mother with passions and hobbies and projects and plans that aren't only related to "mummy" things. You don't want to be someone who says they can't remember life before their darling child was born: that's like erasing the past, and why would you want to do that?'

I nodded along.

'I love Bella with all of my heart and would die for her.' Christie looked me straight in the eye. 'But having her doesn't mean I lose *me*. Where the only conversations you have are about sleep cycles, nappy changes or Peppa bloody Pig. If I could give you any advice, it would be to make sure you don't lose your identity. Don't let the baby *always* come before everything and don't feel pressured to do *everything* the books tell you. It's hard. The hardest job you'll ever do, but you will do it and you will love it.'

I nodded along, thinking about this dose of reality being served to me by this plain-talking stranger.

'Right, we'd better be off. Nice talking to you, Georgia, and good luck.' Christie got to her feet and smiled at me.

'Thanks, I think I'll need it.'

CHAPTER 23

*Futile (adj.) – Incapable of producing any
useful result; pointless*

I'd eventually found my route out of the never-ending gardens when my phone buzzed. I fumbled with it in my bag, thinking it would be Ben asking why I'd dragged him out of his hangover pit to meet so urgently and then kept him waiting. When I looked down at the phone screen, I realised it wasn't Ben but Shelley calling. Without thinking if she was ringing to have another go at me, I pressed answer.

'Georgia?' She sounded as if she was out of breath.

'Shell?' I frowned. 'Everything all right?'

'Oh, Georgia, I'm *so* sorry for our row!' she garbled.

'Shell, are you okay? Where are you?'

She sniffed loudly. 'It's all gone tits up!' She was full-on crying now.

'Take a deep breath. What's happened?' I asked, firmly but calmly.

'He's gone. He's fucking gone!'

I suddenly had this rush of saliva fill my mouth. 'Jimmy's gone?' Oh my God! He'd really jilted her before the big day. I felt dizzy and buzzing with anger at the same time.

'No! Not Jimmy,' she eventually said through a sob.

I let out a breath. 'Who then?'

'Lars! Lars has left. Apparently his wedding-planning business has gone into liquidation and it's all over.'

This was bad. The wedding was tomorrow!

'Tell me where you are right now. I'm on my way.'

I reached the nearest road and flagged down a taxi to take me to her. As we drove through the streets, I hurriedly sent Ben a text apologising that I wasn't going to make our coffee date. All thoughts of babies and pregnancy faded from my mind as I had to help my best friend out. Telling Ben could wait, for now.

*

I found her slumped on the sofa. The television was blaring out an old episode of *The Bachelor*, stained mugs peppered nearly every available surface, and dirty laundry was piled by the washing machine. The seating plan organised with military precision was almost falling off the cluttered coffee table, sheets of papers, formal-looking files and wedding magazines had exploded like debris around her curled-up body.

'Shell?' I tentatively stepped over the box of favours she'd been hand-tying the last time I saw her.

'Oh my God. I'm cursed!' she wailed. Her eyes were red and blotchy, her chin had a couple of spots claiming their territory and her pyjamas were covered in tea stains. I tried not to let my face show how shocked I was at the wedding war zone she was in.

'Sit up and tell me everything. I'll put the kettle on.'

After flicking the switch and rinsing out some of the less skanky mugs, I brewed up as she started telling me that Lars had done a runner with the money and royally left them in the shit.

'I've called the venue and thank goodness they had a note of our booking, but they were missing all the details of numbers, dietary requirements and things like that. I gave all these to Lars to give them weeks ago.' She rubbed at her face and accepted her mug of tea, shifting herself to make some room for me on the sofa.

'Right, we need a list,' I said, decisively.

'It's pointless. The wedding is tomorrow and there's still so much to do. None of the things Lars said he'd done have actually been done.' She scrunched up a tissue in anger. 'Even my no-chip nail varnish has chipped!' She thrust her trembling hands in my face. Her nails that had been perfectly painted at the salon were now tatty and chewed.

I took a deep breath. 'We just need to ring around and see what's been done and then sort what hasn't. We can do this.' I stared at her, needing her to be on board with fixing this, rather than allowing herself to sink into her own filth and ignore it all. 'We might not have time to redo your nails, but I'm sure Cara will have some polish that can touch them up.'

'That's not all.' She took a deep breath, fidgeting with the hem on her jumper. 'You know you asked me if we were okay for money?'

I thought back to the start of the road trip when we'd briefly chatted about budgets. 'Yeah…'

'Well, I lied.' She sniffed as I tried to catch up. 'Johanna didn't pay for Lars, I did.'

I raised my eyebrows in surprise. Wedding planners did not come cheap.

'But then why did you say she did?' I thought back to the meal with her parents. I had known she was being shifty about something!

Shelley shrugged, colour rushing into her cheeks at admitting this. 'I didn't want to confess that I'd blown so much money on such an extravagant thing! But that's not all. I've been getting myself further and further into debt trying to make this day perfect. Why do you think I had to get my dress from a sample sale and why I've suddenly got so crafty at the last minute?'

I shook my head blankly.

'There's no more money left in the pot. There hasn't been for ages. I've maxed out our two credit cards and dipped into the savings fund we'd started for a house deposit.' She started to cry. 'There was a reason I planned our hen do to be a taste of our backpacking lifestyle, because I used the money you and Cara chipped in to pay for our flowers. I had to do it on the cheap! I even resorted to trying to win some bloody competition hoping I'd get lucky.'

I sat back, letting it all sink in. 'What competition?'

'A photo competition. Whenever I posed with the wedding magazine, it wasn't for a memory scrapbook, it was for this competition to win $1000. I didn't win.'

'Shit, Shelley.' I was in shock, taking this all in.

'I just got caught up in it all, wanting to keep up with the Joneses. You can see how living here does that to you.' She wafted a trembling arm around Cara's interior-magazine-inspired home.

'But why didn't you ask Cara or me for some help? I could have loaned you some money.'

At this, Shelley sat upright and violently shook her head. 'No way. I was too proud to admit it was getting out of control, but too foolish to stop spending.'

It all made sense – the stress and worry wasn't just about making her day perfect, it was about being able to pay for it, and then how to break the news to Jimmy that his bride had blown the budget and sent them spiralling into debt.

'Come on, we need to get as much sorted for tomorrow as we can right now. Figuring out how to get you out of this financial mess will have to wait. We will work something out though.'

'Thank you, Georgia.' She looked up at me through wet eyelashes and choked on a sob. 'Cara's at work, Jimmy's still recovering from his bucks' night and my parents are taking Jimmy's parents out to show them the city. I've not told anyone else about this as I couldn't bear admitting it's all gone wrong.'

'Hey, don't worry. Now pass me everything you've got on this wedding and let's get cracking.'

She handed over one of the files that had tumbled to the floor; tear splatters smudged some of the writing on the first page.

'I am really sorry about what I said the other day,' she mumbled, as I picked up a pen, wanting to help her and put our fight behind us. It would also help take my confused mind from what was going on in my own life right now.

'Did I pull you away from anything?' she asked, catching her breath and calming down. 'Were you and Ben sightseeing?'

I shook my head. 'Nothing that can't wait.'

She nodded gratefully and then leant forward slightly. 'Did you mean all you said the other night?' she asked in a quiet voice. 'It's just … a few things have stayed in my mind.'

I stared at her. 'Shelley, I can't remember half of what I was going on about!' I couldn't exactly tell her that it must have been the early onset of baby brain causing me to spew such shite. 'Every girl is entitled to her big day and I am so sorry that I made you feel like you shouldn't have your moment. I guess, in the worst possible way, I was trying to make sure you didn't focus all your energy on the one day and

ignore the years of married life that lie ahead of you.'
I shrugged.

'It's fine, I get it, and I'm sorry for not being more
thoughtful of your feelings, of how hard it must be for
you to dive into wedding world again.'

God, we were a right pair.

'I do believe in marriage, and that if you work hard
at it then you can spend your life with this one person
who makes you feel like the best version of yourself,'
I admitted. 'I just don't think that has to come at the
cost of everything else, like losing your sanity before
the big day.'

I started to sniff back the tears. I wanted to be
happy, and one day I wanted Ben to be my husband;
maybe I was scared that Alex had tainted weddings
for me. That, in a way, I felt as though I was a fraud
for putting on a big white dress and having my own
special day. I didn't have to have the traditional
wedding day that I'd previously organised but never
got to experience. Maybe we could elope or head to
the registry office in our jeans? It didn't have to be this
big show. We could declare our love in our own way.
Without co-ordinated invites, table numbers and debt.

'Georgia! What's wrong!' Shelley asked, pulling out
a handful of tissues.

I dabbed my eyes and waved my hands around.
'Nothing. Sorry, I just feel so happy for you marrying
Jimmy tomorrow!'

'Thank you, hun. God, I love him so much. I'm not a
fool to think that it won't be without its difficulties. But
I also know that I've never met anyone like him. He is
kind, patient, hilarious – honestly, he has me in stitches
at these ridiculous impressions he does.' She shook her
head, trying to wipe the smile off her face. 'For me,

getting married is about placing this protective bubble around us; we become this proper team. It gives us a sense of security, I guess. Jimmy gives me this feeling of happiness and contentment whenever he's around. That's not to say I'm not slightly nervous about the joining our worlds together for ever more amen.' She smiled softly. 'I am so sorry for our falling out.'

I patted her arm. 'Shell, don't worry. I know you're sorry and I am too. So your parents and Jimmy's parents are hanging out, eh?'

Shelley winced too. 'I know, right? There may not even be a wedding if they don't all come back in one piece.'

I laughed. 'Right, first things first, let's see what you do have …'

'Thank you,' she repeated, placing a cool arm on mine.

'So, dress?'

'Sorted.'

'Suits, bridesmaid dresses, shoes, accessories …' I listed on my fingers.

'All done, and thankfully the guys have got their suits and all our dresses are hanging up in the wardrobe.'

'Excellent. Okay, cake …'

Shelley chewed her lips. 'I know which bakery I chose but I have no idea where that's up to.'

'We'll call them first. You said the venue is sorted?'

'Yeah, they just need our information.' She cast a hand over the tumbling table plan and sheets of paper. 'Then I need to check about hotels, the photographer, flowers, the registrar, transport …'

'We've got this,' I said reassuringly.

Thankfully Shelley had been anal about keeping spreadsheets with lists of the suppliers she'd arranged with Lars, so we were able to confirm that most of the things were still going to plan. A few asked for payments that Shelley was positive she'd already paid, and others seemed slightly blank until we described Lars and then instantly they remembered him coming in and sorting something. We were both scrolling on our phones and her laptop, looking for some more details, after our second mug of tea and half the packet of Tim Tams that she'd cracked open, when she turned to me.

'So, how have things been with you?'

I flicked my eyes up and tried to remain cool. 'Oh, you know, fine,' I said, looking back down at the website for ferry timings for the guests. 'What about this crossing?' I pointed to the laptop screen. 'That should get your guests over in enough time?'

Shelley slowly took her eyes off me and onto where I was pointing. I really didn't want to stress her out with my own news, not when she was in the process of re-planning a wedding in a day. I hated keeping secrets from her, but as we'd only just made up, I didn't want her to think I had purposefully got knocked up to steal her limelight, as Marie had said.

'Yeah, that looks fine. Actually, I know what we need to help with all of this – wine! I'm sure Cara has some nice bottles in one of the kitchen cupboards. She usually hides them from us behind her packets of super-grain crackers.' She laughed and rushed to the kitchen.

'No!' I shouted before realising it.

She stopped and spun round, a confused look on her face. 'Why not? It's not too early, is it? And after the day I've had, I need a drink – screw the wedding detox!'

'Erm, because we still have loads left to do.' I said.

'Oh, right.' She paused. One hand was clutching a wine glass, the other was holding an empty packet of healthy crackers. *Please don't interrogate me*, I willed her. 'Yeah, I guess you're right,' she eventually said, going to flick the kettle on once more. 'Save it for tomorrow, right?'

I nodded and smiled at her. 'Good idea. Right, come and help me with this…'

How was I going to get away with not drinking tomorrow?

'I can't believe it's almost over.' She shook her head at the wedding paraphernalia spread out around us.

'But it's only just beginning.' I smiled at her.

She nodded forcefully. 'You're right. You are *so* right. Tomorrow will be what it will be. Even if I don't get my popcorn station or arch of hand-tied flowers, I will be marrying my best friend.'

The wedding planning took longer than I'd expected, so I texted Ben to say I was going to stay over at Cara's to keep Shelley company on her last night as an unmarried woman. I'd picked up my stuff from the hotel room and got re-settled in the enormous bed I'd been given in Cara's guest room. I just hoped that we'd done enough to make sure everything went without a hitch tomorrow. The baby news would have to wait.

CHAPTER 24

Sanguine (adj.) – Cheerfully optimistic, hopeful or confident

'I'm getting married today!' Shelley woke me up by racing into my room, jumping on the bed and performing such an energetic dance routine I thought she'd do herself an injury. She then raced out making a squealing noise 'Ermagerhrddddd I'M GETTING MARRIED TODAY!'

I yawned and sat up in the crumpled bed sheets and rubbed my eyes. Instinctively, my hand went to my stomach. I was growing a baby in there and no one had the faintest idea. Well, no one apart from Christie and Marie. It felt like such a delicious secret that I basked in the enjoyment of being in this small club of three who knew. I also had to face facts that today was going to take all my powers of secrecy and deception to avoid booze, not feel nauseous *and* fit into my dress without popping the zip. That was before I'd figured out a way to tell Ben he was going to be a daddy.

Shelley sped into the room once more, pulling me from my thoughts. 'Get up, get up! We've got so much to do because I'M GETTING MARRIED!' she screeched.

'Okay, okay, I'm up.' I half-groaned, flipping back the covers.

'Great. Go and wake Cara up too!' Shelley ordered, as she sprayed an ozone-layer-melting amount of deodorant, making me cover my mouth to avoid being gassed by the artificial scent of freshly washed linen.

I stumbled to my feet and did what she said; I needed Cara up for the moral support. After padding over the soft carpet and hearing Shelley open the door to welcome people in to help her get ready, I knocked on Cara's bedroom door. But there was no answer.

'Cara? Time to get—' I pushed open the door and was faced with an empty bedroom.

'Shell?' I called. 'I don't think Cara came back last night.'

We'd gone to bed early. I'd barely been able to keep my eyes open and Shelley had wanted her beauty sleep.

'What! You'd better be joking! Call her and get her to come home from whichever man she shared a bed with last night,' Shelley fumed from the other room, as I picked up my mobile to call her AWOL cousin.

Cara's phone just went straight to voicemail. Even though I knew she would probably be walking in the door at any moment, it wasn't like she could have forgotten about this bloody wedding, I hurriedly left her a message.

The flat soon became a hive of activity as the hairdresser, photographer, make-up artist and florist arrived to work their magic and drop off essentials. Shelley was sitting on one of the kitchen chairs having her eye make-up expertly applied.

'Do you not have two bridesmaids who need their make-up doing?' the lady with poker-straight hair and gappy teeth asked.

'Yeah, we've got Georgia here and my cousin Cara. Is she not back yet?' Shelley asked, as I went to make everyone a cup of tea for the second time.

'Erm, not yet. Let me check my phone again.'

I could see Shelley shift in her seat slightly before being told to sit still whilst the woman applied false lashes. Her carefree demeanour had changed as the time passed. Where the hell was Cara?

'You want me to try anyone else? Maybe your mum's seen her?' I offered as her cousin's phone continued to ring to voicemail.

Shelley hurriedly passed over her mobile to scroll through her contacts list. 'Shit, we can't have a bridesmaid who's gone AWOL,' she seethed, trying to balance her emotions between anger and worry.

'At least it's not the groom,' the make-up artist said unhelpfully.

Shelley's mouth dropped. 'Oh my God, what if Jimmy doesn't show!'

I tutted and shook my head. 'Jimmy will be there. Cara will too. I'm sure she's on her way right now. Let me call Ben and double-check everything is okay at their end. At least that will put your mind at ease?'

Shelley nodded. 'Good idea, then we need a drink. My nerves can't take this. I'll bloody kill her when she turns up. Georgia, can you get the Prosecco open?'

I nodded and felt my stomach do a faint flip at the thought of a drink this early in the morning.

'Sure, give me a minute.' I wandered out of the room and into the bedroom, dialling Ben's number.

'Hey, you,' he replied. Just hearing his voice made me bite back the emotions rushing around my chest. As soon as today was over I wanted the rest of our time here to be purely about us, the three of us.

'Hi, I just wanted to see how everything was going?'

'Fine, yeah. Jim's in the shower, his dad has popped by for a drink and we've had a fry-up.'

'Sounds a lot more relaxed than things are here. I'd kill for a fry-up right now.' I paused. 'You haven't heard from Cara at all, have you?'

'No, why?'

'Oh, she's not come back from wherever she was last night. Just a long shot that she might have got in touch with you or Jimmy. Shelley's starting to freak out a bit, that's all.'

'Nope, not heard from her. You worried?'

'Not yet, I'm sure she'll be here soon enough. I'd better go and calm Shelley's nerves with a stiff drink. I can't wait to see you later.'

'I can't bloody wait either.'

I padded back into the kitchen after sending Cara a private Facebook message asking where she was. She hadn't been online for at least twelve hours. This was getting weirder by the minute. I decided not to call and worry Patty; the least amount of panicking, the better.

'What did they say? Did you find her?' Shelley hurriedly asked through a fug of hairspray and perfume.

'Jimmy is fine and getting ready, so no worries there, and Cara is on her way,' I lied, mid-cough. I didn't want Shelley to stress when Cara would turn up any minute, hopefully.

She breathed a sigh of relief. 'I'll bloody kill her when she gets here,' she muttered, receiving a sympathetic glance from the make-up artist. 'Where the hell has she been? She'd better have a flaming good excuse.'

'Oh, err, she didn't say, only that she'll be here soon,' I lied again.

'Right, well, I'll crack open the drinks as it's your turn to get your make-up done,' Shelley instructed.

I went and sat in the chair as the make-up artist
tutted at my face. My forehead had this sheen that
would need all the blotting paper in the world to fix.
If this was a side effect of being pregnant, I didn't like
it. When was that blooming radiant glow supposed to
happen?

'Here you go. Lord knows we need this!' Shelley
lifted her champagne flute into the air and chinked the
one she gave me. Just the smell of it made my stomach
turn. 'Cheers!'

I gingerly lifted my glass to hers and pretended to tip
it to my lips as she closed her eyes and took a large sip.
I then poured a mouthful or so into a half-empty mug
of cold tea while Shelley's back was turned. I saw the
make-up artist looking at me with a raised eyebrow.

'I'm on painkillers,' I mumbled, with as much sass
as I could. She nodded, blatantly knowing I was lying,
and went back to her array of palettes spread out on
the kitchen table.

'Shelley, if we could get some shots of you on the
balcony?' the photographer asked, taking her outside.
This gave me a few precious minutes to hurriedly
type another Facebook message to Cara in shouty
capital letters, when the door bounced open and she
stumbled in.

'I'm here!' she sang, her legs twisting in different
directions as she tried to figure out how to get her
door key out of the lock. Her arms fumbled against
the wood as she managed to remember this basic
skill. The stench of alcohol trailed in behind her as she
dramatically slammed the door shut. 'Has someone
messed with my door?'

I leapt up out of my seat, ignoring the make-up
artist grumbling that she'd have to redo my base again

now, and went to grab Cara. Thankfully, Shelley
was oblivious to the late arrival, as she was too busy
grinning at the camera lens on the balcony. I pulled
Cara's skinny and sweaty arm and led her to the
bathroom before telling the make-up artist we'd just
be a minute.

'What the fuck are you doing! Where have you
been?' I hissed, locking the door behind us. Cara was
struggling to stand up. She was completely wasted.

'It's fine. I'm here, ain't I? Now, let's get married!'
She fell into a fit of giggles as her legs gave way and
she tumbled into the bathtub, pulling the shower
curtain down on her. I winced at the state of her. My
nostrils felt like they were on fire at the burning stench
of booze in the small room, the pathetic fan whirring
away stood no chance in purifying the brewery fumes.

'Look at me! I'm a bride!' she sang, giggling as she
pulled the shower curtain over her messy hair like a
veil.

'Cara! Stop it, you need to sober up. How could you
get into such a state?' I breathed through my mouth,
and tried to lift her out of the bath so I could run her
a cold shower to wake her up. Although she was built
like a bendy coat hanger, she weighed a hell of a lot
more than I expected. She wasn't listening to me;
instead she was faffing with the bottle of expensive
shower gel, looking utterly perplexed about how to
open the thing.

'Cara!' I hissed. She looked up at me woefully. Her
eyes were bloodshot; deep purple bags pulled them
down – she resembled a Hush Puppy dog that was
about to cry.

'Cara, what's happened?' I softened my tone, I needed
to find answers, but I also needed her to get her

shit together before Shelley freaked out that neither of us were currently getting our hair or make-up done.

'Hey!' She changed her expression as a thought came to her. 'You were banned from the wedding. What are you doing here?'

'Well, I'm now back in the team. A team that is one member short because of you. Now, come on, tell me why you've got yourself in such a state?'

She sniffed loudly. 'I can't do it!'

'Can't do what?'

'The wedding. This!' She flung her arms as if pointing to herself. 'I can't pretend any more.'

I heard footsteps behind the door before a loud knock thumped against the wood.

'Are you nearly done? We *really* have to be getting a move on,' the make-up artist's voice shrilled under the closed bathroom door.

'Nearly,' I replied breezily, with a hint of piss-off-can't-you-see-I'm-busy undertone.

I turned back to Cara, who was pulling at the toilet paper, rolling out sheets to dab her eyes and blow her nose. She looked a world away from the glam, put-together version I'd met in Melbourne. Her skin was grey, angry-looking red blotches had broken out on her neck, and her hair needed a good brush. She looked tragic.

'What can't you do?' I repeated, more firmly.

'I've been seeing this guy. This older man,' she began, with a loud sniff. Bits of toilet paper were stuck to a splodge of snot on her chin.

'Wait – I thought you were single?'

She shook her head. 'I've been seeing this guy, in secret.' She paused and took a deep breath. 'I thought he was the one. I thought he loved me too, but it was all bullshit!' She started to sob again. 'I went to see him last night, I wanted to ask him to be my plus-one for today. I'd been asking him about it for ages, but never got a solid answer out of him. When I got there he was…he was…with another woman. Why does this always happen to me? Why?' She began howling, painfully like a wounded animal. I couldn't believe Shelley hadn't heard.

Shit.

Getting dumped right before spending a day surrounded by love and happiness and smug other couples was not going to be easy. But, unfortunately for her, having such an important role to play meant she had to man up. Shelley was already back into bridezilla mode and would hardly be sympathetic to her cousin's plight right now.

'Cara, I know how awful it is to be dumped. I get it.' I bent down to her level, gently moving a strand of slicked-down hair from her forehead. 'But today is about Shelley. I promise that tomorrow we will go and find this shitbag and give him what he deserves, or spend the day in our pyjamas, eating ice cream and singing power ballads, but today, today you have to bring your A game.' I tried to give her my fiercest look.

She remained silent for a moment. 'I don't know if I can, Georgia,' she said in a whisper.

'You can and you will.' I nodded determinedly. 'Now come on, get up, take a shower and I'll make you a very strong cup of coffee. I'll say that you weren't feeling well or something.' I smiled at her gently.

Looks like it wasn't just me who was going to have to struggle through the rest of the day. I left her with the shower running and the promise that she would brush her teeth and wash her hair as quickly as possible.

'Everything all right? Is that Cara? I'll bloody *kill* her for being so late!' Shelley screeched the minute I stepped from the bathroom, quickly shutting the door behind me.

'It's fine. She's not feeling great but I'm sure a shower, a hot drink and some toast will sort her out. Speaking of which, have you eaten anything yet?'

Shelley pulled her narrowed eyes, which had been glaring at the closed bathroom door, to me and shook her head.

'No, I'm too nervous to get anything down me. I'll be fine.' She glanced at the clock and at the make-up artist, who gave an over-the-top dramatic sigh and started tapping her foot.

'You need to get a move on,' Shelley snapped at me before banging a fist loudly on the bathroom door. 'So does she!' she shouted, then stomped off to top up her glass of fizz.

I slumped back into the make-up artist's chair, ignoring her complaints that she would have to start all over again, and closed my eyes. Trying to get the bride to the church on time was harder than I ever imagined.

CHAPTER 25

Sagacious (adj.) – Shrewd. Showing keen mental discernment and good judgement

An hour and a half later and we were ready to go. Cara looked remarkable now she was fully made up, coiffed and had a stomach full of coffee and buttery toast. The team deserved a medal for transforming the girl from *The Ring* into the glamour puss who was standing – well, swaying – in front of us. Shelley had snapped that she didn't need Cara's shit today, but then softened when she realised Cara was in no mood to fight back. The gift of a delicate rose-gold charm bracelet from Jimmy, which had arrived in the midst of this, had helped relax the mood too.

Shelley looked resplendent. The make-up artist had added colour to her previously pale cheeks, covered up that nasty breakout of spots and made her eyes sparkle with a fine dusting of shimmering gold eye shadow and peach glossy lips. Her pixie cut hair had been blow-dried into a glossy sleek style, with a thin, rose-gold, boho headpiece artfully sitting centre stage of her forehead, the delicate chain trailing down the back of her slim neck.

Shelley's phone buzzed to life as we posed for some group photos.

'I'll get it!' I shouted and picked it up. 'Oh, hi,' I said to the chauffeur. 'We're running a little bit late but almost ready!'

'Ah.' The thick Aussie tones of the driver made my heart stop.

'That's okay, isn't it?' I glanced up at the clock. 'You are coming, aren't you?' I asked, hoping Shelley couldn't hear me.

'Sorry, darl, I'm on my way but there's been a massive smash on the A8. It's chaos out here. All other routes are totally blocked. Unless you can push your wedding back a few hours, I doubt you're going to make it by car.'

Noooooo! 'What can we do? We need to be on Shelly Beach by 2 p.m.!'

He let out a deep sigh. 'Your best option is to jump on a ferry. The fast boat will get you there in twenty minutes.'

I hung up and took a deep breath to break the news that Shelley's plush motor had just been swapped for a diesel-splattered, chugging boat.

'Um, Shell.' I headed over to her. 'There's a slight problem.'

She snapped her head up at me so fast I thought she'd done herself an injury. 'What?'

'The roads are blocked. We need to get a ferry over to the ceremony.'

She closed her eyes and pressed her fingertips to the bridge of her nose. 'Fine. Can you just sort it?'

I was both shocked and pleased by her reaction. 'Course, I'm on it.'

*

Shelley had decided to carry her dress to get changed into once we were off the ferry to make sure there was no chance of it getting dirty en route. To save time, both Cara and I were wearing our spectacular bridesmaid dresses and were under strict orders not to mark even one crease. Thankfully, the alterations to my dress had been done and long billowing folds of fabric covered any slightly perceptible bump. We both had our stupid floral garlands on our heads, which were attracting a lot of annoying little flies around our faces.

Shelley's dad, Keith, was waiting at the ferry terminal for us. 'Afternoon, ladies, well, aren't we a treat for sore eyes!' he said, shaking his head as we made our way over to him.

I did feel a bit of a numpty, walking past the crowds of tourists, but I was less concerned with myself and more worried about how Cara was holding up. A short but unsteady boat crossing with the hangover from hell could be the next potential nightmare today.

'Where is the damn ferry?' Shelley muttered under her breath, tapping her foot in impatience. 'I'm going to miss my own wedding at this point!'

'Now, don't fret,' Keith offered, bobbing his white-haired head past the crowds of people milling around us. 'There's bound to be another one soon.'

Thankfully there was; only much later than we'd meant to be on our way. We awkwardly clambered on board.

'Will you call Ben and tell him we're running late?' Shelley asked me.

I nodded and rummaged through my handbag for my phone. 'Crap,' I muttered.

'What?'

'I left my phone at the flat. We were in such a rush to leave I didn't think to check that I had it. Cara, you got yours?'

Cara lifted her head from the seat back and slowly shook it.

Keith mumbled something about not needing a phone, so Patty had taken the one they jointly owned.

'It'll be fine, we're on our way, and I'm sure it's the bride's prerogative to be a little late?' I added brightly.

Keith nodded. 'If he's the one, then he'll wait for you.'

'It's not Jimmy I'm worried about. The bloody registrar has another wedding to get to after us!'

'There's nothing more we can do; I'm sure as soon as we get off this thing, we can be there in no time.' This wedding was going to take place if it killed us.

'Can this morning go any worse?' Shelley moaned into her hands before worrying she would smudge her make-up.

She didn't even know the half of it; that was before I'd told her about my pregnancy news and what had happened with her heartbroken, drunk cousin.

'You've not got a thing to worry about. You're going to have the day of your dreams, I know you will.'

The ferry eventually pulled up to Manly and we all traipsed off, Cara lagging slightly behind and clutching her water bottle like a lifeline.

Keep it together, *keep it together*, I willed her.

'Right, I need to find somewhere to get changed ASAP,' Shelley announced, peering around the cute and slightly kitsch ferry port. Billowing flags waved in the breeze, smells of salty chips and sugary candy floss wafted along in the warm air. The place was packed with tourists enjoying the sunny autumnal day. I think Shelley secretly enjoyed the stares from men who were chided by their wives as they saw her and Cara strut past. Okay, Cara was less strutting and more swaying, but her hair and make-up were on point.

'Let's make our way down to the beach front; there are bound to be hotels along the way. We'll just nip in and ask politely if we can have a room for ten minutes. I'm sure it won't be a problem,' I told her calmly, crossing my fingers.

'Lars mentioned some places down here as potential alternative venues.'

'See, it'll be fine.'

Turned out that Lars had been bullshitting about that too. There weren't any nearby hotels lining the small stretch of beach where we were heading. To have gone back into town to find an alternative would have added even more time, and we were late enough as it was. Poor Jimmy must be beside himself with worry that we weren't going to show up at all.

'The registrar is only there for the next twenty minutes,' Shelley gasped, looking at the battered watch her dad was wearing, poking out of the sleeve of his suit. 'I'm going to miss my own wedding by the time we find somewhere!'

Keith looked on helplessly, Cara was seemingly trying not to vomit in a nearby bin due to the overwhelming smells of fish and chip batter floating through the suntan-lotion-perfumed air.

'What about just walking to the venue like this and getting ready there?' I suggested.

Shelley shook her head in horror. 'No! I'm not having any of the guests seeing me not properly dressed.'

I peered down the beach. 'We're going in that direction, aren't we?' Shelley nodded. 'Look, there's a toilet block. If we're careful we can help you get into your dress in there and walk down the path to Shelly bay? You may need to change into your shoes at the last minute, but we can hide you from everyone seeing that.' I tried to stay as upbeat and positive as I could.

'I think she may be right, Shel,' Keith said, peering at his watch. 'We don't have time to mess about here, girl.'

'Oh God, this is just all going to shit,' Shelley moaned, but she picked up her speed, heading to the public beach bathroom, realising that she had few other choices if she wanted to not miss her own wedding. 'I'll kill that bastard Lars if I ever see him again,' she seethed as she stomped past tourists and huddles of old people enjoying ice creams on the stone benches.

'Not before I kill him first,' Keith muttered, trying to keep up with the power-walking speed his daughter was doing.

'Right, you girls, head in and I'll wait here,' Keith said as we got to the deep brown 1970s-style concrete loo. Two kids wandered out wearing swimming costumes, trying to fix on a pair of goggles.

'Cara, you try and keep anyone out and I'll help Shelley get into her dress. Just don't let it touch the floor,' I ordered, taking charge and peering at the suspicious wet puddles on the grubby tiled surface.

Suddenly, Shelley started to laugh hysterically, her face was pink and almost manically twisted into a smile as she hurriedly stripped down to her underwear. 'For fuck's sake, Georgia, I never thought I'd be getting changed for my own wedding in a stinking dunny,' she managed to say, in between wheezing with laughter. 'So much for everything being perfect!'

'It'll be fine. Just don't, whatever you do, let the dress fall to the ground.' I tried to keep her steady as she gently dropped the gown over her outstretched arms. Her skinny body was rattling with each burst of giggles escaping. I couldn't help but laugh too.

'They say expect the unexpected, but this…' She waved an arm after eventually managing to get it into the right sleeve. 'This is ridiculous.'

With a final tug, she was zipped up and ready to go, carefully holding the hem as high up from the scummy floor as she could. Taking a step back, I looked at her.

'Wow,' I breathed. She looked incredible, even in the harsh strip lighting of a public bog.

'What?' She panicked. 'Is there a mark on the dress? Have I got some stranger's poo stains on me?'

I shook my head. 'You look bloody amazing!'

Her face relaxed. She came forward and tried awkwardly to hug me whilst still holding her dress up. 'Thanks, Georgia. Let's do this!'

After a quick last peek in the cloudy, cracked mirrors, we headed out into the sunshine and began following the path leading from Manly Beach to Shelly Bay. Seeing her striding forward, desperate to get to her man, I found myself growing more nervous about what I was going to say to Ben. The drama and excitement of this morning had meant I'd had little time to contemplate how I was going to tell him that his world was about to change too.

Cara remained silent throughout the flustered hike, past the rocky sandstone cliffs, letting Keith witter on about some facts on the local area and how he'd read that Japanese knotweed was a problem somewhere around here. Shelley seemed to have lost her sense of hearing as she strode forward, not seeing the kind stares she was receiving; all she cared about was saying 'I do' before she lost her chance. Rounding another corner, I smiled at the cheers from a group of enthusiastic swimmers who were doing laps in the specially roped-off section. Shelley grinned and waved back, pausing slightly to catch her breath and savour these moments.

'You want to put your shoes on?' I asked her. She was wearing knackered-looking ballet pumps and I had the sparkly heels she'd asked me to carry.

Shelley shook her head. 'I don't want to delay things even more; I'll go barefoot instead.'

I nodded and tried to keep up with her; amazingly, even at this speed, she wasn't breaking a sweat. At least in one way it avoided her going into panic mode at what else was potentially going to come her way. I had a feeling we weren't out of the woods yet.

CHAPTER 26

Perspicacious (adj.) – Having strong insight into and an understanding of things

The small, half-moon bay was just ahead of us. Golden sand glinted in the sunlight against the gentle lapping waves where a couple of people were snorkelling. The trees lining the edge of the semicircle had been draped in white satin streamers, which were billowing in the slow, warm breeze, and bunting was tied up between branches with colourful ribbons wrapped around their trunks.

The small number of wedding guests were seated on white wooden chairs laid out on either side of a section of sand to make room for an aisle. Huge church candles in gleaming silver lanterns dotted the sides and rose petals had been artfully scattered around. At the front, under a willow arch with chunky flower heads poking through and blue glass baubles hanging from the top, stood a very nervous-looking Jimmy, an angry-looking registrar and my Ben.

He looked bloody gorgeous. He was wearing a deep blue suit, a creamy white shirt open at the top and flip-flops, which, for some reason, all seemed to work. He grinned at me as soon as he saw us approaching, while Jimmy kept his eyes trained on the water ahead. People started to clap and wave, and thankfully Cara seemed to perk up at my shoulder. Shelley slowed down to take it all in.

Music was playing as we got closer, a soft string version of a song I recognised but couldn't place.

Behind the guests were some small groups of sunbathers who'd sat up on their towels to enjoy the show, and children who had previously been playing bat and ball stopped their game to gawp at the pretty woman in the wedding dress. The music changed and the traditional wedding march song rang out of some invisible speakers over our heads. Keith gripped his daughter tightly by the arm and shook his head to stop himself from tearing up.

'Here we go!' Shelley grinned and gave us the nod, gently patting her dad on his tense forearm.

Cara was the first to go up the aisle; she was either hiding her hangover remarkably well or had made a complete recovery on the journey here. Either way, she glided up to the front without fault and smiled kindly at all the guests who were now on their feet and peering back at us with their camera phones trained in our direction.

'Georgia, your turn!' Shelley whispered, and nodded her head in the direction Cara had just gone.

I took a deep breath and smiled back at her and her dad. 'Good luck.'

As I started to take slow steps along the aisle, I suddenly felt this rising emotion of wobbles grip me. I could feel the eyes of everyone focus on me. I felt myself skid a little on my footing.

'Fuck,' I muttered under my breath. Picking my head up high, I forced myself to get to the end, to reach the front where my boyfriend was waiting. Jesus, why was it taking so long? Why did I feel so hot and sick under the scrutiny of everyone? Why did I agree to this?

I'd walked up the aisle in my own head hundreds of times; I'd daydreamed about what the guests would say to me, how they would compliment me on my dress or the decorations that I'd spent months hand-making. I'd used up so much of my brain space thinking about the big day that I never got to experience. Seeing the effort and stress that Shelley had put in for her wedding brought it all back to me. The squabbles between families, the need to please everyone, the worries about budgets, the fear of missing out, the desperation for it to be perfect because you only got one shot at this. I practically raced the last part to stand in front of the chair beside Cara, hoping that my hammering heart would calm down. I couldn't even look at Ben, couldn't bring myself to focus on Shelley, who was now taking her time to walk down the aisle behind me. I just felt like I wanted to vomit.

I glanced around. A few skinny trees lay to one side and the rest was the open bay. The reception venue was a good few minutes' walk over the hot sand to get to, and there were no other toilets or enclosed areas around to secretly throw up in. *Breathe, just breathe*, I told myself, realising that Shelley had now made it to the front and was kissing her dad on the cheek before he came and sat to my right. The registrar tapped his watch with a sigh and then began.

I let out a small burp that was mercifully blocked out by the music still playing and continued to manically smile at the soon-to-be-wed couple. As the registrar wiped his reddened forehead and beckoned for all the guests to sit back down, I gratefully sunk into my chair and told myself to breathe in through my nose and out through my mouth. This was not the time to start experiencing morning sickness.

The nauseous feeling eventually passed and I lifted my gaze from the stubby tufts of grass shooting from the edges of the sand ahead of me to Shelley and Jimmy, who were about to exchange their rings, with not a bird of prey in sight. I realised that Ben had been staring at me this whole time, his eyebrows knotted together, probably because of how green my skin had turned.

He was mouthing something to me. 'Are you okay?'

I nodded and gave him a weak smile, feeling my stomach flip once more. It was as if this morning's drama to get Shelley here had subsided and now the secret baby wanted its moment to shine too.

Ben caught my eye for a second longer, looking as if he didn't fully believe me, then nodded and turned away. I tried to focus on the registrar, who was loudly droning on about marriage being the most important step a person can take in their lives and how sacred this bond was between these two people. I felt Cara flinch beside me.

'What joy this union brings to these two people who have mutually decided to take the path of true love, light and happiness towards a better future. A future that contains never-ending promises of honesty, respect and commitment. Their vows to cherish and love each other are the most wonderful and important steps in the world,' the registrar explained, in his monotone voice.

'Pfft, a load of bullshit,' Cara grumbled. I heard the person in the row behind us tut, and prayed that her Uncle Keith hadn't heard her. 'So, if you're single you're just useless?' she said, a little louder, until I nudged her in the ribs and gave her a look.

Soon after he'd proclaimed that they were now man and wife; everyone was back on their feet, clapping, whooping and taking photos of the couple. Once they

broke for air from their first kiss, Jimmy pumped his arm
and Shelley wiped away the happy tears from her eyes.
I had a feeling that Jimmy was as ecstatic about marrying
the woman he loved as he was that she was no longer a
bridezilla. They practically skipped back down the aisle,
shaking hands with friends and family members who
were congratulating them. I linked my arm through
Cara's and hissed that she needed to smile and act like
everything was fine as we followed them down the aisle
and over to the restaurant opposite the bay.

Tissue pom-poms were strung on invisible threads
between whitewashed beams, pastel-coloured
flowers bloomed from vintage birdcages, and huge
lit-up letters spelling out 'LOVE' glowed from the
back of the airy room. There was a selfie station set
up in the corner – a compromise on a photo booth;
chalkboards with beautiful handwritten messages
telling guests to say cheese and use the hashtag
#Smileforthenewlyweds were artfully propped on tall
tables. Wicker baskets full of flip-flops – sorry, thongs
– were placed at the edge of the dance floor for later.
Looking around at the room that could have come
from one of Shelley's many wedding magazines, I felt
this strange feeling of pride that she'd pulled it off.

'Hey, beautiful, nice flowers.' Ben sidled over to me
with a glass of fizz in each hand. *Oh God, here we go.*
'I got us both a drink.'

'Yeah, it's something hey?' I shook my head;
my neck was starting to ache under the weight of
this stupid crown. 'Oh, I'm good for a drink thanks.
I've just finished one,' I lied. 'Think I'm going to
pace myself.' I caught his downturned mouth. 'But,
thanks.' He nodded and placed one of the full flutes
on a nearby tall table trussed up in ruffled paper and

confetti stars that were catching the light. 'It's still going to be a long day, and who knows when Shelley will need me to help her with her dress or whatever maids of honour do at the actual wedding.'

Ben smiled. 'You look absolutely fantastic, you know. Flower headpiece and all.' He cast his eyes over the golden-coloured dress, drinking me in. I self-consciously placed a hand over my stomach, knowing too well that the material was a lot tighter than it should have been.

'You don't look so bad yourself.' I smiled and pecked him gently on the cheek, inhaling his familiar citrusy aftershave.

'What a morning eh? I heard about the wedding-planner dude doing a runner. Was that what you were doing when you couldn't meet me yesterday?' he asked, quickly stepped out of the way of a young waitress who was scuttling past, struggling with a heavy tray of beer bottles.

'Yep!' I squeaked, forgetting that I'd almost broken the baby daddy news to him then. I knew we needed to talk, we had *a lot* to discuss, but not just yet.

'What a shit.'

'Don't remind me.' I rolled my eyes. 'First, he went AWOL, then the car to bring us here was caught in traffic so we had to jump on the next ferry over, then Shelley had to get changed in a public loo, and not to mention the drama with Cara.' I glanced around to see where Shelley's cousin was hanging out. I spied her leaning on the bar, twirling a straw around her full cocktail glass, giggling to the barman who must have been at least ten years younger than her.

'Jimmy was convinced that Shelley wasn't going to turn up,' Ben admitted, taking a long sip of his drink.

'Well, we were cutting it very close.' I winced with a smile.

'I mean he was worried that she'd been listening to you.' He dropped his voice to a whisper.

'What. Me? Why?'

Ben let out a deep sigh and finished his glass before continuing. 'Apparently she told him about the row you had.' *Oh, that.* 'You never told me that you two had fallen out.' He raised his eyebrows, as if waiting for me to explain.

'Just the stress of the wedding was getting to her and…' I trailed out, it was all in the past now, what did it matter?

'And you thought it was all bullshit. Marriage, I mean.'

I felt a blush dance on my cheeks. It was so warm in this room and I needed to get something to eat soon. I didn't want another repeat episode of feeling like I was about to vom during the ceremony.

'I don't get it, Georgia.'

'Get what?'

'You and weddings,' he said, running a hand through his dark locks. 'I mean, you came over here to help your mate out, but then have been blowing hot and cold over what you think of it all. One moment you're acting almost jealous that she's having this big fancy day, and then the next moment you're scoffing at how ridiculous and over the top it is.'

I stared at him. Had I been doing that?

'Oh, well, no, I…' I bumbled, then took a deep breath. 'What does it matter anyway?' I looked up at him. Why did he care what I thought about getting married; it wasn't like either of us had brought up that as a possibility in the near future? That was before this baby bombshell I was soon to be chucking his way.

'No reason, I just find you hard to keep up with.' He gratefully picked up another flute of fizz as a waiter sauntered past. 'You want one?'

'What, a wedding?' I scoffed.

He shook his head. 'No, I meant a drink.'

'Oh.' I smiled weakly. 'Erm, no, I'm good thanks.'

I needed to tell him. I wasn't sure where this conversation was going, but I needed to tell him that he was soon to be a dad. I took a deep breath. 'Well, actually there is something I need to—'

'Ladies and gentlemen, if you would kindly take your seats for the wedding breakfast.' A loud booming voice rang through the room, instantly hushing the chatter that had been going on around us and silencing me from sharing my secret.

Ben glanced at his watch. 'Thank God for that, I'm starving.' He took my arm, leading me to the top table where we would be sitting at either end. 'Wait, sorry, babe, what was it you were going to say?'

'Oh, nothing. I'll tell you another time.' I brushed it off and let him gently move us past the other guests, who were scanning down the seating plan to find their spot for the meal, trying to work out what had just happened. Was Ben on the verge of proposing? Had I been putting him off from doing that by being such a wedding phobic? I didn't have time to think as I was squashed in beside Keith and Johanna at the long table at the top of the room. Speeches were first on the agenda.

Thankfully, both Jimmy's and Shelley's parents were on much better terms than when they'd all been in that restaurant together. After spending yesterday exploring Sydney, they'd bonded over overpriced coffee and a mutual hatred of traffic jams. I mean, who *didn't* hate traffic jams? But I wasn't going to complain – the animosity had been eclipsed by this happy day. The meal went without a hitch, as did the speeches. Jimmy said all the right things about his new wife looking lovely, and Ben had the room in his hand as he told jokes from their childhood. We were given a break in the timetable for the band to set up and the evening guests to arrive. This meant that everyone went to grab a few more drinks or went out to smoke.

'How are you doing, hun?' I sidled up to Cara, who was sitting on a high stool at one end of the bar.

'It's all crap,' she exclaimed a little too loudly, considering the looks she received from Jimmy's parents nearby.

'Shh,' I hissed at her.

'What?' She turned around to face me, swaying on her diamanté heels. God, she was still half-cut. Either that or she'd topped up her hangover with the hair of the dog. 'I thought you'd have loved this. Being proved right.'

I jolted back slightly. 'What? What do you mean "proved right"?'

'About marriages being a sham. About it all being pointless.' She was slurring her words by now. 'You said that no one can make a promise that they'll be able to keep for the next fifty-odd years. And you're right.'

'Cara, I *never* said that.' I felt my cheeks heat up as I denied the allegation. I would have remembered this, surely.

'Well, whatever, either way you're right. Weddings suck.' She pouted.

'Come on now, you know that's not true. Look at how your and Shelley's hard work has paid off!

Everyone is loving it.' She ignored me and muttered something under her breath. 'I know it's hard for you, but you have to see that it will soon get better.'

She glanced up at me under her false lashes and bobbed her head gently. 'I know. I'm okay. Well, I'm not okay okay. But I'll be fine.'

I didn't get it. Here was this stunning woman with a great career, amazing apartment; apart from being a little high-maintenance, she should still have men flocking. 'If you don't mind me asking, why did you tell everyone that you were single and loving it?'

Cara sighed. 'I couldn't say that I was seeing that guy.'

'Why? Oh God, he's not related to you is he?'

She laughed for the first time today. 'No! Eurgh! He was just a guy I met at the gym, of no relation to us at all. I just meant that I couldn't tell anyone as it was complicated.'

'Complicated?'

Cara sighed. 'Shelley would go mad if I told her I'd been with a married man.'

'He was married!' I gasped.

'Sshh.' It was her turn to hiss at me to keep my voice down.

'Wait – so the woman you walked in on him with…'

'That was his wife. He's gone back to her.' She sniffed and tried to pull herself together, flashing a megawatt smile at the young barman before turning her attention back to my shocked expression. 'What does it matter now anyway?' She brushed a strand of hair from her face and glanced over her shoulder at the happy couple dancing in the centre of a busy dance floor. 'I mean, both you and Shelley have got it made.' She nodded at Ben, who was laughing over in the corner with two men in dark blue suits. 'In fact, you probably don't know how lucky you are.'

I realised then that it had all been an act. She didn't have her life together as I'd thought she did. She was desperate for her happy-ever-after ending like we all were.

'That's the reason I don't want Shell and Jim to move out. I hate living in that huge place by myself. I hate being the last singleton on the shelf. I hate that every time people mention fucking weddings and children they give me this patronising sympathetic look.' She tilted her head to one side and moved her mouth into a sad smile, to demonstrate. 'I may be living in one of the best cities in the world, but that doesn't mean meeting men is any easier. All the good ones are married, or in long-term relationships. The ones left are either too young and immature, thinking that dick pics is the way to charm a woman, or that romance means "Netflix and Chill". I'm scared of dying alone and being that straggly-haired old lady who pushes battered shopping trolleys down the street with junk piled inside, whilst waving a bell or singing some weird, out-of-tune song.'

'At least you'd be pushing a trolley full of *nice designer* things.'

She laughed weakly. 'Yeah, but it would be so good to share this all with someone – not pushing trolleys down busy streets cackling, together; I mean, sharing my life with someone.'

'I'm sure you'll be planning your own big white wedding sooner rather than later.'

She gawped at me. 'What, me do all this? Pfft, no thanks. The stress, the family politics, not to mention the pressure on every single thing being perfect or else your whole day, sorry your whole *marriage*, will be doomed from the start.' She shook her head. 'I wanted to help Shelley because I guess I realised that it was my only chance to be a part of this bonkers world of weddings.'

I shook my head in disbelief. She'd seemed so organised and full of knowledge of the wedding world that I'd expected this to be the test run for her own spectacular day.

'If it were me I'd elope with my other half.'

I raised an eyebrow. 'What? You?'

Cara nodded. 'Why not? It's so romantic, just you and him running off to tie the knot in a ceremony full of secrecy and intimacy.'

At that moment, the DJ played a classic Jackson 5/ Stevie Wonder mega-mix. Cara groaned. 'See what I mean? Why spend thousands of pounds and have a bloke like him ruin it by playing shite like that?'

I laughed. 'Maybe so, but come on, you. Let's dance anyway. You never know, the man of your dreams may be the bloke playing this shite.' We peered around past the happy moving bodies filling the dance floor. The DJ was at least eighty years old and had a cowboy hat and long stringy grey goatie. 'Oh, well, maybe not.'

Cara laughed. 'I wanted to speak to you actually.'

'Oh yeah?'

'I hate myself for being weak and always running back to this guy. I know I was a little grouchy at the start of our trip, but that was because he was playing his usual games with me.' She let out a deep sigh; it was still raw. 'I actually loved that small taste of travel and it's made me want to push myself even more.'

I tried not to gawp at her in shock. I thought she was hating every minute of our low-cost basic backpacking trip.

'You work in travel, don't you?'

I tried to find my tongue. 'Yep, yes, I have a travel business.'

She scrunched up her face a little. 'See, I didn't want to join a tour group, too restrictive with dates and a set route. I was thinking of doing something a little freer.'

'Solo travel?'

'I'm not sure, that sounds pretty scary. I was thinking more of a dating trip? You know, around the world in eighty dates or something.' She flicked back her hair as one of Jimmy's mates walked past, giving her the eye. 'Anyway, I'm just mulling it all over, but I wanted to see if you had any ideas.'

If I hadn't been holding on to the bar, I would have fallen over in shock. 'Erm, I'll have a think.'

'Come on,' she continued, 'you can think *and* dance. Let's show these guests how to really get the party started!'

CHAPTER 27

*Taciturn (adj.) – Reserved or uncommunicative
in speech; saying little*

After some energetic dance moves, the music slowed
right down to a smoochy, romantic number.

'I think I'd like the next dance,' Ben gallantly asked,
taking my hand that was clammy from being spun
around by Cara. She winked and danced off to find
one of Jimmy's gym friends who'd been loitering near
the bar for most of the night.

'I think I need a sit-down after that.' I smiled and
pushed the sweaty strands of hair from my face. My
feet were killing me, my mouth was dry and I was
sure I was developing unsightly sweat marks under my
armpits.

'Just one dance with me, please?' Ben asked and
wrapped an arm around my waist. I tried to ignore
the worry that he was bound to rub his wrist against
my slightly swollen stomach and instantly know
something was up.

'Now I definitely know that you've had a few
drinks,' I laughed, as he did a silly little pirouette on
his toes.

'What? I love dancing, I don't know what you're
going on about. Now come here you.' He nuzzled his
head into my neck and left a series of soft kisses on my
warm skin.

As he gently spun me around, I caught Shelley and
Jimmy lost in their own world, swaying to the music.

'Look at them,' I mused, nodding my head at the newly-weds. 'They look so happy.'

He planted a kiss on my forehead. I could smell whisky on his warm breath as he spoke. 'I've been thinking...' He paused and gently held me back so he could look at me properly. 'Why don't we do this?'

'This?' I wasn't sure if it was the drink making his speech hard to understand or if I was just too hot to follow along. 'Dancing?'

'No, you muppet. This... getting married.'

I stopped dancing. 'Are you proposing?'

Ben flashed a lopsided smile. 'No, not yet...'

I suddenly felt very awake compared to him, as I took in the happy, drunken glaze on his slightly squiffy face. My heart was pounding so hard I was sure he could see it through the fabric of my dress.

He wafted a hand in the air, now swaying thanks to the many whiskys I'd seen him and Jimmy neck earlier. 'Like I said, you've been blowing hot and cold about weddings, it's kind of hard to keep up.'

'Ben, I need to tell you something.' I forced myself to blink under his hazy gaze. 'But not here.' I took his warm hand and attempted to get off the dance floor. 'Here, drink this.' I grabbed a bottle of mineral water from the side of the bar and hoped he would sober up enough to understand what I was about to reveal.

'Aww, you're so good to me, Georgia!'

'Yeah, yeah, just drink it all.'

I led him down the stairs, out of the restaurant and onto the beach. The evening light had dropped to a deep blue, speckled with faint stars visible through the low clouds. The cooling breeze instantly soothed my warm skin. I kicked off my shoes and held them in my hand as my bare feet sank into the grainy sand, waking me up for what I was about to do.

'Where are we going?' he laughed, struggling to keep his footing straight as I tugged at his arm to follow me.

'I think we need to talk,' I said quietly, leading him to a wooden bench not far ahead, grateful that there was no one else around. All the sun worshippers had long since packed up and gone home, and the other guests were all getting stuck into the free booze inside. I heard the music lift in tempo once more as cheers and whoops from the happy and tipsy guests floated on the evening air.

I let out a heavy sigh, grateful to sit down and rest my feet. 'Sit down.' I nodded to the space next to me. I stretched my legs out in front of me and dug my bare heels into the sand, convinced that my ankles had already ballooned.

'Why are we not dancing? Was I that bad?' He laughed.

I took a deep breath, wishing that we didn't have 'Come on Eileen' as a background song filtering from the packed room behind us. How did you break this news to someone? Especially as he'd seemed so resistant to the idea when Jimmy's parents had grilled him about it. I'd always imagined both of us excitedly crossing our fingers and looking at the lines develop on the pregnancy stick, not me telling him that I was keeping a child he didn't want.

'Wait.' He flicked his head up to mine, faster than he'd intended judging by the way his eyes shot into focus. 'I know what this is about.'

'You do?' I whispered. How the fuck did he know? Oh my God, maybe Lars was right. Maybe I did give off a pregnancy aroma.

'Yeah, I really wished you hadn't brought it up today though. I mean, it's Jimmy and Shelley's big day,' he said, with a straight face.

'Oh, well, I didn't exactly plan when to talk to you about it.' I fiddled with my dress strap, unable to look him in the eye. 'How do you know?' I was half tempted to sniff myself to see if there was something I was missing.

'Because you told me!'

'What are you going on about?'

'You lurve me,' he said, sinking back against the cold wooden back of the bench, roaring with laughter. 'You L.O.V.E me!'

I rolled my eyes. Boy, he was way too drunk to cope with this news.

'Yes.' I cleared my throat. 'That's what I wanted to speak to you about.'

'Aww and I love you toooooooo, Georgia!'

'Hey, guys. There you are.' Jimmy was staggering over the sand, holding a bottle of bubbly, with a wide grin on his face.

'Jimmy! My man!' Ben called out, acting as if he hadn't seen his best mate for the past year.

Jimmy's cheeks were flushed and his eyes looked a little glassy; he must have enjoyed the Prosecco station more than he thought he would. 'The fireworks are just about to start. And then, Georgia, I need you to help me with, erm, that thing I mentioned to you.' He blushed but Ben was too drunk to pick up on his best mate's weirdness. I was never usually the sober one; this felt very strange and I didn't like it. 'Err, sure, yeah.'

'Great! What are you two doing out here anyway?' He raised his eyebrow.

'Just telling her how much I love her and how perfect she is,' Ben slurred, wrapping a thick arm over my shoulders.

I nodded and fixed on a tight smile. I could only hope he would think things were so perfect when he knew the full truth.

*

The fireworks were spectacular. I could now see how Shelley had lost control of the wedding budget as they must have cost a bomb, but watching the glittery pops of colour fill the night sky, hearing the guests ooh and ahh with every loud explosion and flash of bright light, it was all totally worth it. Well, for everyone else here. I was struggling to focus on the streams of neon-rainbow darting across my head as my mind was lost in my own thoughts.

I'd been watching the show wrapped up in a blanket that Shelley had gently placed on my shoulders. She kissed my cheek and thanked me for all my help before being whisked off by Jimmy to get the best viewing spot. I hadn't seen Ben since he left with Jimmy to get everyone off the dance floor and outside to watch the show. I kept glancing around at the guests huddled up, gazing up at the sky, to see if I could spot him. But it was too dark to make anybody out in the cluster of people around me.

'How's it going, hun?' I turned to see Patty by my side.

'Oh, hi. How are you doing?'

Her face lit up and it wasn't just the cast of light from the fireworks. 'It's all been so wonderful, hasn't it?'

I nodded and swallowed back the lump in my throat. She reminded me of a mix between Trisha and my mum. Two people who would be overjoyed by my pregnancy news. 'You girls all look utterly beautiful. I'm so pleased Shelley has a friend like you. When she was off travelling, I'd be worried sick about her, but then hearing she met lovely people like you, Ben and Jimmy, really put my mind at ease.' I smiled back. I guessed she didn't get to hear about our recent falling out then. 'I know it is a long way for you all to come for the wedding, Lord knows Johanna has mentioned it enough times, but I really think that being here shows what a good friend you are.'

'Thanks, Patty.'

'And your chap seems lovely too.' She winked.

Don't cry, *don't cry*, I willed myself under her kind gaze. 'Yeah, he is. Sorry, do you mind, I just need to nip to the loo,' I said, turning to go back inside, as she patted me on the shoulder and continued to look up at the entertainment.

I headed into the venue expecting to find my boyfriend slumped at the bar. Instead, the room was empty except for some staff quickly cleaning up for the evening buffet and the band preparing to warm up for their next set.

'Georgia!' Jimmy shouted over the room, as guests started spilling back in. The fireworks must have ended and now it was his turn to perform his surprise for his new wife. He gave me a look as Shelley began chatting to the women who'd been at her flat on that night of our row. I'd purposefully avoided them all day but had felt their eyes on me.

I nodded and went to move Shelley out of the room so Jimmy could get on stage and into position without her noticing.

'Can I just steal you a second,' I asked, as she looked up at me. Her face was flushed with the heat in the room compared to the chilly evening air outside.

'Georgia! You okay?' She tried to fix her eyes on me but they were also heavy with the look of a few vodka and oranges.

God, this not drinking lark was harder than it seemed, and I still had months to go.

'Yeah, great, well, not really, I need to have a word.' I nodded my head to the ladies' bathroom. The women perked up as if there was some more gossip they could be part of.

'Sure, I'm bursting for a wee and could do with your help in this dress.'

I steered her out of the room as she babbled on about how the guests had been saying how pretty it all looked, and winked at Jimmy to get ready.

'So, what's going on? You and Ben all right? I haven't really seen you together that much,' she said as I helped her into the cubicle.

'Fine,' I replied, having never before thought I'd feel pleased to have my face burrowed away from her view by helping her hoist her dress up.

'You sure?'

'Mmmhmm.' I nodded, staring at a crumpled tampon wrapper on the floor. I couldn't say anything to her, not on her wedding day. Tomorrow I'd be able to have a proper chat and let her know what had happened, but today was hers.

'Georgia.' Her voice grew firmer. 'There is something going on and I know it.'

She finished having a wee and I helped her to stand back up again, making sure the bottom of her dress didn't end up in any wet patches.

'Everything's fine. Right, come on, let's go and find that new hubby of yours and get a selfie.'

She kept her gaze on me, unsure if she believed me. 'I thought you needed to talk to me about something?'

'Oh no!' I laughed. 'I meant that I just wanted to talk to you, to see how it was all going.' I wafted an arm in the air. 'I know how busy you are and I just wanted a moment to make sure you were happy with it all.'

'How can I not be? It is the best day of my life!' She laughed and pulled me into a hug. I smiled at her and took her hand, leading her back to the party. I hoped that it wasn't about to be ruined by her husband making a show of himself and embarrassing her with his awful voice.

I kept straining my neck as we walked down the corridor decorated with enormous beach shells and old fishing nets to see if I could spot Ben anywhere.

'Georgia?' Shelley asked, as I'd stopped walking without realising it.

'Yeah, yeah, sorry. Come on.' I pulled myself together and led her into the large room. She immediately took her concerned eyes off me as soon as she saw Jimmy standing on the stage in front of the microphone.

'What's going on?' she asked quietly, as the other guests clapped our arrival. 'Jimmy? What are you doing? We've done the speeches!'

'This is just a little something I've planned for you,' Jimmy said into the mic, winking at his unsure-looking bride. 'And a one, and a two, and a one, two, three, four,' he called out to the band patiently waiting behind him with their instruments at the ready.

He was surprisingly good. The lessons had certainly paid off and everyone was soon dancing to the song that made Shelley well up, lost in some shared memory together.

It was perfect, the whole day had been perfect. Not because it had all gone to plan, but because Shelley and Jimmy were happy, they were married, and they had their whole lives together ahead of them. After all, wasn't *that* the point of a wedding?

CHAPTER 28

Ruminate (v.) – To think deeply about something

I'd been out most of the morning, walking around the streets trying to get my head together. It was pointless staying in bed and attempting to get some sleep. I'd spent the night tossing and turning as Ben punctuated the air with drunken snores next to me.

Glancing at my phone, I realised that he should be on his way by now. I'd left a note asking him to meet me at the Opera House at midday. I turned off the main street and wandered down a path cut through what looked like it used to be a churchyard. The overhanging trees on each side seemed to meet and fuse in the middle over my head, forming a ceiling of leaves with sunlight shining through. A boy with bright blond curls, wearing red shorts and a blue t-shirt with a dinosaur on the front, was walking along and holding his dad's hand, zigzagging in my direction.

'Hey, Noah, watch out of the way of that lady,' his shaven-headed dad said, giving me an apologetic 'you-know-what-they're-like' type of smile.

'We're getting sicks!' Noah said, planting himself at my feet and looking up at me with enormous blue eyes framed by pale blond, almost white, eyelashes.

'Oh,' I said slowly. 'Cool.'

His dad ruffled Noah's hair, making the curls glint golden under the sunlight. 'He means sticks.'

I smiled politely and went to step around the pair of them when I felt a pull on the bottom of my top. Noah had a small pudgy hand grasped around some of the material.

'Do you have any sicks?' he asked.

His dad shook his head in mirth. 'Noah, let the lady get on her way. Sorry about him, he has an eye for the ladies.'

I smiled and then squatted down to the same height as Noah and his mesmerising eyes. I wondered what colour eyes our baby would have. The thought gripped me tightly in my stomach.

'What are you getting sticks for?' I asked him.

He looked up at his dad, squeezing his brow tightly as if trying to remember.

'Have you forgotten already?' His dad laughed.

Noah shook his head after a long pause. Just seeing this small human, this person created by two people probably as normal as Ben and me, a collection of cells and DNA and love and personality and a soul, which was currently developing in my womb right at this moment, who would eventually turn out to be a child in front of another stranger, I felt a flip of excitement. We had done something pretty awesome in making a baby – sharing half of ourselves to create a whole new character, was ruddy incredible when you thought about it.

'We're going on an adventure,' Noah eventually remembered and grinned at me proudly.

'Oh, is that so?' I smiled and glanced up at his dad. 'An adventure, eh?'

Noah nodded and placed his arms against his small tummy, sticking it out proudly.

'Well, I saw some sticks back where I just came from.' I pointed up the path. 'They would be perfect for your adventure.'

Standing to full height again, I said goodbye as Noah took his dad's hand once more and excitedly scampered off to find the promised sticks. I closed my eyes for a second and inhaled the heady air of the woods, the scent of perfumed flowers, cut grass and the warming breeze, and made my decision. I was about to go on my own adventure too.

Being pregnant and having a child didn't have to mean the end of the world. I felt foolish for being so dramatic. It just meant things would change again. It was the start of a new life, not just one for the baby, but for Ben and me too. The initial shock had died down slightly and in its place was this buzzing anticipation for the start of something exciting about to happen. Adjustments would have to be made, but that wasn't necessarily a bad thing. I'd managed to grow up in every other area of my life – this would just be the biggest test of them all. Being pregnant gave me nine months, well, slightly less than that, to get my shit together. It was like the ultimate deadline to prepare myself for the future and focus on another human being. It might take time to adjust to being a mum, but surely I could be a mum and still be Georgia? Travel didn't have to be totally forgotten about, just altered slightly. If I had to learn how to ask whether the cheese is pasteurised in another language, or avoid travel to places prone to malaria, Zika virus, Ebola virus and other terrifying diseases, then so be it. I was only going to fail at being a mum if I set myself unrealistic expectations of what a mum should do.

I just had to get Ben on board.

*

Walking around Circular Quay was like no other place
on earth. Apart from the happy smiling locals and the
excitable tourists, there's the view that totally sucks
you in. The imposing steel of the Harbour Bridge on
one side crossing the gently lapping water, and then
the iconic white sails of the Sydney Opera House on
the other. It was a view you could never get tired of
seeing. Ferries and smaller boats chugged lazily across
the waves as tourists took selfies with the two impressive
landmarks. Winding my way through crowds gathered
to watch street performances – Aboriginal men playing
didgeridoos and young lads balancing footballs on their
noses – I padded up the promenade to the steps of the
Opera House.

It's actually a lot smaller close up than I'd imagined.
The segments of an orange style sails domed over like
silver containers you find at all-you-can-eat buffets.
A grinning family were doing the peace sign in every
photograph they could possibly fill their phone
memory with, and nearby a group of older tourists
were being told about the design of the building and
how it took sixteen years to finish. The late-morning
sunshine on the harbour water sparkled like a hundred
paparazzi bulbs going off under the surface.

Ben was already waiting on the steps as I walked up.
Even with a hangover he still looked bloody gorgeous.
His face creased into a wide smile as he saw me.

'Hey, you.'

'Hey, yourself, how's the head?'

'Surprisingly not too bad. It must have been all that
water you were feeding me.'

I smiled, surprised he'd remembered that.

'Anyway, where did you run off to this morning?'

'Oh, I just wanted to get some fresh air.'

'Ah.' He gave a knowing smile. 'Feeling a little delicate yourself, are we?'

I forced myself to laugh. 'Something like that. Shall we go and grab a drink?' I started to walk off and realised he wasn't following me. 'You okay?' I turned back, wondering what the hold-up was.

'Yeah!' he said, a little too brightly. 'I just thought it would be nice if we took a photo first, seeing as we both finally made it here.' He rummaged in his pocket for his phone.

'Oh right, you want to use mine?' I asked.

'No! I mean, no thanks, I'll take it. I swore it was in here.' He patted down his pockets. 'Ah, got it,' he said, pulling his phone out. 'Right, let me ask someone to take a nice photo of us both.'

'Can we not just get a selfie?'

It was sweet that he was trying to be romantic, but my head was swimming with what I needed to tell him and this was just delaying the inevitable. However Ben had wandered off and was looking purposefully around. There were plenty of people to ask but he acted as if he was searching for someone in particular.

'Wait here a sec!' he said, and jogged down the steps to a man who was pushing a small food cart selling ice cream and sugary pastries.

I sighed and dropped to sit on the warm stone step, placing a hand in front of my eyes to shield them from the sun, enjoying the heat spreading on my face. I was too busy basking like a contented house cat, I barely heard Ben call out that he was ready and needed me to come over there for the photo. I flicked my head and spotted him deep in conversation with the man working at the food stall. They were both pointing further up the steps, probably planning where best to take this photo he was so eager to get.

'You ready, babe?' Ben asked, as I walked over to him. He was sweating slightly and wringing his hands together. Why did he look so nervous? I was the one who had to break this bombshell.

Okay, deep breath. You can do this. It was now or never.

He was nodding at the bloke at the food cart before flicking his face back to me. 'I reckon that's a good spot, over there!'

'Ben?'

'Do you reckon that works?' he was saying to the impromptu photographer.

'Ben, you're not listening to me,' I said, more firmly. 'I need to tell you something.'

'Come on, we don't have much time.' He was trying to get me to move and head over to have this bloody photo taken.

'This is important,' I snapped. He ran a hand through his hair, messing up the dark brown curls. Wait – was he making some hand signal to the man who was going to take our photo? What was going on?

'And so is this…'

He dropped to one knee and pulled out a ring box.

Oh my God, he was proposing!

'Georgia Louise Green,' he began. 'I have loved you since the moment I met you—'

'Wait!' Ben looked up, a flash of fear on his face that I was about to say no. 'I'm pregnant,' I blurted out.

'You're pregnant?' I thought his eyeballs were at risk of snapping from the optic nerve and rolling across the concrete. Not an inch of his body moved as he waited for my answer. I was about to say something when the man he'd given his phone to sheepishly walked over.

'Shall I take it now?' he asked Ben, holding the phone up to take a photo. I wanted to laugh at the absurdity of it.

'Err, no, it's fine thanks, mate,' Ben said on autopilot, taking his phone back as the man jogged down the steps.

'You're really pregnant?' he repeated, still not moving, still on a bended knee.

I nodded. 'Yes.'

'Like, pregnant, pregnant?' he uttered, remembering to blink and take a breath as I nodded again. 'Oh, shit, I mean, oh …' He trailed off.

'Here, sit down.' I crouched down and pulled him to join me on one of the steps, his legs looking like they might give way on him.

He placed his head in his hands and rubbed his face roughly. I was willing him to wrap his arms around me, to tell me that it was all going to be okay, but he stayed in that same hunched-over position, as if he should have a brown paper bag to suck air through.

'Ben?' I asked, after what felt like an eternity of silence.

'How do you feel?' he asked, eventually facing me. The colour had drained from his face and he was biting his lower lip so hard I thought it would start bleeding.

I fidgeted. 'A little bit nauseous, but it's not as bad as I've been reading that other women have it.'

'No.' He shook his head. 'I mean, how do you feel about us having a baby?'

'Well, it was a shock and—'

'How long have you known?'

'A few days.' I felt bad that it seemed like I was totally fine with this when inside I was still panicking as much as he looked like he was. 'Ben, are you all right?' I asked softly. *Please give me a hug, please stroke my hair and realise this is the biggest shock to me too,* I willed him.

'Yeah, err, yeah,' he said slowly. He was lying; of course he wasn't all right. This was huge. He also forgot that I knew him well enough by now. I knew that his chin wobbled ever so slightly when he was not telling the truth. How do you expect a guy to react to the news that you're expecting a baby that you weren't expecting?

'I completely lost my shit too when I found out,' I admitted. 'I'm still freaking out right now.'

'Really?' He shot his head up. 'You are?'

I nodded and smiled gently at him. He looked as terrified as I felt. 'Yeah, but I've had a few days' start on you.' I held his clammy hand. 'I just didn't know how to break it to you, especially when you don't want children.'

'What?' He straightened up and puffed his chest out. 'I do want children! I just thought you didn't.'

I pulled back and looked at him funny. 'What do you mean?'

'Well, when you came back from Marie's you were pretty adamant that kids weren't for us at all.'

I thought about that evening, how knackered I'd been, and how all I'd done was moan about the children. 'Really? So from that you thought kids were off the agenda for us?'

'Well, I know in the past we've joked about kids' names but never really had *the* chat. Then you seemed so traumatised after looking after Cole and Lily, I figured you were trying to tell me that you didn't want a family of your own.' Both of us had totally got the wrong end of the stick.

'Why did you say you didn't want to be a dad when Johanna asked you about it at the restaurant that time?'

'For you! I didn't want you to be interrogated and have to defend your desire to stay childless. It's much easier for a guy to say that than it is a woman.'

I started to laugh. 'Well, Mr Stevens, I do want children, I always have done, I just didn't know when. Everyone says there's no right time to have them and with the business expanding and the move to London …' I paused. 'We may not be ready and this may not be the perfect time, but when would it ever be the perfect time? We already lead such busy lives, maybe this will force us to slow things down a little!' Ben kissed my forehead. I noticed that his eyelashes were wet. 'You do want it, don't you?'

'Do I want to be the father of your child?' he spluttered. 'Hell yeah!'

I laughed and let out a breath I hadn't realised I'd been holding. 'This will change everything, you know?'

'I know.'

'Like, *everything*. My body, our jobs, our social life, our relationship, our sex life.'

That last one made him pause. 'I don't care, I'm ready.'

I looked up. 'Really?'

'Really,' he said decisively. 'I also still want you to be my wife.'

'You're not just doing this because you've knocked me up?'

He shook his head, laughing. 'Georgia. I've wanted to do this for months.'

'Sorry. Carry on.' I grinned at him.

He took a deep breath and dropped back down to one knee. 'Georgia Louise Green. I have loved you since I met you. You will never know how happy you make me and how wonderful you actually are. In a way, that is what I love most about you. You are clumsy and hot-headed and passionate and sometimes drive me mad, but I need you to challenge me, to make me a better person and I am so grateful to get to call you mine.'

Tears pricked my eyes; my breath was caught in my throat.

'So, will you do me the greatest honour of marrying me?'

'Yes!' I squealed as he got to his feet and spun me round. A crowd I hadn't noticed had built nearby, watching the show, and the smiling audience began to clap.

'You don't think Shelley will mind?' I whispered, admiring the ring he placed on my trembling finger. It was incredible.

'Pfft, her wedding was yesterday. Now this is all about you.' He glanced at my tummy. 'Well, us.'

I couldn't let go of him; strangers were coming up to shake our hands and share the photos they'd taken of the moment. I was being passed a tissue for my streaming eyes and running nose as I kept laughing at the fact this had actually happened. I don't think I'd ever felt this happy before.

'Right, Champagne!' he suggested, taking my hand and kissing it firmly. 'Oh, sorry, shit. You can't drink!'

I shook my head. 'I don't need alcohol to give me a buzz.'

We wandered to a bustling coffee shop overlooking the harbour waters.

'This is beautiful.' I couldn't stop looking at the glinting diamond on my finger. 'I knew you had good taste, but this…'

'I may have had a little help,' he admitted. 'Marie. But, actually, I found this one when she wasn't with me. I just asked for her advice on the style you might like, but I chose it all on my own.'

'Well, you did an excellent job.' I grinned, reaching up to kiss him and never wanting to let go.

CHAPTER 29

Intrepid (adj.) – Resolutely courageous; fearless

Before we went to break the news to everyone else, there was someone I wanted to meet. I'd filled Ben in with what had been simmering in the back of my mind and he loved the idea, so now it was time to see if I could put it into practice.

'Georgia?' I glanced up from the notebook I'd brought with me where I'd been jotting down what I wanted to speak to Terry about. This guy, who hated crying babies on planes, who was going through marital problems, and who thought I was this irritating non-stop talkative traveller he'd been unlucky enough to be squashed next to on a long-haul flight, could possibly be the boost Lonely Hearts Travels needed.

'Hi! Thanks so much for arranging to see us at such short notice.'

He wafted his beefy arm. 'Not a problem. I was just going to be killing time before a meeting later, so at least this way I feel a little useful. I have to say, I'm very intrigued by what you want to talk about.'

I'd been a little cryptic when I'd called him and asked to pick his brains over a coffee. I'd looked him up online and used his mobile number from the business card he'd given me when he thought we wouldn't make it out of the turbulence.

'Ha, well, I'm still working it all out in my head, but I wanted to use your expertise for some advice. Sorry, this is Ben, Terry, Ben.' I did the introductions as the two men shook hands and we ordered drinks.

'Ah, the business partner boyfriend, I take it?' Terry's face creased into a wide smile as Ben nodded. 'Your girlfriend helped me out with a little problem on the plane. And now she can't keep away from me!'

'I'll have to keep my eye on her in the future,' Ben joked.

I smiled, accepting a herbal tea from the waitress. 'We've had this idea.'

'Tell me all.'

I wasn't sure where to begin. 'How easy is it to create an app?'

Terry took a long sip of his flat white. 'Super easy, depending on what it is you want to create. The more technical it is, the harder it gets. What are you thinking?'

I took a deep breath…

'Since we last met, I've made my way from Melbourne to Adelaide via the Great Ocean Road and had a taste of what it means to be a backpacker today, which was eye-opening to say the least. Frankly, as a business, we are not doing enough. The traveller today wants super-fast broadband, they want the world at their fingertips, and they want to combine their interest in seeing new countries with the security that their phone gives them. We're living in a modern age where it's normal to share your feelings via emojis rather than words; life is moving faster than ever before, but what is being left behind is the travel industry. We need to change and modernise with the times.'

I paused to see if Terry was keeping up. I'd been tossing and turning this idea in my head since being here, noticing the sheer volume of time backpackers spent on their phones or tablets in the hostels we'd visited, then at Shelley's wedding hearing Cara's ideas about mixing solo travel with dating and meeting others. I'd had a brainwave.

'We already offer incredible travel tours for broken-hearted backpackers. However, thanks to their time with us, our customers will move on from their heartbreak but still keep that urge to travel, to make the most of this new-found confidence they've picked up. So...' I took a deep breath. 'I was thinking of creating an app that offers our tour services, but for solo travellers who have found themselves and are looking to date again with someone who shares the same interests as them: travel.'

Ben squeezed my knee under the table, encouraging me to continue.

'We want to create an app that can be used as you travel in order for you to meet and hang out, or even hook up, with other backpackers. Like a mix of Tinder and TripAdvisor, with real-time reviews of the people you've met and the experiences you've shared. This way you get the independence and freedom that comes with solo travel, but also the comfort of knowing you're not alone and can easily meet other people like you.'

I felt like I was rambling and probably should have created some fancy-shmancy presentation with PowerPoint or pie charts, as I really wanted him to get on board with this, or at least tell me that I was on to something. A wave of worry washed over me, thinking back to the pitch presentation I'd given at the bank. What if this idea wasn't as good as I'd built it up to be in my head? What if baby brain was making me jump the gun, yet again?

I gulped at my drink and waited for his reaction. True to form, Terry had been eating a plump pastry, getting flakes of croissant over his jeans as I'd been jabbering on. A slow smile grew on his rubbery lips, which were glistening with buttery oil.

'I love it!' he enthused, slapping his hands together.

I let out a sigh of relief. 'Really?'

'I mean, we would need to create a watertight business plan, but, as an idea, you think it would work?' Ben asked.

'One hundred per cent. If you piggyback this onto your tours, offer paid-for content perhaps on a subscription model, and we nail the design and development, then I don't see why it wouldn't. When you asked to meet me, I did some research on you guys and I like what it is you're trying to do. I could have done with being on one of your tours when I split up with my first wife. I just spent the whole time hanging out in the nearest bar when I went travelling back then.' He rolled his piggy eyes at the memory. 'The only company I found was the sixty-year-old barman who wasn't the slightest bit interested in seeing some Mayan ruins with me.' He was a completely different person to the stressed-out grumpy guy who'd sat next to me on the flight here. Today had been the best day ever.

I couldn't stop my smile from spreading. I saw Ben was beaming at this too.

'I'm so sorry, but I need to go or I'll be late for my next meeting. But call me when you're back in the UK and we can sit down and work out some more details. I think this is just a fantastic idea and something that my team can definitely get behind!'

We shook hands and said goodbye, and I felt this glow inside of me. This could be the idea we were all waiting for. I couldn't wait to tell Conrad and Kelli. First, I needed to let Ben in on the next part of my plan.

'Well, that went well.' He leant back in his chair watching Terry waddle off.

'If we can make it happen, financially and practically, then I want Shelley to head it up for us.'

He looked confused. 'Er, yeah, if you want. Is this because of the baby? Because I'm sure we can jiggle stuff around with your packed diary and—'

I shook my head. 'No, although that's a whole other conversation. No, this is because she could do with a break, and I think she would be awesome at the marketing and collaboration as it's going to be a big project.' I didn't want to tell him about her money worries. Instead, if she could get her teeth into this for us, surely she would be back on track soon.

'Fine by me. Speaking of the new Mrs Priors, shall we head back and break our news to them?'

Our news! Even with the excitement of sharing this new business idea, I kept stealing glances at my ring finger. I was going to be Ben's wife!

When I was meant to make the life-long commitment to Alex, I was a totally different person to who I am today. Back then, I'd never developed a sense of myself, or an idea of who the future Georgia would be and what she wanted from her one and only life. I now know who I am. I'm not this desperate, timid girl who thought she needed a man and a big fancy white wedding to complete her. When I do walk down the aisle, it will be for the right reasons, not because I felt a little lonely, or jealous, or because everyone else on my Facebook timeline was tying the knot. This would be because I wanted to commit to one person for the rest of my life. Ben.

'Wait, one more thing – what time is it back in England?' I tugged on his arm as he tried to catch the waitress's attention to pay our bill.

'I need to tell my parents!' I pulled out my phone and tapped open the FaceTime app. Within seconds, the black screen filled with their confused-looking faces, peering way too close down the camera lens.

'Is it on, Sheila?' I heard my dad mutter. 'I can't hear a thing.'

'We're here!' I smiled and shouted, making them both look up. 'You might need to hold the iPad a little further away from your faces though. Dad, we've got a very nice view of your nose hair.' I giggled as my mum tutted and Ben stifled a laugh from beside me.

'Ah, there. Much better. So, how are things?' my mum asked. She was hugging her hands to her chest and blinking rapidly.

'Good,' I said, trying to stay calm and control the smile on my face. 'How are you both?'

My dad started to speak but my mum wafted him out of the way and leant closer to the microphone. 'No, no, we want to hear all *your* news…'

I glanced at Ben. They knew about the engagement.

'What?' Ben said, leaning back and placing both hands in the air defensively. 'I had to get your dad's permission, didn't I?'

I smiled.

'So…?' my mum asked expectantly.

I flung my hand in the air and screamed. 'We're getting married!'

My mum began crying happy tears instantly. My dad just nodded his head, as if choking back the emotion. 'Oh, how wonderful! Congratulations!'

'Thank you!' Ben chimed and kissed my hand.

'I'm guessing this isn't much of a surprise?' I asked, wiping away tears at how happy they both were.

'Well…' My mum couldn't lie to save her life. 'Not really. We were kind of in on it from the start. But I'm so pleased you said yes.'

'Thanks, Sheila,' Ben said. 'And thanks, Len, for letting me finally ask the question I've been waiting to ask for ages.'

'You did well, son,' my dad nodded.

'Oh, Georgia. The ring is stunning. Tell us all. How did you pop the question?' My mum half-pushed my dad out of the way to sit closer and hear the juicy details she would no doubt be sharing with everyone in her slimming class tonight.

'Let's just say it was everything I wanted in a proposal.' I grinned.

'Well, it is a lovely surprise,' my mum cooed.

I rolled my eyes. 'You knew he was going to ask me!'

'Well, yes, but we didn't know *when*,' she said, pulling herself upright.

'Or if you'd say yes,' my dad chimed in with a chuckle and a wink.

'There is some other news we have that may come as more of a surprise,' Ben said, checking with me if it was okay to spill. I nodded.

'Oh no, you're emigrating to Australia, aren't you?' My mum clutched at her necklace in horror. 'Lynne's son, you know Lynne from the chippy on the corner? Well, Lynne's son went to Australia on holiday and never came home again. He got a job, got a girlfriend and stayed there!'

'Don't panic, we're coming home. Anyway, you said you'd meet our flight from the airport, remember?'

At that she let out the breath she'd been holding. 'Oh yes, well, thank the Lord for that.'

My dad shook his head at her dramatics. 'What's this other surprise then?'

I grinned at Ben; we shouldn't really be telling lots of people, especially as I was still so early on, but we couldn't help ourselves.

'We're having a baby!'

'What!' my mum shrieked and then clapped her hands together. My dad sat back in stunned silence with the biggest smile on his face.

'Now, it's still early days...' Ben tried to say, to help manage their excitement levels, but it was pointless. My mum had her hands fanning her tear-stained cheeks and my dad had pulled his trusty hankie from his jeans pocket to blow his nose and dab at his eyes when he thought we weren't looking.

'Oh wow, oh my days, oh, Len!' my mum was clucking, not knowing where to put herself. 'Are you sure?'

I nodded and gratefully took a tissue Ben passed me to wipe my own eyes. Stupid hormones. 'Yep, like Ben says, it's early on, but we couldn't wait to tell you.'

'Oh, are you going to be okay on the flight home? It's an awful long way to travel in your condition, isn't it, Len?' Mum grew concerned.

Ben grinned at me. Oh God, protective grandma had happened already.

'We'll be fine.'

'I'll take care of her, Sheila!'

'Well, you must get lots of rest and don't be rushing back to work as soon as you get back,' Mum ordered, then shook her head in wonderment. 'Oh, Georgia, we are so utterly delighted for the pair of you.'

'Thanks, Mum, thanks, Dad,' I said, sniffing back the tears. 'That means a lot.'

We hung up and clinked our coffee cups together.

'You okay, babe?' Ben asked, pulling me into a warm hug as I put my phone away.

I nodded. 'More than okay. I never expected that this trip would end with us announcing our engagement *and* our pregnancy!'

He kissed me heavily on the lips. 'I'm so happy that it has. It's hands-down the best trip I've ever been on.'

'Ditto.'

I wouldn't be a mum who made organic baby food with the array of vegetables growing in her garden. I wouldn't be a mum who swaddled her child against her floral Joules maxi-dress and glided around the city attending things like baby yoga, baby pottery and baby opera. Imagination creates expectation, so I needed to have a strict word with my imagination and bring it back down to reality. I would probably be the mum with porridge in her hair, the mum who stays in her pyjamas until the very last moment – and not swishy satiny ones, but crusty and comfy Primark ones – and that is totally okay. I didn't know exactly what lay in store for us but I'd had the strength not to let my past define my future – that was how I got this wonderful life after all. I was proof that taking chances, saying yes and overcoming deep fears, could *seriously* pay off.

'I've heard that pregnant women get a little friskier, you know?' Ben winked as he called for our bill.

'Oh, is that so?' I teased, raising an eyebrow.

'Yep.' With that, he leant over and I let his kisses wash over me, enjoying the burst of love and happiness fizzing in my chest. I knew better than most that some of the best things happen when you least expect them, and that life has a funny way of giving you what you need when you aren't looking. I'd survived being a jilted bride, being the boss of my own company and learning to both trust and love again. Now I was going to survive the next step: motherhood. And do you know what, I couldn't bloody wait!

THE END

Acknowledgements

I had no idea when I was writing the first draft of *Chasing The Sun* that life would literally imitate art. For all of you who have followed my writing via the 'Lonely Hearts Travel Club' series or via my blog (notwedordead.com) and social media (@Notwedordead), you know the journey that I've been on. To be writing the acknowledgements for my fourth novel, married and expecting our first child is utterly bonkers but so incredible! I am proof that second chances exist. The support from family, friends, and readers old and new as I approach this next stage in my own life has been overwhelming. Like Georgia, I'm not sure where this new adventure will take me, but I cannot wait to see what happens and, of course, bring you along for the journey too!

To the Goughs, Gants, Hothersalls, Lethuilliers, and Blakes for your never-ending love, encouragement and all round awesomeness. Mum and Dad (or should that be Grandma and Grandad!) in particular, I couldn't have done any of this without you. To the Siddle family, thank you for welcoming me to the clan. Shout out to Dorothea for making sure nothing is lost in translation and championing my novels among the Polish community.

Thanks to Jen Atkinson for her business know-how and endless support; you are the yummiest mummy I know. One day I want to grow up and be just like you. Thanks to my Australian guru Laura Hughes for our unforgettable Oz road trip. Driving down the Great Ocean Road discovering grotty hostels, 'I think he's broken', epic sunrises (and some not so epic) and deep chats as we got eyed up by kangaroos, inspired much of this tale. Thanks also to travel blogger and Sydney tour guide extraordinaire, Jayne Morris

Mega thanks has to go to John Siddle, my husband (!!!), who from the very beginning accepted me for me and completely changed my world for the better. The past twelve months has felt like something out of a rom com and this Backpacking Bridget Jones couldn't be happier.

Shout out to the Katy Colins crew – seriously, where are our matching t-shirts? – consisting of Juliet Mushens, Nathalie Hallam, Victoria Oundjian, Lydia Mason, Jennifer Porter, Hannah McMillan and all at Caskie Mushens, Midas and HQ Digital/Harper Collins. Thanks for waving the pom-poms in mine and Georgia's honour.

Thanks to all the new writer friends I've made along the way. You cheer me up and spur me on by being fabulous and super inspiring. Shout out in particular to Isabelle Broome, Miranda Dickinson, Adele Parks, Cesca Major, Kat Black, Rachael Lucas, Holly Martin, Emily Kerr, Helen Redfern, Kirsty Greenwood and Lisa Hall for your insight and incredibleness.

Hello *waves* and thanks to the lovely online chums who read my rambling blogs, comment on my Instagram images or drop me inspiring emails sharing your journey going from lost to wanderlust. There are many real-life Georgia Greens out there who refuse to let being dumped be the end of their world and, for this, I salute you. Keep on trucking and flying the flag for travel as a way to heal heartbreak.

Most of all, thanks to you reading these words right now. For picking up this book, giving it a chance and hopefully sharing it with your friends once you realise it is the Best Book Ever means I get to live my dream of being a writer. They haven't figured out I'm totally winging it, just yet…If we could keep this pretence gong a little longer by you helping me out and writing a review, sharing via social media (don't forget to tag me in – @notwedordead) or buying a copy for everyone and anyone you know. then that would be great! Seriously though, I never, not even for one tiny second, take your support for granted.